D1264002

EVERYWHERE I ROAM

BEN LUCIEN BURMAN

EVERYWHERE I ROAM

Drawings by Alice Caddy

DOUBLEDAY & COMPANY, INC., GARDEN CITY, N. Y.

The characters and the incidents in this book are entirely the product of the author's imagination and have no relation to any person or event in real life.

PRINTED IN THE UNITED STATES

For Elizabeth Patterson

CHAPTER ONE

THE rolling Cumberlands stretched in endless ranges to the horizon, with no break in the dark forests hiding their slopes to mark where Tennessee began and Kentucky ended.

A log cabin lay at the foot of a saddle-like mountain, its roof glistening with a recent shower. Shallow pools stood here and there in a depression of the yellow clay, and muddy rivulets raced down to a creek that wound into the distance. The tall pines growing along the bank were dripping musically. Overhead the spring sun was already shining again with vigor, as though eager to draw back to the sky the water just cast upon the earth.

Before the cabin a graying man of unusual height was hurrying back and forth, carrying bundles and an occasional piece of furniture into the ungainly, horse-drawn trailer standing before the door. Two pretty young girls and a lanky youth, from their manner toward him obviously his children, aided in the labor.

As they continued loading the vehicle, overalled mountaineers passing along the creek would stop and call out to the father, addressing him as Captain Asa.

A broad-hatted individual wearing the badge of a deputy sheriff drove down the stream in a mud-spattered car. He waved a hand marred by a deep bullet scar on his wrist, and halted for a moment.

"You ain't going to find no place, Asa," he called in amiable warning. "All you're going to find is trouble."

Captain Asa knocked off some mud clinging to the trailer's blue-painted sides. "I'll find a place all right, Rafe," he answered cheerfully.

The other shifted his wide hat. "Anyway, you be careful with them two girls. Taking 'em around all them big towns and places. I see a-plenty going on down at the sheriff's office."

Captain Asa shook his head. "Ain't anything going to happen to 'em, Rafe. All three of these children of mine's good children."

The car sped off.

Captain Asa climbed behind the ancient horse standing patiently in the shafts, to put a box on the driver's seat. As he stood there a moment, he seemed an American pioneer setting out in a covered wagon for the West. His body was bony, gaunt; his graying blond hair showed clearly the marks of home cutting. Except for this blondness, his appearance was reminiscent of the angular Lincoln who had come from the same area over a century before. His mouth was warm, friendly, his blue eyes often lighting in a twinkle. But it was nevertheless a thoughtful face, like that of the pioneers or any rustic dweller accustomed to constant struggling with inhospitable nature. To the traveler familiar with the Southern hills he would have been instantly recognized as one of those picturesque figures still to be found in a piny hollow or drowsy village store—an extraordinary combination of self-taught wisdom and childish simplicity.

His clothes were not remarkable, a shabby blue coat, shiny at the edges, and a pair of baggy trousers, both bearing the signs of frequent repair.

The loading was finished at last. Captain Asa fastened the door of the cabin with a rusty padlock.

Soon after he climbed behind the horse again. The girls mounted at his side. A large, brownish sheep dog with a grave, troubled expression scrambled awkwardly after them, and stretched out at the driver's feet. The lanky son, so straight and dark he resembled an Indian, took a post as a sort of rear guard on the trailer doorstep.

Captain Asa flicked the reins. The awkward vehicle began to lumber down the creek. Over the stones it jolted and bounded. Sprays of water shot out from the wheels, occasionally turning to rainbows in the brilliant sunlight. As it swayed across the green countryside, it semed an azure ship tossing on an emerald, mountain-bordered sea.

Past fields where straw-sombreroed farmers were hoeing corn they rattled, past cabins where sunbonneted women were working in their gardens. The two girls hugged their seats. The lean youth at the rear clung tight to a metal handle near the door.

The trailer gave a violent leap as a wheel dropped into a deep hole. There came a dull cracking.

The younger daughter looked in the direction of the sound. Her voice grew worried. "It's broke the Chinaman," she said.

She lifted from behind the seat a large basket filled with cheap, freshly painted statuettes of the sort given as premiums at carnivals—impossible bulldogs and preposterous ducks, intermingled with potbellied policemen and grotesque caricatures of heroes of the day. At the top lay a pigtailed figure with a wide break running down its middle.

Captain Asa's bronzed face was touched with regret. "That was a mighty pretty Chinaman."

The girl placed the damaged statuette at one side. "I'll hold 'em in my lap."

"Guess you better, Fernie."

She was a quiet, gentle girl of perhaps sixteen, clad in an awkward-fitting, once pink dress that like her father's barbering plainly showed the marks of a home pair of scissors, and did much to obscure her natural beauty. Her hair, falling below her shoulders, was so light it seemed almost the color of the silvery birch trees growing in the forests farther to the North. Her face was pale, giving a striking quality to the dark brows and lashes that framed her large gray eyes. There was about her that air of deep humility, of wistfulness, so common to the mountain girl who as a child often knows all the suffering and hardship that her sister of the city knows only when twice the age. She was wearing a pair of brown cotton stockings, carefully mended, and a pair of worn black shoes.

A pile of factory-made bedspreads lay nearby, of the sort now common in the South, with a gaudy design to be finished by hand.

She took one of the coverlets, and packing it around the statuettes to prevent their jarring, set the basket on her knees.

Everywhere on the rocky slopes the spring flowers were blooming, the pink-touched laurel, the chaste dogwood. Blackbirds and cardinals flew past in jeweled flashes. Overhead a faint wind whistled softly in the mysterious melody of the pines.

The trail left the creek bed and began to run along the bank, with an occasional patch of pavement, as though they were nearing a town. A lofty column of smoke became visible over the crest of a hill. There came the far-off rumbling of machinery.

The older daughter opened a cheap vanity case, and hastily made up her face. There was a difference in age of perhaps three years between the sisters, and they were cast in such a different mould it seemed impossible there could be any kinship. The hair of the elder girl was a lustrous black, and cut in a short bob, held in place by a green-jeweled pin. Where the younger daughter was subdued, she was vivacious, with a pert, turned-up nose that increased the impudence of her flashing black eyes.

Her clothes differed in similar startling fashion. She was wearing a dress spotted with flamboyant red poppies and shiny red shoes and red belt to match. Resting at her side was a handbag of white imitation leather, topped with a showy gilt frame.

She finished her beautifying, then with a sudden movement leaned back in the seat, and putting up her feet on the dashboard, began to whistle a jazzy tune.

Captain Asa turned quickly. "You stop doing that, Ula. Ain't a nice thing for a girl to be whistling."

She made a wry face. "Golly, Pa. You just see something wrong with everything a person wants to do."

She continued to whistle under her breath.

The rumbling of machinery grew louder.

They rounded a bend, and the creek ended, flowing into a narrow river that lay at the foot of the dark-timbered hills. The trail became a highway, built along the bank of the swift-running stream.

In one direction lay a huge steel mill, its giant stacks belching volcanic clouds of smoke and flame, with the dingy dwellings of the laborers strung for half a mile in its shadow. The buildings of a little city showed beyond.

Captain Asa's face grew somber. He drove the trailer onto the concrete, then turned the horse where the road led off toward the open sky. Even though they were moving away from the mill, for some time their route was bordered by ugly walls of slag from which steam was still rising. The pines growing nearby were seared and blackened, their branches hidden under a thick layer of ashes.

The monstrous smoking structure dropped farther and farther behind. The ant-like workers, scurrying about as though devotees at the altars of some fiery gods, were lost in the distance.

The somberness of Captain Asa's face vanished.

Ula took out her vanity case again, and retouched her lips. The younger girl selected an unfinished bedspread, and began knotting the threads to make a fringe.

The son jumped down from the trailer, and walked alongside, inspecting the brakes and the creaking wheels.

Captain Asa leaned beyond the driver's seat. "How's she doing, Vergil?"

The son moved nearer. His hair, black like that of his elder sister, was straight and shiny. With his aquiline nose and his high cheekbones, he clearly possessed a strain of the Indian ancestry so common to many of the dwellers of the Cumberlands. His gaunt face was quiet, dreamy, giving him an air older than his seventeen years. When he answered his father's question, it was in a slow, abstracted voice, with a slight hesitation between each few words, as though with a suggestion of a stammer. "Looks like she's going to run pretty good, Pa."

He went into the trailer again.

A truck rumbled near, loaded with bags of cement. The driver saw Ula, still busy with her lipstick, and saluted.

She waved at him, and turned to her sister gaily. "We're sure having fun, ain't we, Fernie?"

The younger girl glanced back in the direction from which they had come. "I'm worried about my chickens. Marty's mother said she'd look after 'em. But she's too old to take care of chickens right."

The road narrowed and began to wind tortuously through the dark hills. Gigantic rocks lay everywhere, rolled down from the overhanging peaks by some tremendous earthquake. Often the highway was a thin ribbon of concrete, hung at the edge of a stony precipice. Occasionally a mine tipple came into view, huge, forbidding, like the dwelling of some sullen giant. From it there arose a continuous wheezing and groaning as the metal buckets carried their loads of coal to the black cars waiting on the railroad track below. Above them the pines towered into the sky, stark, solemn, like mountain men attending a funeral.

They passed a natural bridge linking two perpendicular cliffs of limestone, with a tiny stream flowing beneath. Beyond it a cabin appeared, shaded by a spreading oak tree. On the porch was sitting a white-bearded old man with one of those parchment-like faces of the mountains, marked with the passage of so many years no further time can be measured.

A water trough made of a hollowed log stood at the roadside. The horse whinnied as it drew near.

Captain Asa halted, and with the old man's permission, began to fill the trough from a creaky pump. Vergil came hurrying to aid. The dog climbed down and followed close at Captain Asa's heels, watching him constantly out of its grave eyes.

The horse drank noisily.

At the old man's invitation, Captain Asa took a seat on the porch. Withdrawing two crudely-rolled stogies from his pocket, he presented one to his white-bearded host. "Make these myself," he said.

They smoked a moment in amiable silence. The air became thick with the odor of uncured tobacco.

The snowy-bearded one gazed at the two girls standing near the trailer. "You going up to Lexington with them children?"

Captain Asa chewed the end of the stogie in an attempt to make it draw. "I ain't figuring on Lexington."

"Going over towards Louisville?"

"It's a good place. But I ain't heading that way."

"Then I reckon maybe you're going to Berea to put 'em in the college."

"I ain't making Berea neither."

The snowy beard gave a quiver of slight exasperation. "Then there ain't no place left for you to be heading except Virginia."

"I'd like to see Virginia. But I ain't got any call." A shower of tiny sparks fell from the stogie, here and there alighting upon his baggy trousers. He brushed them away. "Fact is, brother, I don't know where I'm going."

They sat in silence once more, lost in clouds of overpowering smoke from which now and then a new fiery wave descended.

Ula stood at the roadside, watching the great trucks

speeding past. With her gay-colored dress, and her dark, impudent face, she seemed almost a gypsy, just emerged from the doors of some cigarette factory in Madrid, ready to exchange volleys of spicy repartee with the male loungers in the street outside. She began to whistle a tune again.

Captain Asa called to her sharply.

The parchment face of the host wrinkled further in disapproval. "A crowing hen and a whistling girl always comes to a bad end."

Captain Asa grew troubled again. "Fact is, it's girls a-whistling and smoking cigarettes and things that's making me go away."

The snowy beard nodded in agreement. "Things today are mighty bad."

Captain Asa did not reply for a moment. When he spoke his voice was tense with emotion. "Things are getting worse and worse. It was bad enough when the coal mines come around Clay Creek where I've always been living, cutting up the hills and ruining the timber. And now they've got the steel mill, I don't want to stay any more. Bums hanging around pool halls playing them juke boxes, and everybody getting drunk and shooting and cutting all the time. I could stand it, I reckon. But it sure ain't a place for my children."

The wrinkled eyes, set far back in the parchment face, grew dim, as though looking off into a vanished world. "Used to be mighty fine living in the hills before the roads come. Never had no lock on your door. And if you was hungry or sick, you knowed there'd be a neighbor to bake you some corn bread or give you some herb medicine to get you well. Now if you're a old man like me, you know maybe you'll die by yourself, 'cause don't nobody care what happens to you. Everybody's so busy making money. And next year maybe they'll throw you out of your grave to open up a new coal mine."

The wrapper of Captain Asa's stogie loosened, allowing some bits of broken leaf to drop to the floor. He wet it with his lips, and pressed it back in place with a finger. "It was a sorry day they found coal in these hills. And it's sure right what you said about the roads. It'd have been better if they'd never had built one of 'em. People kept hollering and hollering for the highways. And the politicians gave 'em what they wanted. And now you can see what it's done everywhere. World's the worst off it's ever been. What people needs to do is get back to living the way they did when I was a boy. Those times people were living right."

Captain Asa kicked off a bit of tobacco fallen onto his shoe. "Worst thing's the way it's got families to breaking up. All you hear 'em talking about in the paper and over the radio is about the way there ain't any more families today. I took care of these three children ever since they were babies, when their mother died a-bearing the last one. I love these children. They're all I got. I brought 'em up. And I want to keep 'em with me, way a family ought to be. I knowed if I stayed around Clay Creek, way things are going today they'd be spoiled mighty quick. So I got to studying about it, and I fixed up the trailer. This here's a big country. There's sure plenty of places where people's still nice, and living way they used to do. I'm going to keep looking. And maybe when I'm going around, I can find me a good wife to help make a home for my children, too. Then when I find the right place, that's where I'm stopping."

The snowy host studied the blue vehicle where the dilapidated horse was munching the sparse grass. "Looks to me like you're going to get into plenty of trouble, with all them hitchhikers and escaped convicts and holdup men that's traveling the highways. Ain't a week goes by around here, seems like, a hitchhiker don't hit somebody over the head, and throw their body in the woods."

His wrinkled eyes seemed to draw back into the past again. "I'm a old man now. I got eighteen grandchildren. I seen the war over the darkies, and the fellows that come after, riding the horses and wearing the sheets, and I seen the war over the ship they blowed up in Cuba. I seen the German war over the ship that hit the iceberg, and the other German war over the fellows wearing the shirts. And I ain't never seen times like they are today. . . . How you going to make a living while you're traveling?"

Captain Asa found a match and relit his defunct stogie. "I'll get along all right. I sold my two cows. And the girls are making the bedspreads and painting the statues. I guess you seen the fellow drove through selling 'em. The bedspreads come pretty near finished. You buy the statues for a dime, and after they're painted up you sell 'em for fifty cents. There's Washington and Napoleon and a thermometer on an alligator. The thermometer's fifteen extra."

The old man moved stiffly in his chair. "I went to Pineville once and a fellow in a drugstore give me a thermometer free. It was on a calendar."

Captain Asa arose to take his departure. "I'm going to try other ways to make some money, too. If I don't do so good first time, I'll start something else. Right now I'm going to try handling them new Home Knowledge Books they're talking about all the time on the radio in Memphis. I've knowed a lot of fellows come through here handling sets of books and 'cyclopedias and maps and things. And I always figured I'd like to be doing it, 'cause there ain't nobody anywhere, I reckon, reads more books than me. I seen a piece in one of them true magazines saying the Home Knowledge company was wanting people to go around selling. So I wrote, and they told me I'd make a pile when I got things to going right. There's three books and it costs a dollar a book. I bought ten sets, though 'course I didn't have to pay no three dollars. You get one of these charms with each set free. Like you did the thermometer."

He held up a cheap watch charm dangling from a vest pocket, a tiny aluminum globe representing the world with the phrase engraved upon it, "Knowledge Is Power." "You wouldn't need none of the statues or the spreads or the books, would you?"

The snowy beard recorded a negative.

The travelers took to the road once more.

For several hours they journeyed without ceasing, while an irregular parade of vehicles rumbled past, giant motor trucks loaded with sheets of iron that clattered like broken bells, and huge logs from the forests that covered the hazy mountains. Occasionally along the side of the road a coal miner walked on his way to the pits, an unlit lamp fixed to his grimy cap.

The son jumped down from the trailer, and joined the others at the front.

"Getting kind of hot," he remarked.

He climbed into the cramped space behind the seat, and stretched his long legs over the boards. He spoke little as he sat there, uttering a few sentences now and then, always with the same dreamy air and in the same abstracted voice that held a faint suggestion of a stammer. Occasionally at some remark or some sight in the road his thoughtful eyes lighted; his lips would curve in a luminous smile that spread slowly over his dark countenance.

As though in compensation for his quiet manner, he was wearing an old sport coat with large black-and-white checks of the sort affected by the jauntier youths of his age everywhere in the area. From one of its pockets he took out a popular scientific magazine, and began to read. At times he would pause, and laboriously underline a passage with a pencil.

They neared a counterfeit of a log cabin decorated with wide red stripes and bearing a sign "Dew Droppe Inne" over the doorway.

Ula gazed at it with pleasure. "That's a pretty place, Pa. Let's go in and get a drink of soda."

Captain Asa pulled at the reins. "Some soda pop 'd be mighty fine."

At Ula's urging, her brother put down his paper, and moved off with her to the roadhouse.

Captain Asa called after him. "Get me and Fernie a strawberry, will you, Vergil? I'm going to take the horse under them trees."

The younger daughter walked off with her father, and waited while he fed the dilapidated animal some oats.

Vergil came out from the roadhouse carrying several bottles, and set them on a table under the trees. But there was no sign of Ula.

The raucous music of a juke box came drifting through the open window. Captain Asa hurried onto the porch, and looked through the door.

He saw his daughter, near the juke box, dancing with a young man wearing a flashy shirt and imitation collegiate trousers. The stogie in Captain Asa's mouth quivered. He went inside, and waited at the entrance.

The girl relinquished her partner, and with a shame-faced air, followed her father out of the roadhouse. "He's a wonderful dancer," she remarked nervously. "He works in a garage over at Pineville. He wanted me to go dancing tonight. I told him we was just passing through."

Captain Asa did not answer. He sat down at the table under the trees, and drank in silence.

The travelers rode on again. The father's spirits soon brightened.

They pulled off the road for the night at the edge of a fragrant pine grove. Captain Asa and Vergil tied up the horse, then blocked the wheels with heavy stones. They went inside the trailer.

It was a pleasant though cramped interior, the tiny windows hung with bright-flowered shades. At one end was a minute, curtained-off section like a Pullman berth for the girls, with neat built-in bunks along the walls. The remainder served as sleeping quarters for the male members of the family, and living room for all. On shelves above Vergil's bunk were several volumes filled with pictures of railroad locomotives and more scientific magazines, a few comic books and detective weeklies, together with a baseball glove and a ukulele. Opposite was Captain Asa's corner, with shelves holding a variety of objects. There were records for a battered phonograph, and a glass ball enclosing a red-cloaked girl in front of a church, which when shaken became the center of a snowstorm. There was also a stuffed dove under a transparent dome; a bronze paper cutter and a volume of photographs, both marked "Souvenir Of The St. Louis World's Fair"; and a worn Bible.

Ula unfolded an old bridge table and set out some dishes. She went into the little alcove furnished with an oil stove that served as a kitchen, and with the help of Fernie, began to prepare supper.

The elder daughter's mood had changed now. She left her cooking a moment to gaze at her father with an air of impudent proprietorship, then reached out to straighten his hook-on tie which had wandered widely from the perpendicular. "Going to cut your hair pretty soon," she declared.

They all sat down to eat.

Vergil studied a road map as he ate a dish of ham and turnip greens. "We ought to be making Corbin tomorrow, Pa. Which way you figuring on heading from there?"

Captain Asa munched his corn bread happily. "Over towards Memphis, and then South, I reckon. Further South you go, more it gets like old times, they says. I'll bet there's plenty of people down there feels the same as me."

CHAPTER TWO

THEY set out again in the morning. All day they traveled and many days thereafter, the blue wheels creaking as the ancient horse trudged without complaint over the winding roads. Past Red Bird they lumbered, and Marrowbone, and Summer Shade, past Bowling Green with its pretty girls, and Paris in Tennessee. Beyond Corinth in Mississippi they rolled, and Rienzi, and Tupelo, past Egypt, and Winona, and across the muddy Yazoo.

The landscape had altered gradually, the pine-covered mountains becoming low, grassy hills that in turn gave way to fields of cotton. Plantation wagons passed them, piled so high with the white fibers they seemed loaded with snow. Often there came the whirring of a cotton gin.

As the country changed, so did the occupants. Negroes were everywhere, hoeing in the fields or driving herds of cattle. Often when the travelers stopped at night beside some rustic settlement they could hear the voices of the black worshipers in a nearby church chanting a sorrowful hymn.

The rivers they crossed were growing wider. The tangled trees along their banks were festooned with Spanish moss. Great cranes began to drift overhead, floating without apparent motion, as though they were bits of cloud detached from the fleecy masses in the sky. The air was growing warm, lazy.

The traffic of the road continued to sweep past them in endless procession, the blood stream flowing between the cities of the Mississippi Valley. Occasionally a peddler's truck appeared, or a trailer like their own, with its driver taking orders for groceries or selling patent medicines. Now and then a rickety auto rattled along with a family of gypsies crowded near the wheel, waiting to reveal for a piece of silver the fortunes of the gods.

Several times carnivals passed on the move from their warm winter quarters to the North. Once a caravan of a dozen weather-beaten vehicles paused nearby for a moment, with heavily-rouged girls sitting beside the bored drivers.

Ula and the others gazed in fascination.

They stopped one night at a trailer camp, a collection of cars and tents and children and dogs encircled by a wall of blaring radios.

Captain Asa went with Vergil to the little building that served as restaurant and camp office to purchase some tobacco.

A row of slot machines stood against the wall. Vergil studied the painted symbols with close attention, then dropped a nickel and pulled down the handle. He played several other coins, losing with each new experiment.

Captain Asa looked on unhappily. "You ought to know you can't win nothing playing them machines, Vergil."

The dreaminess of the son's Indian-like face heightened. "If you study long enough you can learn how to beat 'em. Some day I'm going to win plenty. I knew a fellow come from Pineville hit the jackpot once. He got over a thousand nickels."

They walked back to the trailer. Captain Asa ate his supper and started the phonograph, then sat on a whitewashed bench outside to enjoy the evening air. In the sky the stars shone brilliantly. A pale moon was just becoming visible above the horizon, seeming covered with cobwebs for an instant as it was veiled by a long pendant of moss hanging from a tree.

Captain Asa wound the phonograph. A ballad singer began to chant in a curious nasal fashion the verses of *Sparrow On The Mountain.*

Over and over the record played dolefully:

Sparrow on the mountain,
A sparrow trying to crow.
A dead man trying to shave himself,
And a blind man trying to sew.

A dilapidated automobile piled high with painted willow chairs was parked a few feet from the trailer, with a frayed tent erected alongside. Beneath the canvas the owner was sitting, a short little man wearing a cheap green suit and shabby but still lurid socks and tie. As the music continued, the stranger came over to listen.

"It's a good song, *Sparrow,*" he declared in a jerky voice. "Got plenty of trouble in it."

Captain Asa nodded. "All them old-fashioned songs are good songs."

The newcomer paced up and down a moment, then took a seat with Captain Asa on the bench. His movements were quick, electric; his black eyes shrewd, penetrating, with a little of the uneasy air of a pitchman on the street corner, watching for the approach of the police. His hair, black like his eyes, was shiny with some oily preparation that kept it flat against his head. His speech was swift as his movements, and was generally touched with cynicism.

They talked, slapping at the mosquitoes buzzing about their faces and ankles.

The green-suited little man pulled up a drooping sock. "You been in the Army, or is Captain your born name?"

"It's my born name."

"They sure got funny names in them hills you come from. But a good name 'll help you if you work it right. I know a fellow whose born name was President. And he got himself a fine job tending bar in a big saloon in New Orleans. . . . What you selling?"

"We're a-selling the statues and the bedspreads. And I'm trying to start the Home Knowledge Books."

The little man glanced at Captain Asa in quick appraisal. "You sure don't look like a selling man. . . . Got anything good in the Knowledge Books?"

"About everything, I guess. I ain't read 'em all yet. Book One's what they call the Nations Of The World and the New Wonder Atlas. And Book Two's what they call Science And Discovery. And Book Three's what they call the All Round Volume, that's How To Be A Public Speaker, and How To Be A Doctor At Home, and How to Make Your Wife Happy, and How To Keep A Dog From Running Away, and things like that. They're mighty fine books."

"I'd get 'em if I had a dog."

Captain Asa arose to change a record. On the road nearby giant trucks roared past like intermittent thunder. Their headlights starkly illuminated the whitewashed trees, scarred with the marks of wildly driven autos. From the restaurant shack there came the blaring of a juke box, mingled with the scratchy playing of the phonograph. There drifted out the pungent odor of frying hamburger.

The green-suited man dipped into his coat pocket, and pulling out a handful of flattish black grains, offered them to his companion. "Sunflower seeds. Good for your stomach," he announced.

Captain Asa nodded. "When I was a boy people eat 'em plenty."

The green-suited man cracked a seed between his flashing teeth. "If a fellow didn't eat nothing but sunflower seeds, he'd get to be old as a parrot, they says."

They continued talking. Captain Asa told the other of his problems and his plans.

Far down the railroad track that stretched in back of the camp the headlight of a locomotive flashed, and a bell clanged in the distance. There came the rumble of an approaching freight train.

The little man chewed a seed in meditation. "You ain't going to find no place," he remarked.

"How you meaning?"

"I'm meaning you ain't going to find what you're looking for. You can't find it, 'cause there ain't no good old times any more. Fact is there never was no good old times."

Captain Asa's bronze face was touched with stubbornness. "That ain't the way I figure it. Things was fine when I was a boy. Maybe you didn't live as long, but you were happier when you were living. I was reading in the paper everybody's worrying so bad today, it ain't going to stop till half the people's in the crazy asylums, and the other half's taking care of 'em."

He paused an instant while the approaching train whistled shrilly. "Some of my kinfolk went to the St. Louis Fair, and they gave me a book about it. I got it there inside. It says that if everything on earth had blowed up, and just the Exposition was left and they'd have started the world over from it, things would have been the finest they ever was since the Lord throwed Adam out of Eden. I've read plenty, and I've talked to plenty of people. And way everybody says, ever since the Exposition things has been going down and down."

The freight train thundered past, so close the trailer rocked with its vibration. The air was filled with an invisible curtain of cinders.

The little man rubbed an eye with a bandana. "Them was good times, and it was a good Exposition. But people was worrying then, and things was changing. Just the same as now. Things is always changing. That's nature. And you can't beat nature noways."

The cindery shower ended.

The little man chewed a seed once more. "You ain't going to keep your family from growing up and leaving you, neither. Won't make any difference where you take 'em. Any more than won't nothing keep you from getting hungry, and cold, and even killing somebody if you get mad enough. 'Cause all that's nature, too. Nature and trouble, them's the same thing."

"That ain't what it says in the Bible."

"It's there if you look for it. You just ain't looked right."

A frog jumped out of the shadows onto the edge of a cement pool, and began a loud croaking.

The little man shot a seed toward it. "Way you got to do nowadays, instead of looking for the old times, is to keep up with the new ones. Or better than that, get ahead of 'em. Take these here willow chairs I'm selling. It ain't my regular line at all. It's a old-fashioned way of living. I figured if I painted 'em up nice, I'd sell a-plenty. But I'm starving pretty near. Soon as I get these chairs sold, I'm going back to show business. That's an up-to-date business—carnivals like them that's heading North now, and pinball machines, and photographing, that's my line. I seen a fellow down along the Gulf Coast last year knew how to do show business right. He was riding a big bull all the way from California, and photographing people a-sitting on it. He was getting his picture in the papers everywhere, and people come to sit on that bull till it was pretty near wore out. These here's advertising times. All you got to do is get your name in the papers, and you don't have to work no more. If I can get me a little money, I'm sure going to buy me one of them bulls."

Captain Asa's lips hardened with stubbornness again. "If you get yourself hung, you get your name in the papers easy. You don't need no bull."

"It's them old-fashioned people that get hung. Up-to-date people just get the gravy."

The little man arose from the bench. "I know a place if you want to live quiet. You go and stay with the people out in these swamps around here. There's a whole town of 'em at Spanish Lake, where I buy these chairs before I paint 'em. Ain't but fifteen miles from here, down by the river. Them people at Spanish is so old-time they think when we get in a war, it's to fight the Indians. But you go there or anywhere else, and you'll see if I ain't right."

He shot another seed at the croaking frog. A greenish shadow flashed through the darkness, and there came a sound like the uncorking of a bottle. The croaking ceased.

The little man's face lighted with ironic satisfaction. He spat jerkily. "About them children of yours. I ain't a family man. But I've kept my eyes open. If you want to keep 'em with you, handle 'em easy. I know a man had a fox stayed with him a year till one night he got scared and locked it up. Next day it ran off, and he never seen it again. Children and a fox acts the same way."

He disappeared into his tent.

Captain Asa entered the trailer. He turned to his two daughters, busy drying the dishes. "We'll go and look at Spanish Lake tomorrow," he announced. "Maybe we ain't got much more traveling."

They set out with the rising sun. The country was changing once more. Houses and travelers grew rarer and rarer. The road ran across a tangled swamp in whose moss-hung trees gloomy buzzards were roosting, like prophets of doom. White cranes drifted overhead, their motionless, outstretched wings casting giant shadows on the white highway.

The road turned, and the Mississippi came into view, winding through the luxuriant valley like a muddy carpet laid over a greenish floor. A towboat was moving down it, pushing a great convoy of barges. A puff of steam arose above its pilot-house. A whistle sounded, mournfully. A dredge was anchored at the shore, with a long pipe thrust far out over the water, like the neck of some river monster searching for its prey. The steady sucking as it brought up the mud of the bottom echoed weirdly across the green wilderness.

They left the highway and took a narrow trail leading through a tangled grove of cypresses. Moss hung everywhere in long streamers from the branches, like funeral pennants marking the death of some lord of the countryside. Moccasins and an occasional young alligator crawled off into the brush as the trailer lumbered near. The river was still close. Often through a break in the trees they could catch a glimpse of its brown surface. At times they could hear a rhythmic chugging, as some unseen vessel labored to bring its cargo up the stream.

The trees thickened and closed overhead in a somber canopy. The path became a tunnel, silent, ghostly, the only sound the dull whine of the trailer wheels or a pistol-like cracking as the top struck against an overhanging branch.

The tunnel merged into another and another. They seemed to be moving through some silent subterranean world, the trailer a blue boat again, floating through endless caverns.

The last tunnel ended. They saw a wide greenish lake, bordered by rows of drowned cypresses.

Captain Asa's face lighted. "It's Spanish," he declared.

They drove along a stony road that circled the water. Tiny cabins showed everywhere on the bank, with clothes drying on makeshift lines. Here and there a shanty boat lay anchored at the foot of a gnarled cypress tree. On the lake tall men with deep-tanned faces were rowing flatboats or dugouts, running their fishing lines, or pulling down Spanish moss from the overhanging trees. Grizzled trappers sat on the porches of their cabins, chewing tobacco and curing muskrat skins. Sunbonneted women, smoking corncob pipes, bent over wooden washtubs, and gossiped with their neighbors.

In the center of the settlement was a tiny church, and an unpainted frame warehouse belonging to the sawmill whose single smokestack rose at a little distance. Before the warehouse some muddy mules and horses were standing, harnessed to crude jolt wagons. A crowd of rustic figures, celebrating a wedding in their Sunday finery, milled back and forth between the vehicles and the wide doorway. From inside the bare-walled structure there came the sound of a fiddle playing a quick country tune. As the trailer drew near, the travelers could see the bride and groom, sitting awkwardly on a bench, while booted men and stiff-clad women hopped about in a fast square dance. Above the scraping of the violins rose the voice of the sweating leader, calling out the swift-changing steps. The dancers bowed and swung in merry obedience.

Captain Asa reined the horse. He sat for a moment watching, then turned to the two girls at his side. His blue eyes were gay.

"Looks like we'll be stopping," he said.

CHAPTER THREE

A RICKETY frame store with a tin-roofed porch showed beyond the warehouse. Before it some high-booted figures were gathered, talking lazily.

Captain Asa drove toward them, and tying the horse to a rail, went inside the building with Vergil to make some inquiries.

A trio of swampmen sat near the doorway, where the storekeeper was bargaining in amiable fashion with a trapper over the price of some muskrat skins. The sitters examined the newcomers with curiosity.

The proprietor, a large, hearty man somewhat overflowing his wide overalls, halted his dickering a moment, and greeted Captain Asa cordially.

"There's plenty of places around here you can settle," he remarked in answer to the visitor's questions. "We're old-fashioned folks around here, and everybody gets along good. These swamps are big enough for everybody, just so long as you don't get tangled up in somebody else's fishing lines. That's about the only thing 'll get you in trouble around here. If I was you, I'd go out by the lake to where old Luke Maney lived. Fishing and trapping's good. And if you want to farm a little, you can do that too. Used to be a house there, but it blowed away in the big tornado hit here last year, so there ain't nowheres much to stay. But you got a trailer, so that won't bother you none."

He took down a plug of tobacco for one of the swamp-men. "You try a-living there a few days, and then if you feel like staying you can pay me a little rent, or maybe buy it if you want to. Luke kind of blowed off with the tornado to Texas. And he give the handling of the place to me."

They drove along the water for perhaps two miles, halting at a strip of land where a stone foundation overgrown with weeds marked the site they were seeking. Beyond the vanished house lay an unfenced cornfield reaching back to the endless swamp that formed the somber horizon. Everywhere the earth was rich, black, exhaling the heavy, damp smell of the region that meant extraordinary fertility. The stalks of corn, the melons growing in scattered patches, were fat, succulent.

Along the shore tall reeds arose, over which great butterflies were drifting. Near their drowning roots a fringe of purple water hyacinths was floating, like a gorgeous carpet laid out for some royal ceremony. Beyond the flowers the lake stretched in emerald beauty under a cloudless sky. Black fish leaped in long arcs, like flashes of dark lightning.

From a log two cranes arose and began flying in odd patterns, as though they were scouts signaling the presence of the visitors to the flock of ducks bobbing on the green surface a quarter of a mile away.

They unhitched the horse, and let it graze in the luxuriant grass. They walked about looking over the property, the well with its bucket still fixed to a fraying rope, the chicken house which had survived the storm, its high wire fence now enclosing only a few frightened lizards.

The inspection completed, Captain Asa and Vergil set about making some delayed repairs to the trailer. The girls stretched a line from the tree and began to wash the soiled clothes accumulated from their long traveling.

They were busy at their task when a sunbonneted woman came from a little cabin up the road, carrying a basket covered with a towel.

She set it down beside the trailer. "Seen you coming in," she declared. "Thought maybe you could use these for your supper."

Ula removed the cover, exposing a roasted chicken, and a loaf of fresh-baked bread.

The bonneted figure hurried off to escape their thanks.

As the day wore on other neighbors arrived, bringing a ham, a huge fish, and the bountiful vegetables of the countryside.

A tall, grizzled trapper wearing a coonskin cap rowed up in a flatboat. He took out the rifle lying in the bow, and made the vessel fast to a tree. "Pop Masters that runs the store was a-telling me maybe you was settling for a while," he remarked. "I brought you this boat of mine case you was staying, till you build your own. I got two of 'em. You can't get along here without no boat."

He stalked up the road.

Captain Asa gazed after him with delight. "People around here sure are mighty fine."

They were busy with various duties until it was nearing sunset. Captain Asa went off with the dog to the store to inform the hearty proprietor that they were remaining. He had paid the small rental for a month, and was returning in the twilight when he neared a bare little cabin set back from the road in a clump of gloomy cypresses. From it there came the sound of chanting voices.

He stopped at the edge of the path leading toward it to listen.

He had been standing there a moment when a thin, fine-faced figure wearing a miner's cap came through the shadows, carrying a heavy stick. Beside him were walking a sad-eyed woman and two neat-aproned little girls. By his careful tapping of the cane, and the way he gripped the woman's arm, it was apparent that he was blind.

He reached the path, and sensed the other's presence. He spoke gently. "We're churching here tonight, brother. Maybe you'd like to come to the meeting."

Captain Asa called the dog, who was sniffing at the blind man's heels. "You hold with the dipping, or do you sprinkle?"

"We don't do nothing but the dipping."

"I hold with the sprinkling. But I'd mighty like to come and set with you a while."

Captain Asa followed the blind man inside.

About the bleak room a dozen booted men and poorly-clad women were gathered, sitting on chairs and boxes before a dwarfish fisherman who was praying in low tones.

The fisherman finished his supplications. With a worried air he made his way to the back of the room, and returning, set an unlit lamp on a table.

A gaunt woman in a stiff calico dress went about taking up a collection.

Captain Asa's sightless companion counted out a few pennies with awkward fingers. "It's to buy coal oil for the lamp," he explained. "I can see the Lord in the dark. But them others can't have no services till we get the oil for the lamp."

His sad-eyed wife nodded. "Ain't enough oil in it to last more'n just a little while. And Lord wouldn't like no meeting broke off in the middle."

Captain Asa added a coin.

The gaunt woman took the money she received, and put it in the hands of a freckled boy waiting eagerly near the doorway. The boy darted away.

The finely-chiseled face of the blind man grew troubled. "A fellow went through here on a gas boat once was a-running for Governor or something. Give away cigars and candy and everything, and said he'd give us a whole barrel of coal oil. But he didn't get elected, so it never come."

The boy returned, bearing the oilcan. The lamp filled the room with a flickering yellow glow. The worshipers began to sing in quavering chorus.

Captain Asa lingered awhile, then returned to the trailer.

They ate supper. The girls took out some unfinished statuettes, and began to paint them in vivid colors. Vergil picked up a book of railroad locomotives and studied it intently. Captain Asa found an old ball of fishing tackle, and set about unraveling the tangled strands.

Far down the lake a whippoorwill called in eerie tones, followed by an answering cry so close it seemed almost inside the trailer.

Ula grew restless. Putting down the striped pig she was painting, she glanced into the mirror of her vanity case.

Rouging her lips, she put a flower in her hair, increasing her gypsy-like appearance, then peered out the window into the swampy blackness.

Her dark eyes grew anxious. "Hope it ain't going to be too lonesome around here. I ain't seen any place to go dancing."

Captain Asa untied a knot in the tackle. "They were dancing at the wedding."

She turned on him in quick reproach. "That ain't real dancing, Pa. . . . I wish we'd have gone off with one of them carnivals or something. I know a girl come from Corbin joined a show, and she said they didn't do nothing but have fun all day long."

An enormous red moon climbed suddenly above the black-pennanted trees in the distance. A rooster somewhere down the shore crowed with a lusty voice, as though mistaking it for the rising sun.

Fernie listened. The wistfulness of her pale face deepened. "Maybe we can get some chickens again. I miss my chickens mighty bad."

Captain Asa nodded. "We'll get you the chickens. I'll start working on this place tomorrow and get it fixed up right. I'll go down to Pop Masters' store first thing, and buy some of those big nets I saw there tonight. I always wanted to be a fisherman and live by a lake. And way fish are jumping here, with fine fishing and farming both, looks like there ain't going to be no place like this anywhere."

The moon mounted higher. A wave of great white moths drifted out from the trees. They settled on the screens, their delicate wings fluttering, their graceful bodies quivering. At times a huge June bug floundered among them, battering noisily against the wire, like a drunken man among beautiful, white-robed ladies.

There was a crackling in the bushes. The grave dog moved to the door and began an ominous growling.

It bounded outside as a shadowy fox sped across the road.

Captain Asa called sharply. "Come back here, Ruby."

The dog paid no attention, but disappeared into the brush. It returned soon after, its tail hanging low in dejection, its ragged body covered with briars.

The crimson moon turned golden. The surface of the lake began to shimmer as though with the reflection of countless hanging lanterns that stretched off to infinity. A large night bird flew past, catching the moonlight on its feathers for an instant, like a luminous ghost. Far down the water where a lamp twinkled, there came the muted voices of the worshipers in the cabin, singing a hymn. In the settlement beyond there floated up the occasional sound of violins, still playing for the wedding guests. A golden stillness spread over earth and water.

Captain Asa's face seemed to glow like the moonlight. "This here's the way things ought to be," he murmured. "Just trees and birds and natural living people, like it was in the mountains before the road come. We don't have to look for a place any more."

The days passed in pleasant procession. Each day Captain Asa and Vergil would row out in the flatboat with their nets, returning with gleaming hauls of catfish and buffalo. Often they would anchor beneath the overhanging trees and pull down the long strands drooping from the branches, to await the coming of the moss-buyer. Occasionally Vergil took the boat alone to inspect their lines. As he stood in the stern, wielding an oar, he seemed a young Indian on a lake far to the North piloting his canoe off to some new encampment. At times when his work was done and he had enough of his science magazines or detective weeklies, he would put on his leather glove and play baseball with a youthful fisherman, or take up the battered ukulele and pick out a labored tune.

The girls busied themselves with the duties of the tiny household, Ula by turns gay, impudent, and tender; Fernie always quiet, gentle, taking each task with deep seriousness, whether the embroidering of the bedspreads or the feeding of the hens and the four baby chickens that now paraded up and down the wire run.

Often Captain Asa would go for a visit to the blind man who lived a short distance up the bank. At irregular intervals he would take the statuettes and spreads the girls had finished off to Pop Masters' store, in the hope of finding an appreciative customer.

They had been at the lake for perhaps a month when a sudden change became noticeable in Ula's manner. She was always restless now, her eyes straying absently as she made the beds or stood setting the table. At times she would leave the trailer and be away for several hours. Once she missed the supper she had helped prepare, and did not return until long after darkness, giving as the reason a visit with an ailing old woman who lived down the road. Captain Asa paid no attention.

He went on his periodic journey to the store one morning, carrying a basket that held half-a-dozen newly painted statuettes and a lurid bedspread.

The regular high-booted loungers were sitting on the counter, chewing tobacco and sending out carefully-aimed volleys in the direction of the spittoons set at strategic intervals on the floor.

Pop Masters twisted his heavy body uncomfortably inside his cramping overalls and glanced at the statuettes with his usual good humor. "Reckon I can sell these here dogs and cats and the funny duck for you, Asa. But them Washingtons and Napoleons you give me ain't been moving. Looks like people around Spanish ain't interested in no politics."

"You want one of them Hawaiian girls or them Mexicans riding a donkey, maybe?"

"They don't like no foreigners neither."

He moved down the counter until he was some distance from the others, then leaned over so that they could not hear. "I been thinking I ought to tell you something, Asa. It ain't none of my business. And that's why there's so many old men in Spanish, they minds their own business. But you just come, and I thought maybe you ought to know. That girl of yours has been seeing a-plenty of one of the young fellows around here. Some fellows'd be all right. But this here fellow, I hate to see a nice girl a-going with."

Two irregular whitish patches appeared in Captain Asa's bronzed cheeks as the blood slowly left his face. He stood motionless. "Who's . . . the . . . fellow?"

The storekeeper looked onto the porch where a half-dozen figures were standing, lazily exchanging the gossip of the day. "He's out there right now, case you're interested. Leaning on the barrel of potatoes. Pretty Boy, they calls him."

Captain Asa followed the other's glance. He saw a sallow, blond young man with a weak mouth and a feeble chin, dressed in a giddy sport shirt with a red handkerchief tucked around the collar, and tight-fitting riding pants thrust into embroidered cowboy boots—the costume affected by the more dandified young swampmen of the area. On one finger was a ring bearing a bulldog with a pair of ruby eyes; serving as the cuff links in his shirt was a pair of imitation dice.

The storekeeper continued in low tones. "Pretty Boy's always a-going with the Starkey gang, Asa. Them boys never do no honest work. Just steal logs other people cut, and make moonshine whisky. They're going to get into plenty of trouble one of these days. I wouldn't want nobody that run with them going with no girl of mine."

The patches in Captain Asa's cheeks had spread widely. His face was gray as the statuettes in the basket where the paint had been scraped away. "When . . . does she . . . meet him?"

"About five o'clock. Pretty near every day lately. Right in front of the store." He turned to serve a sunbonneted customer. "Yes'm. You buy some of that new feed for your horse, Mrs. Caney. I give my horse some and he run so fast, his shadow got too hot and had to set down and rest."

Captain Asa walked with numb steps out the door, and returned to the trailer.

The day passed slowly. Ula went about her tasks in high spirits, whistling and singing, her mood changing at times as she would be seized by a sullen spell of abstraction.

Captain Asa watched her with foreboding.

At four o'clock she ceased her work and put on her dress of the flaming red poppies, with the shiny red shoes and red belt to match. Fastening to the dress a cheap silver pin in the form of a deer, she arranged a new flower in her hair, and touched a lipstick to her mouth.

She looked with approval at the pert face that gazed back at her in half-a-dozen places from the defective mirror hanging near the door.

"Going to the store, Pa," she remarked gaily. "I'll get what we need and then go over to Dodie Johnson's. Her ma's been took kind of bad again with her stomach, and Dodie wants me to stay with her a while. I reckon I won't be back for supper."

She kissed him with hasty affection, and flounced whistling down the road. Captain Asa waited a moment, then followed, keeping in the trees so that he would not be visible. The dog attempted to come after. He ordered it back with a sharp command.

He left the main road when he neared the settlement, and took a short cut that brought him to the piles of lumber opposite the store, where unobserved he could watch any visitors. He saw the weak-mouthed young man leave his fellow loungers as Ula came hurrying down the street. Together they walked to a side road, where a muddy car with a raccoon tail hung over the radiator was parked under a tree. Captain Asa followed through the bushes.

Pretty Boy helped her into the car, keeping up a constant fire of flippant repartee. He was about to climb in beside her, when Captain Asa stepped into the roadway.

Ula started with fright, then grew rigid. Pretty Boy drew back in sullen defiance.

Captain Asa's face was ashen again, bloodless. His lips moved dully. "Where . . . you . . . a-going?"

They made no answer, staring at him in silence as though they were part of a plaster trio fashioned by the hand of some odd sculptor. Only the silver deer on Ula's dress rose and fell with her tense breathing.

A giant truck went past loaded with logs for the sawmill. An old Negro woman followed, leading a goat in the shafts of a child's wagon. Still the girl and her companion remained motionless.

The spell was broken at last. Pretty Boy fingered the rim of his cowboy hat and shifted uneasily. The defiance in his sallow face heightened. "I'm taking her over to Cypress. We're going dancing."

"Not as long as I'm a-living."

Pretty Boy's weak mouth curled in a sneer. "You can't stop her from going. She's nineteen. And a girl nineteen in this state don't have to listen to nobody."

He put his foot on the running board of the car.

Captain Asa took a step toward him. "I said she ain't going."

The trio grew rigid again as a boy with a ragged dog went past, carrying a homemade fishing pole. He gazed at them in wonder, and vanished down the road.

Ula came to sudden life. She tossed her head in anger. "Guess we won't go tonight, Pretty Boy."

She climbed down from the seat. Her companion shrugged his shoulders and mounted behind the wheel. The car sped away.

Ula began to walk with wrathful steps down the road. Her father came sternly to her side. Beneath the trees they made their way without speaking, Ula's dark face flushed with suppressed passion.

They reached the trailer.

Captain Asa's lips were grim. "Ain't any girl of mine going to run around with a no-count fellow like that. You ain't going to the store any more."

She turned her fiery black eyes upon him an instant, then swept without answer through the door.

Several weeks passed while he watched carefully for some sign of their meeting. He saw nothing, and heard no further reports of their being together. His anxiety passed. The episode seemed ended.

He returned near sunset one afternoon with Vergil from a fishing expedition, and saw to his surprise that Fernie was cooking the supper alone.

"Where's Ula?" he asked.

Fernie looked up from the batter for the corn bread she

was preparing. "She said she was going up to Miss Nettie's to get some eggs, Pa. Guess she'll be back in a little while."

Her voice was touched with nervousness. Captain Asa did not notice.

Half an hour passed. Ula did not return.

Captain Asa strode to the doorway, and looked up the muddy road. "She's taking a mighty long time with them eggs, ain't she, Fernie?"

The younger daughter drained the water from some steaming turnip-greens, and avoided his glance. "Miss Nettie always likes to keep you a-talking, Pa."

The sun set in splendor over the water. On a distant island two tall trees were bathed with unearthly light. Magnified by some odd reflection, they seemed like the entrance to a golden heaven. A flock of cranes hovered round them, with dazzling white wings, like angels awaiting entrance.

Captain Asa began to grow worried. He turned to his son, who was cleaning the barrel of his rifle. "Go up to Miss Nettie's and bring her home, will you, Vergil? I don't like her coming through the swamps in the dark."

Vergil nodded dreamily. "Plenty of things happen in them swamps."

He put away the rifle, and went up the road with the same long, shambling steps of his father.

Captain Asa began pacing up and down, at times toying with the glass ball where the red-cloaked girl stood before the church, waiting for an ever-threatening fall of snow.

Soon after Vergil appeared in the doorway.

The hesitation in his voice was more marked than ever. He spoke with obvious reluctance. "Miss Nettie says she ain't been there today."

The ornament in Captain Asa's fingers quivered, obscuring the red-cloaked figure and the church with a sudden feathery deluge. Round and round the tiny flakes whirled, settling lower and lower until only a few were left, revolving in ever-narrowing circles near the edge of the glass. He watched them as though hypnotized.

The last drifting flake sank into the white carpet at the bottom.

Captain Asa's lips moved numbly. "She's run off with him."

He stood staring into the twilight.

The son and the younger daughter, schooled in the stoicism of the mountains that represses any show of emotion in times of crisis, kept silent. But as they turned at intervals to glance toward him, their eyes were marked with the awkward helplessness of the young when confronted with tragedy.

Darkness fell, the heavy palpable darkness of the swamps, that seemed to cling like wavering veils about the trunks of the cypresses.

Fernie lit the lamp hanging overhead. Its rays brightly illumined her silvery hair. She stood near her father a moment as though without touching him she might warm him with her presence. She spoke in a gentle voice. "Maybe she's just gone to town, Pa."

He made no reply.

She went back to her cooking.

Some Negroes rowed past in a flatboat, with a flare sputtering at the stern. Soon after several other vessels followed, bound for a rendezvous across the lake, a church social or a catfish fry. The singing of black men and women drifted over the water, low, plaintive.

Fernie set some dishes on the table. "You better come and eat, Pa. You ought to be eating."

He continued to stand as though he did not hear.

Vergil put down the net he was repairing. The gauntness of his Indian-like face was accentuated in the shadows. "You got to eat, Pa."

The brother and sister took places at the table and waited, helpless again, unwilling to begin the meal.

Outside the insects gathered on the screens once more. Each window became a curtain of fluttering wings.

Two hunters strolled along the road, with lighted miners' lamps in their caps to catch the gleam of their quarry's eyes in the darkness. A wagon rattled past, filled with young girls bound for some festivity. Their merry voices echoed through the night.

Captain Asa's long body shifted at last. Stonily he moved to the doorway. "I'm going out to find 'em."

Vergil rose in haste from the table. "I'll go with you, Pa."

"I don't want . . . anybody a-going. . . . This ain't for nobody to do . . . but me."

He strode outside. The dog gazed at him a moment in hesitation, then followed.

Down the road he walked beside the lake, a giant golden bowl in the moonlight. He reached the settlement, deserted now, and saw the darkened store. Two figures were sitting on the porch. He questioned them, his words dull, toneless.

"I seen 'em, Asa," drawled the nearer of the two figures, a skinny little swampman with a wide patch of gauze taped onto one cheek, the result of a fight or an accident. "She come here about five o'clock, and they went off in his auto towards Cypress. He was carrying a suitcase. Way they acted they was up to something sure."

Captain Asa stared down the empty road. His eyes were glazed, lifeless, like the eyes of a man gone blind. "Anybody here . . . that'll get me over . . . to Cypress?"

The bandaged man shook his head with emphasis. "Ain't but half-a-dozen people drives that Cypress road in a auto, and they all went before six o'clock. Reckon there ain't nothing for you to do but walk it, unless you want to go back and get that nag of yours. It ain't but thirteen miles. That ain't nothing for a hill fellow like you."

"I'll walk it." He stepped from the porch into the road.

The other arose lazily. "I'll go with you to Alligator and pick up one of my traps. Lent it to Jap Perry and he ain't brought it back."

They set off into the night. The dog, delighted at the unexpected excursion, lost much of his gravity. He stood up at his full height to put his ragged brown paws on Captain Asa's chest a moment as though in thanks, rolled in a patch of grass before the sawmill, then followed with heavy playfulness at his master's heels.

They took a trail formed by two wagon ruts cut deep into the spongy clay. Dense canebrakes and groves of cypresses showed everywhere in the moonlight, with circling bats squeaking weirdly. Here and there a cabin appeared at the edge of a field of cotton, or a pasture where some cows munched in the darkness. Mosquitoes buzzed about their heads, and locusts shrilled in excited chorus. Crickets chirped in a crazy tremolo, and bullfrogs boomed in solemn accompaniment, like the beating of a thousand drums. Every leaf, every blade of grass seemed alive, vocal.

A giant turtle crossed the path and waddled off toward the underbrush.

The swampman tossed a pebble to hasten its progress.

"These here's sure funny times," he remarked. "People and animals acting mighty queer. Caught a turtle a couple of weeks ago and cut off its head and throwed it in the chicken yard. And before you could turn around pretty near, the head killed every chicken I had. Cut their throats just like it was a butcher knife."

He pulled out a few fraying threads from the patch of gauze on his cheek. "Everything's acting funny. Turtles and girls and everybody, I reckon. You just can't figure on anything. . . . Tell your dog to git his nose out of my hip pocket, Asa. He's a-trying to steal them gumdrops a fellow give me at the store. That dog looks like a preacher. But he's the stealingest hound I ever seen."

Captain Asa made no reply. His glazed eyes were fixed ever before him; his long legs swung in steady rhythm, as though they were the legs of an automaton with a new-wound spring.

The swampman grew silent. There came only the sound of the four tramping feet and the occasional rush of the dog as it crackled through the brush in pursuit of some unseen animal.

A cabin showed at a crossroads. Before it some beehives were silhouetted beneath a lofty pine.

The man with the patch burst into speech again. "This here's where I get off, Asa. Hear Jap's having plenty of trouble with his bees a-leaving. Guess it ain't as bad as the other side of Cypress, though. Hear them people lives over by the IC tracks are losing all their bees since them new fast trains they call the screaming lions started coming through. Bees'll follow a fast train or a fast auto every time."

He took a step toward the wooden gate. "Looks like bees ain't the only one'll follow an auto, neither. Looks like girls does it, too."

He vanished into the cabin.

Captain Asa plodded onward.

Mile after mile he trudged, his feet sometimes sinking into the sticky clay until it was above his ankles. His shoes, coated with endless layers of mud, had lost all trace of their former appearance. They seemed giant rolls of dough, ready for baking in some outdoor oven.

He was growing weary now, for he had been laboring since morning. His steps shortened. His feet began to ache painfully. A nail suddenly seemed to appear from nowhere in one of his shoes and began stabbing at his sole. He sat down at the roadside and hammered it with a stone. The pounding aided little. He walked slower and slower.

The trail led onto a highway, a narrow ribbon of concrete shining in the moonlight. He followed it with dull tread. Automobiles whirred past, and huge trucks with dazzling headlights that shadowed him monstrously against the pavement. The drivers honked in irate warning.

The lights of Cypress showed at a little distance. The highway became a street with a canvas sign stretched overhead, "Welcome To Cypress. Heart Of The Moss Country. But No Moss Grows On Us."

He reached the center of the little town, almost asleep at this hour, for it was nearing midnight. A single traffic light hung over the middle of the wide roadway. But it was dark, like the useless eye of a dead man, its functions ended. Here and there showed a scarlet glow marking a late restaurant or filling station. A stocky foreigner without a hat stood in a dim doorway, awaiting customers for the blackened bananas and the dusty soft-drink bottles on exhibition in the dingy window alongside. Before the shop was a peanut wagon with a thread of steam issuing from the top, whistling sleepily.

From a short distance down the road there came the playing of a raucous swing band. Captain Asa trudged toward it. The music was drifting out of a garishly illuminated two-story building that seemed to be a lodge room.

Cars were parked everywhere before it, black and blue and red and green, like giant colored beetles attracted by the light.

Captain Asa's lips tightened. His pace grew quicker.

He searched the street for the car of Pretty Boy, without success. Slowly he mounted the drab stairway, littered with burnt matches and cigarette stubs, that led to the dance hall. He stopped before a bored young man collecting tickets at the entrance, and looked beyond. A dizzying procession whirled past him; heads with short-clipped hair and heads with long flowing tresses, vivid-checked shirts and bright-flowered dresses; a merry-go-round of gay-clad young men and women, their arms and legs flying in every direction. A long time he watched and saw no familiar face. The dog waited beside him, looking at the dancers with solemn interest.

He trudged downstairs again.

A flickering neon arrow on a small building adjoining lit up the legend "Nick's Nook—College Cut Eats."

He went with the dog inside the glaring interior where some boisterous youths from the dance were eating, and questioned the squat, dour-visaged figure behind the counter. The other shrugged his shoulders.

Captain Asa ordered a cup of coffee. When it arrived, he sat before it without drinking.

In the corner a crippled old Negro waited on a stool, holding a battered guitar. Occasionally one of the diners would walk toward him and place a coin in a tin cup fixed to the handle. As though the donation pressed a button, the old man would burst into a shaky tune.

Two flashy-clad youths wearing green straw hats, each decorated with a small red feather, came in from the dance and sat down next to Captain Asa. They began to talk in loud voices.

A diner on his way out gave the old Negro some pennies. The musician's withered hand plucked the strings a moment. His high-pitched voice began to quaver out the doleful refrain of *Never Believe*:

You can't never believe
What a young man tells you,
Unless he's on the gallows
And wishing he was down.

The green-hatted youths buried themselves in massive chunks of cocoanut pie, and talked louder.

The elder of the two, his lean face lined with dissipation, winked lasciviously at his companion. "Boy, that was a hot mama I had at the dance last week. Wild one. From back in them swamps. Boy, she was double hot."

His red-haired companion lit a cigarette and let it hang flippantly. "Them swamp ones is the hottest there is when you can find 'em. But you got to do plenty of looking. . . . You going back to the dance?"

"Nope. Didn't see nobody that was hot."

Captain Asa went outside. Down the street he wandered dazedly. The dog, sensing the unusual, began to gaze at him in grave anxiety.

He heard of a tourist camp at the edge of town, and rang the night bell where a torn paper blind afforded a view of the drab office within. A florid woman clad in a cotton bathrobe appeared, angry at being awakened. He learned nothing.

He walked through the streets again. The music in the dance hall had ceased. The neon glows here and there in the town had faded. Only the lights in the restaurant were still burning. The hatless foreigner had locked up his blackened bananas, and was pushing the peanut wagon slowly along the curb in the hope of meeting some prosperous wayfarer. In the quiet of the night the faint hissing seemed loud as the whistle of a locomotive.

The courthouse showed ahead, a shadowy-domed building encircled by some towering cottonwoods. In the basement Captain Asa could see the police station, where a fat officer sat drowsing over a desk. He hesitated, then moved near the doorway to enter. As he did so he caught sight of the bleak detention room at the rear, separated from the officer by an iron-barred door. In the cell a young woman was sitting forlornly, her head bowed on her hands.

He shuddered, and resumed his solitary walking, hurrying forward whenever he saw a group of young men and women returning from a late party, now and then stopping before some tourist home and gazing at the curtained windows.

Dawn began to touch the eastern sky. It grew light rapidly. He was nearing exhaustion. As he trudged on, he found himself in front of the restaurant again, the neon arrow pale in the dawn. He went inside.

The shiny stools were empty now. The dour figure behind the counter was cleaning the coffee boiler. Captain Asa sat down at a table and ordered a hamburger. His eyes followed hypnotically as the counterman's reddened hands moved back and forth, polishing the nickeled metal with a cloth. His graying head drooped onto his chest. He slept.

The dog stretched out between his chair and the door, where it could protect him from any who might enter. A long time it lay there, mounting a worried guard.

A clock somewhere in the town struck the hour. The gloomy counterman walked to the table and shook the sleeper's arm. Captain Asa wakened with a start. He looked out the window.

The morning was well advanced. Cypress had begun its daily activities. Negroes were sweeping in front of the stores and splashing buckets of water over the narrow pavements. A farm wagon, loaded with vegetables, creaked past on the way to market.

Mechanically he ate the hamburger still untouched on the plate before him, and gave another to the dog.

The counterman took his money, and answered his new questions with a grunt. "Try the other tourist camp. Mile and a half from town."

Captain Asa stumbled outside.

He reached the camp at last, a collection of shabby cottages built around a spreading live oak. Before one of the buildings stood the muddy car with the raccoon tail hung over the radiator. His body grew taut.

He approached the cottage, and halted. Within, above the rattle of dishes, he could hear Ula chattering happily and the answering voice of Pretty Boy in his labored repartee. Through the window came the crisp smell of frying bacon.

Captain Asa knocked dully.

The conversation inside halted, and there came the sound of a shifting chair. Pretty Boy appeared in the doorway wearing his cowboy costume, his pasty face framed with a night's growth of stubbly blond hair. He saw the visitor. His cheeks went ashen.

Beyond him Captain Asa could distinguish the seedy interior, the red sofa sagging deep in the middle, the green-upholstered chair, scarred with cigarette burns and countless boot heels.

At a table Ula was sitting in a brilliant flowered kimono, serving breakfast. She looked at the weary figure standing on the step. The spoon with which she was helping some hominy grits dropped slowly to the dish. She arose and joined her companion at the doorway. They stood in silence.

Pretty Boy's dismay suddenly changed to bravado. An attempt at a smile touched his weak mouth.

"You can't do nothing, Pa," he said. "Ula and me's got married."

CHAPTER FOUR

A SUDDEN tenderness swept Ula's dark face. She stepped outside and took her father's arm. "You look terrible tired, Pa. Come in and I'll get you a cup of coffee."

He stood hesitant, a weary automaton whose spring had run down, then plodded with her through the drab entrance.

He slumped into a seat at the table.

Ula filled a cup from the steaming pot on the stove, then put some slices of bacon in a frying pan. Constantly as she moved about the room, she turned to gaze at him with anxiety.

She spoke again, her voice a mixture of embarrassment and pride. "We was married in Cypress last night, Pa. We was coming over this afternoon to tell you. . . . Don't be mad, Pa."

Captain Asa sipped the coffee in silence.

The bacon began to sizzle. The dog, waiting beyond the screen, gave a single impatient scratch on the wire. Pretty Boy let it come inside, and glancing at Captain Asa doubtfully, fed it some scraps from the table. The dog accepted the gift with its usual gravity.

Pretty Boy sat down with some nervousness opposite his father-in-law, and continued his unfinished breakfast. He began making studied efforts at politeness, trying to anticipate the visitor's wants at the table.

He spoke with a labored attempt at jocularity. "You should have been at the wedding, Pa. The fellow that done it was sure a card. He's the one they calls the Laughing Judge. Guess you seen some of them big write-ups about him in the paper. All the time he was doing the marrying he kept saying things 'd make you bust your sides laughing pretty near. 'This hurts you two worse than it does me,' he says. And when he finished, he says, 'You're hooked for life, Adam. Kiss him, Eva.' And 'course them ain't our real names at all. He was sure a card."

Ula set a plate of bacon and eggs on the cloth. "Eat these here while they're hot. . . . You ain't going to be mad, are you, Pa?"

Captain Asa made no reply. But soon after he picked up a fork and began to eat slowly.

Ula watched with pleasure.

Pretty Boy went out to the automobile for a package of cigarettes.

Ula followed him with loving eyes. "You'll like him fine when you know him, Pa. He's a wonderful fellow." She came to her father's side, and studied him a moment. "Don't you go to feeling bad, Pa. Things ain't going to be any different. I'll come over every day and make coffee for you. And I'll cut your hair and everything. Just the same as I done before."

His dreary face brightened a little. "Ain't nobody can cut my hair like you without pulling."

He ate with more appetite.

Pretty Boy appeared with the cigarettes.

Ula's voice was touched with pride again. "He gave me a wonderful wedding present, Pa."

At her request the groom took off the piano scarf thrown over a bulky object in the corner, revealing an ornate juke box enameled in vivid red and orange, with a series of glass tubes fringing the edges. Pretty Boy clicked the electric switch. The instrument became an exploding rainbow. Long bubbles appeared everywhere in the glass tubes and began rising in endless fountains of changing light. The room was filled with musical thunder.

Pretty Boy beamed with satisfaction. "The fellow owns the pool hall in town bought it. But when it come he wanted a bigger one, and he said he'd sell this one cheap. Me and Ula both likes music and dancing. And we was figuring on getting a phonograph. You can't get no finer kind of phonograph than a juke box. So I told him we'd take it."

He played a few selections.

Ula washed the dishes, then went into the bathroom to dress.

Captain Asa and Pretty Boy sat in awkward silence. The son-in-law took a stick and began cleaning some mud from his embroidered boots.

There came a knock outside.

Pretty Boy arose hastily. "Guess that's the fellow I asked to take our pictures."

The newcomer entered, a timid little man with seedy clothes and a shiny bald head. He was carrying a battered camera.

Ula, fully dressed now, came out to join the others.

The photographer set up his apparatus and began bobbing in and out the black cloth covering the camera, like a shabby jack-in-the-box.

He spoke in a timorous voice that carried an air of permanent apology. "We got the plain black and white, they're six dollars for six. And we got what they call the sepia, they're eight dollars. And we got what they call the natural tone, they cost ten. They're all in colors. Everybody in Cypress gets the natural tone for the wedding pictures. I guess that's the kind you're wanting, too."

Pretty Boy drew himself up with dignity. "We don't want nothing but the best there is."

Ula nodded in agreement.

The photographer adjusted the tripod nervously. "How you want to take 'em? Sitting or standing?"

Ula gazed at her husband a moment. Her face lighted with new tenderness. "Mama when she was married had her picture took standing by the wedding present Pa give her—that was her sewing machine. I'd like ours took in front of the juke box."

The photographer arranged them before the instrument and snapped several poses.

Ula turned to Captain Asa. "You get in one of the pictures, too, Pa."

He shook his head.

Pretty Boy urged him on with joviality. He consented at last, and awkwardly stationed himself between the bride and groom.

The photographer departed.

The newlyweds hastened to pack up their belongings. Captain Asa helped Pretty Boy move the juke box to the back of the car.

They set off toward the lake.

Ula's concern over her father vanished as she saw the color returning to his face. As they sat all three packed tight in the front seat, she began to chatter gaily. "We're going to live in Pretty Boy's house back of the sawmill, Pa. He's going to fix it up beautiful. He's going to get me a piano, and a cherry living-room set with what they call a love seat. The love seat's a kind of chair just for two, with two Cupids painted on it, a boy and a girl Cupid, and a big heart on the back. We picked out the set last night in the window of the furniture store in Cypress. We're sure going to be living in style."

They neared the trailer. Fernie and Vergil saw the car approaching, and hurried outside.

They received the news with the stoic acceptance of the mountains.

Captain Asa sat down with the bride and groom in the trailer. He turned to Vergil and Fernie standing near the doorway. "They took me in the wedding picture," he announced. "It's what they call the natural tone."

The newlyweds remained talking for a little while, then drove away.

Several weeks passed. Each day as Ula had promised, she came on a visit. At times Pretty Boy accompanied her, always bringing some showy present, a box of cheap candy or an ornate cushion cover. He was making a determined attempt to win the favor of his father-in-law, as though in fulfillment of some promise to his wife. Dutifully he would listen as Captain Asa took down the volume of photographs of the St. Louis Fair, and explained in detail the Exposition's wonders. All evening he would sit playing seven-up or Chinese checkers with the family, and try to conceal his restlessness.

He was even polite when refusing to join them at church. "Lived till I was fifteen with my uncle up in Arkansas was a Holy Roller preacher," he would remark. "I jumped and I hollered and I talked in tongues ever since I was five years old. I had enough churching for a couple of fellows."

But he would evade all inquiries as to the source of his income. If Captain Asa mentioned the matter to Ula, she would flare up angrily in his defense. Her father soon learned it was better to keep silent.

A few more weeks went by, and a gradual alteration began to take place in Pretty Boy's manner. His old swagger was again noticeable. He grew more and more self-conscious when he came to call. Often there would be long periods of uncomfortable silence. His visits, and those of Ula as well, grew less and less frequent.

It was early summer now. Captain Asa and Vergil went about their tasks, fishing, and occasionally going off to earn a few dollars cutting timber for the nearby logging camps. Fernie took care of the household alone, looking after the little garden, or mothering the hen and her hungry brood.

The lake was at the height of its beauty. Each evening the sun would sink in crimson splendor, till the surface of the water as though by a miracle seemed turned to wine. Often the glow would scarcely have died away when a huge moon would rise over the swamp, touching the tops of the moss-covered cypresses with silvery light, until they resembled white-haired old witches gathered to weave some evil spell.

The lake was dotted with fishermen, chanting in unison

as they raised their nets. The forests resounded with the axes of the loggers. Money flowed freely. And as so often follows in primitive regions, with the money there came crime—an epidemic of robberies in the lumber camps and the nearby settlements. The owners of several crossroad stores were attacked and a sawmill pay roll was stolen. The moss buyer and a trader buying skins had each picked up a stranger asking for a ride, and been almost murdered for their kindness. Ugly rumors began to drift about the lake. The swampmen grew bitter.

Captain Asa went to Pop Masters' store one afternoon to make his usual purchases. The proprietor was serving a gaunt countrywoman. When the customer had gone, he leaned across the counter.

His manner was solemn. "I been waiting a couple of days to tell you, Asa. You better talk to that son-in-law of yours. He's going to get into awful trouble if he don't watch out."

Captain Asa looked up from the dried peas he was examining. "How . . . you . . . meaning?"

"I'm meaning that people around here's just getting tired of them Starkeys, that's all. Everybody figures it's them a-doing all this robbing. About one more holdup and something's going to happen. I'm telling you 'cause I like you, and 'cause I figure Pretty Boy ain't natural bad like them others. He's just a show-off, thinks he's smart 'cause he makes good money moonshining. But if he keeps going with them others, he'll get the same medicine. I just thought you'd like to know."

Captain Asa filled the bag with the peas, and put it on the scales. "He's a-coming to the house tonight. . . . I'll try a-talking to him. . . . But don't look like him and me's doing so good any more."

Soon after he left the store.

The newlyweds arrived after supper. Ula began helping Fernie finish a bedspread. Captain Asa motioned to Pretty Boy to come outside. He spoke gravely as they stood under the trees.

Pretty Boy listened with an uneasy air. He dug the toe of an embroidered boot into the bark of a rotting log. "Don't you worry none about me, Pa. Pretty Boy always gets along."

They went back into the trailer.

At the sight of Ula, Pretty Boy's bravado returned. His glance chanced to light on the phonograph near the window. Lifting out the worn record lying on the turntable, he held it up before the others.

"Show you a trick a fellow done yesterday down at the pool hall in Cypress," he announced.

He whipped out his knife, and despite Captain Asa's protestations, quickly widened the hole in the center until it was the shape of an egg instead of a circle. Returning the disk to the instrument, he cranked the handle. There came the nasal voice of a singer, ludicrous, unintelligible, wavering like the voice of the hero in a Chinese opera.

Pretty Boy chuckled at his accomplishment.

Captain Asa winced with pain. "That there record's *Sparrow on the Mountain*. It's my favorite."

Vergil's Indian-like face flushed darkly. "You oughtn't have done that, Pretty Boy."

A coldness fell over the company. Ula and her husband went off to their home.

Captain Asa shifted the record on the turntable so that its position was normal once more. He played it again and again, listening intently.

He shook his head.

From that time on the visits of the couple became a rarity. Two weeks passed with no sign of Ula's appearance. When she came at last she seemed aloof, distant.

Captain Asa's graying head began to grow ragged. With no word spoken, as he was dozing one evening in a chair, Fernie took the scissors and began to cut his hair.

The wave of crime continued. There came a new robbery and another. The mood of the dwellers along the lake grew ominous. Whenever two fishermen or loggers met they talked in low tones.

There was the tapping of a cane on the path leading to the trailer one afternoon, followed by a knock on the door. Going to answer it, Captain Asa saw the blind man who lived nearby, accompanied by his sad-eyed wife.

They sat down on the chairs Captain Asa brought forward.

With slow-moving fingers the blind visitor laid his stick on the floor, and set his miner's cap on his knees. He spoke with hesitation. "They had a meeting last night, Asa."

The host arranged a bowl of fruit on the table. "What kind . . . of meeting?"

"You know the kind. Out in the swamp. When there's going to be trouble." He felt an orange in the dish, and placed it on the cloth. "It's coming mighty quick, Asa. You'd better tell him to get away."

Captain Asa put down two faded napkins, and waited for the other to continue.

The blind man peeled the orange slowly with a knife. "There's good people and there's bad people around here, Asa, way there is everywhere else. Most of 'ems all right, way I figure it. But when something like this happens, things just go kind of black, I reckon, and they can't see nothing.

Then it's them that's blind. It ain't the people like me."

A bee lighted on a bright-polished apple, and began to sip some hidden nectar.

Captain Asa let it remain. "I ain't seen him for a month . . . pretty near. . . . Nor her neither."

"If I was you . . . I'd go see 'em."

Soon after he fumbled his way to the door.

A great buzzard that had been resting on the steps flew off toward the swamp.

The blind man's wife watched it with sadness. "Going to be somebody dying. When a buzzard sits before your door, that's sure somebody a-dying."

The cane tapped down the path.

Captain Asa sat for a while in reflection, then arose and made his way to the cottage near the sawmill where his daughter and her husband were living. He found Pretty Boy standing on the back porch, talking with two unpleasant-faced strangers. They slunk off as he entered.

Ula had gone on an errand to town. Captain Asa told his son-in-law of the blind man's warning.

Pretty Boy's weak mouth hardened. "Mind your own business, Pa," he answered curtly.

Captain Asa walked away.

He was asleep in his bunk a few nights later, when he awakened suddenly with a consciousness that someone was moving in the bushes. He sat up, and peered through the window. He could see nothing unusual by the light of the full moon shining overhead, only the gloomy silhouettes of the cypresses. He walked to the doorway, his long nightshirt flapping about his legs, and looked for the dog, who generally slept at the threshold. But the animal was away on some nocturnal excursion.

The crackling noise in the brush was repeated, seeming

closer than before. Captain Asa stepped outside. With difficulty he could distinguish a vague shadow crouching under a spreading cottonwood.

"Who's there?" he called sharply.

The shadow advanced a little. A feminine voice called in low tones. "It's me, Pa. Ula."

She hurried forward. Her breath was coming in gasps, as though she had been running.

He let her into the trailer. She stood a moment, unable to speak, her breathing still so agitated it seemed close to suffocation.

Captain Asa moved to the lamp and struck a match.

"Don't light no light, Pa."

He could see her in sharp detail by the tiny flame, her pretty face and lustrous dark hair decorated with a flower. She was gray with terror.

Vergil was awake now, and was sitting in his bunk, his lithe body clad only in pajama trousers. Beyond him at the edge of the curtain that formed her bedroom, Fernie had appeared, wearing a cheap kimono.

The match went out, with an acrid smell of sulphur.

Captain Asa set the burned fragment on the table. "It's . . . about Pretty Boy . . . ain't it?"

She nodded slowly.

"Where . . . is . . . he?"

"He's outside. . . . You got to save him, Pa."

"Why they . . . after him?"

Her breathing came with difficulty again. "It wasn't his fault, Pa. . . . He didn't do nothing. . . . He didn't have no idea where they was going."

"What . . . they . . . done?" His voice was cold, insistent.

When she answered her words were so low they seemed

almost lost in the croaking of the frogs beyond the window. "They held up a store. . . . The man . . . wouldn't give 'em his money. . . . And before Pretty Boy could stop 'em . . . one of the fellows . . . shot his pistol."

Captain Asa's tall body stiffened. In the moonlight, with his long nightshirt, he seemed like a stern-robed prophet of the ancients awaiting some gloomy decree of the Lord. "Who's . . . the . . . shot man?"

"It's Pop Masters. . . . They says . . . he's dying."

The prophet quivered, as though under a blow from the heavens.

A great white moth that had flown in when the door was opened came to rest on Ula's shoulder. For a moment it seemed merely another ornament, like the deer-shaped pin flashing dully on her dress. "You got to save him, Pa. The Starkeys all run away. He ain't got nobody to help him but you."

"I ain't got no call to save a murderer."

The moth drifted off and began fluttering against a screen.

From the settlement down the lake there arose a faint shouting, followed by the excited barking of dogs. Through the window they could see the glare of far-off torches, reflected fantastically in the water. The torches increased.

Captain Asa stared off into the night. "What they a-doing?"

'They're getting ready . . . for a . . . lynching."

The rigidity of the prophet was broken. He lit a candle-lantern, and shielding it on a shelf so that the faint glow would not be visible beyond the windows, took down his worn Bible. He began turning the pages, as though he were searching for counsel.

Fernie came forward soundlessly in her kimono. Her childish face, framed with its silvery hair, was resolute.

"He's her husband, Pa. You can't let your own family be took away for a lynching."

There came a new noise in the bushes. Vergil caught up his rifle and hurried to the door. He saw nothing, and turned to his father, his body, still naked above the waist, gleaming like polished metal. "It's the way Fernie says. He's kin to us, Pa."

Captain Asa continued to thumb the tattered volume.

Ula looked at him with hesitation, then went outside. She returned in a moment, followed by her husband. His tight-fitting riding pants bore a long tear as though from a barbed-wire fence. His fancy cowboy boots were spattered with mud. All trace of his bravado, his flippancy had vanished. The natural pastiness of his skin had heightened. As he stood with Ula near the candle, he seemed the color of the sooty tallow spreading farther and farther over the tin holder.

From the distance there came the barking of dogs once more.

Pretty Boy hurried to the window and gazed fixedly toward the sound. His bloodless lips began a spasmodic twitching.

Captain Asa listened as the outcry of the dogs continued. "They got the bloodhounds?"

Pretty Boy shook his head. "Ain't got 'em yet. . . . They was bringing some . . . from Hardwood."

The torches down the lake grew in number until they formed a wide arc along the shore. Mirrored on the still surface, they resembled the campfires of some invading army, preparing an attack.

The great moth fluttered about the trailer again, and drifted near the candle. Closer and closer it circled, then suddenly flew into the sputtering wick. Its body flamed an instant, then fell to the table a blackened cinder, its burned wings wrapped about it like funeral robes. There came an unpleasant smell of burning.

Captain Asa shuddered.

There was a faint whimpering at the door as the grave dog returned from its wanderings. Vergil let it come inside. A moment later there was a muffled sound of tramping feet. The dog began a low growling.

Pretty Boy's eyes glazed with horror.

Captain Asa extinguished the candle. He strode out beneath the trees. Vergil took the rifle and followed.

Near the water some Negroes were walking in silence. At their head was a wrinkled old black man who lived in a cabin at the edge of the swamp. The Negroes drew back as they saw the rifle, huddling together like frightened sheep before an oncoming storm. A woman began a doleful praying.

The old Negro recognized his neighbors. He came forward nervously. His black skin in the moonlight possessed an odd greenish color, as though his face were coated with sulphur.

"They're a-hunting niggers tonight, ain't they, Captain?"

"They're a-hunting . . . white men."

The torches down the water began to form a circle, as though surrounding some speaker delivering a harangue.

The old Negro followed the movement with anxious eyes. "We better go on up the river way we was figuring. We'll git us a rowboat and go out on one of them islands till they quiets down. Even if they're a-hunting white men, they always ends up killing niggers."

They continued along the road.

Captain Asa and Vergil returned to the trailer.

The dogs down the lake burst into a new uproar.

Captain Asa turned to Pretty Boy, whose face was pressed against the screen. "When the hounds come they'll track you here sure. . . . We'll start a-traveling."

With Vergil he harnessed the horse, grazing drowsily in a patch of grass. The girls hastened to bring in the clothes on a washline. Fernie glanced with indecision at the hen and the three young chickens roosting in the coop, then put them, clucking sleepily, into a market basket, and carried it to the trailer.

Captain Asa climbed into the driver's seat. The girls mounted beside him, with Vergil at the outside, gripping his rifle. Pretty Boy dropped onto the floor behind, where he would not be visible to any passerby. They set off down the road.

Along the shore the vehicle lumbered, the wheels creaking in steady rhythm. The torches vanished. The barking of the dogs grew still. Captain Asa took out a stogie and began to smoke. The face of Pretty Boy lost some of its pallor.

Suddenly from the distance there came a melancholy baying. The dog, stretched at Captain Asa's feet, raised its head and began to howl in mournful sympathy.

Captain Asa took a slow puff of his stogie. "They've got the hounds."

He drove the horse faster.

The torches reappeared down the lake, dancing magically on the water, like lanterns set out for a carnival.

The baying of the dogs changed, becoming quick, nervous. The torches shifted and formed a long, wavering line, advancing from the dark horizon.

Vergil watched with stoicism. "They've done found the trail."

The pallor of Pretty Boy returned once more.

Captain Asa's stogie went out.

The road left the lake, and entering a swamp, approached the first of the gloomy tunnels where the funereal pendants of moss hung down from the mourning trees. The trailer plunged inside. The hoofs of the horse splashed heavily in the muddy road.

The smell of the swamp grew overpowering. Great water lilies lay rotting all about, floating on pools of slime; the twisting cypress knees rose uglily from the mud, like serpents drowned in some oozing flood. Giant toadstools flattened beneath the wheels of the trailer, leaving on the rims a curious odor as of poison.

Overhead the trunks of the trees rose like a grim cathedral for some eerie Devil's mass. Cicadas chanted shrilly, like the voices of celebrants before the Satanic altar. Frogs croaked in metallic chorus, like phantom worshipers beating on bronze drums. In the distance owls hooted, like demon elders chanting their responses.

They entered a second tunnel and another. They were near the river now. Often through a break in the trees they could see the wide stream glowing in the moonlight.

A fox barked weirdly in the distance. A great eagle-like bird, roused from its sleep, flew up suddenly, flapping its huge wings like a monstrous ghost.

Far down the road there sounded the sputtering of an automobile.

Captain Asa listened. "They're a-coming."

Vergil's hand went to his rifle. "They seen the wagon tracks."

Captain Asa lit the stogie again.

There was another gap in the cypresses, affording a new glimpse of the river. Some recently-cut timber lay along the bank.

Captain Asa brought the horse to a halt. He turned to Pretty Boy. "You better do the same as the darkies. Get on one of them logs, and go down the river. Only way the hounds can't track you."

The automobile in the distance came nearer. Pretty Boy rose from his cramped seat, and held Ula in his arms an instant. He vanished in the shadows.

The horse trudged onward.

The sputtering of the automobile was close at hand. The dazzling rays from its lamps began to brighten the hanging moss. The sound of the motor became a deafening roar, echoing like thunder in the moisture-laden air. The car swept past, braking to a sudden halt a few yards down the road. Half-a-dozen booted men descended, carrying rifles. Their gaunt figures were starkly silhouetted against the blinding glare of the headlights. They advanced toward the trailer in silence, the shining barrels of their rifles like the spears of lion hunters circling for the kill.

One figure separated itself from the others, the tall, grizzled man wearing a coonskin cap who had brought the rowboat on the day of Captain Asa's arrival. Slowly he came forward, his eyes glassy now, his skin possessing the peculiar waxiness of ordinary men turned executioner.

He halted at the wheel.

"We done come for him, Asa." He spoke in low tones, in strange contrast with his threatening rifle.

The stogie in Captain Asa's mouth glowed and darkened with his breathing. The dog sat tense, quivering, gazing at its master with a questioning air, as though seeking to know whether to attack these strange invaders. Captain Asa caressed its shaggy sides. A burr entangled in its hair scratched against his fingers. Mechanically he twisted it free. The dog winced a little.

Captain Asa dropped the burr beyond the seat. "Pretty Boy ain't here."

"Where is he?"

"I ain't a-telling."

The man in the coonskin cap went off for a conference with the others.

Captain Asa descended with Vergil from the seat. He stood smoking, watching an occasional spark from the stogie blacken as it struck the wet grass.

The man wearing the coonskin cap came forward again with the others. They strode toward the trailer entrance.

Vergil's grip on his rifle tightened.

The face of the grizzled leader showed no change. "Don't try to stop us, Asa. We don't want no trouble."

At a word from his father, Vergil moved away.

The swampmen tramped inside, directing their flashlights into every corner. Captain Asa looked on grimly from the doorway.

The leader returned his flashlight to a pocket of his trousers. "You done wrong to help him get away, Asa."

"He didn't do it. And I don't hold with a lynching."

"That's what them other two said when we caught 'em, they didn't do it. But Pop's a-dying just the same."

A burly figure with a heavy red beard and red mustache nodded in assent. His eyes possessed the same glassy quality as the grizzled chief. "We'll catch him soon as the hounds come. Then we'll have the three."

They waited near their automobile, its motor still running, its headlights surrounded by twin clouds of mosquitoes. On the water, visible through the trees, the distant river beacons twinkled peacefully.

Two other cars roared through the blackness, open trucks filled with more men in muddy boots and overalls. They leaped to the ground. A moment later a sleepy-eyed rustic descended, followed by a trio of hounds with droopy heads and expressions so melancholy they seemed on the verge of weeping. The animals began to sniff the damp soil, the sleepy-eyed individual encouraging them in drawling phrases. Dogs and master swung down the road, pursuing the tracks of the trailer. The others took torches and hurried after.

The horse in the shafts shied at the leaping flares, and whinnied in alarm. Captain Asa took the reins.

The girls joined their father, watching the hounds as they zigzagged through the bushes. The silver deer on Ula's dress was still.

The dogs halted, and baying hoarsely, sped off toward the river.

The truck pulled close to the trailer, as though to bar any attempt at escape. In the nearest vehicle, Captain Asa could see two young men lying on the floor, their faces hidden by the wide gags tied about their mouths, their bodies trussed with ropes, like captive animals brought in from the wilderness. Only their eyes moved, desperate, imploring.

Two men holding rifles sat on the tail of the truck as guards, one a stunted individual with a pointed, weasel-like face, the other a paunchy rustic wearing a leather shirt whose collar cut deep into his fat neck.

One of the prisoners moved a little. The weasel-like man gave the prostrate figure a vicious kick. He offered the other guard a plug of tobacco. "What you figure they're going to do with 'em soon as they catch the other fellow, Lonnie?"

The paunchy man cut off a generous fragment with his knife. "Take 'em out in the swamp. To the Blue Hole."

The weasel-like figure nodded in approval. "Don't need no rope when you use the Blue Hole."

The paunchy one returned the plug to its owner. "Ain't no chance of them detectives bothering you, neither. 'Cause they can't never find no body."

The weasel-like man pried off the tin star on the tobacco with his fingernail. "The Hole's plenty better than hanging. When they hung that nigger up at Hardwood, them detectives was fooling around for a month pretty near. Things in this state is getting mighty bad."

They chewed steadily.

The baying of the hounds in the distance grew louder. There came the voice of the sleepy-eyed rustic giving sharp commands.

The weasel-faced man listened. His tiny eyes grew bright with expectation. "What about putting all them pairs of overalls on 'em, the way they done with them two niggers up at Whetstone? You put six pairs of overalls on each of 'em, and then you get a bucket of gasoline, and you don't need nothing else but a match."

The paunchy one shook his head. "You just use the overalls when it's a nigger harms a woman. And six pairs of overalls costs a heap of money. Don't cost nothing when you put 'em in the Hole."

The baying of the dogs mounted to a frenzy, then suddenly ceased. There came the murmur of angry voices. The torches began circling back toward the halted automobiles.

The bloodhounds came slinking down the road, staying in the shadows as though anxious to avoid notice, their drooping heads seeming more doleful than before. Their crestfallen master piled them into the truck with the guards.

"Got away on the river," he mumbled in apology.

The animals sniffed at the mute captives on the floor. The weasel-faced man kicked them away.

The moon was down. Only the stars shone in the black canopy of the sky, mirrored faintly in the tree-shadowed water. A towboat drifted past, like a smoky specter. There came flashes of a Negro, naked to the waist, tossing coal into a firebox. The vessel vanished around a wall of cypresses. Somewhere on an island lost in the darkness a cow mooed sadly. There came the faint crowing of a rooster.

The red-bearded man looked off at the sky. "Going to get morning."

The grizzled leader in the coonskin cap nodded. "Sheriff or some of them people 'll be coming over from Cypress. We better take the two we got."

He climbed up beside the guards. The cars roared off into the distance.

The sound of the motors died. There arose again the mournful symphony of the swamp, the calling of the whip-poorwill and the melancholy hooting of the owl, the booming bass of the frogs and the shrill tremolo of the cicadas, the cry of the fox and the grunt of the wild hog, the voices of all the creatures of this lost world where man had yet to prove his mastery.

Captain Asa climbed wearily to his old seat on the trailer. He picked up the reins. "I ain't going to stay here any more," he said.

The others mounted beside him. The vehicle lumbered over the spongy clay.

The river vanished as the trail turned inland. The cypresses ended, giving way to a low tangle of palmetto and cane stretching off to the distance. Far up the road they could see the automobiles halted once more. From the glow surrounding them like a luminous mist fragments of light broke away, becoming torches and lanterns. Assembling in an irregular line, they began moving across the black swamp, like will-o'-the-wisps borne by phantom marchers to some ghostly rendezvous. Slowly they wound off toward the horizon, growing fainter and fainter.

They merged into the stars.

CHAPTER FIVE

MORNING CAME, with the swamp still stretching out to the horizon. The trailer rolled on.

Vergil, who had been dozing a moment, sat up and rubbed his eyes. "Where we heading now, Pa?"

Captain Asa gazed across the somber landscape. He studied the tattered road map in his hand. "We'll go down to Baton Rouge and then out towards Texas. There's plenty of old-time people over that way, they says."

Day after day they traveled, past Tunica and Baton Rouge and beyond the Mississippi, past Plaquemine and Thibodaux and the wild Atchafalaya.

They were in the Cajun country now. Tiny French villages appeared, where bearded old men argued excitedly over cups of pungent coffee. In the fields Negroes sweated beneath the sun, cutting the waving sugar cane. Along the bayous tugboats chugged laboriously, pushing barges loaded with yams and watermelons. Now and then near the shore there arose the curious, too-sweetish odor that marked a sugar mill.

Little by little the shock of the night in the swamps lessened and the old pattern of life on the trailer returned. Captain Asa recovered much of his former cheerfulness. Fernie found it impossible to keep the chickens when traveling, and giving them to a poor old woman along the road, devoted herself to the duties of the household. Vergil obtained an old automobile carburetor from the proprietor of a gas station, and taking it apart, made a close study of its operation. But Ula showed no interest in the concerns of the family. Her gaiety had vanished. Each day as before she made up her dark face, and penciled her already black brows. But the act was now automatic, without meaning.

Occasionally as they stopped before a courthouse in some little town, Captain Asa would see her gaze at the row of handbills tacked up on a board where under the legend, "Wanted—Reward," appeared the photographs of some fugitives from the law, their faces so distorted they bore no likeness to humanity. Each time as she turned from one sullen countenance to look at its gloomy neighbor, she would tremble a little, as though afraid of coming upon a too-familiar face.

The road was running close to the Gulf. Flocks of seagulls drifted over hazy salt marshes, and solitary man-of-war birds flew in stately circles. Now and then a bayou would widen into a great bay, and a ship would rise in startling silhouette as it lay anchored at a dilapidated wharf—some rusty tramp steamer loading cargo for the Indies.

Shrimp fishermen rowed in tiny boats, bringing their catches to the little houses erected on stilts along the shore. Everywhere along the horizon lay spectacular clouds, towering in snowy layers, like mountains of cotton.

Each morning Fernie and her father would take baskets filled with the statuettes and bedspreads and go off to one of the pleasant little cottages that lay back from the road. The men or women who answered their knock were cordial, hospitable, offering them coffee and the rich fruits of the luxuriant countryside. But often they spoke only French. The travelers' sales were few.

Their scanty funds began to diminish.

They stopped at a little grocery where a row of slot machines stood against the wall. Vergil studied them for a long interval, then played three coins, and lost in quick succession.

Captain Asa looked on in disapproval. "You can't beat them machines, Vergil."

The dreaminess of the son's face heightened. "That machine on the end's about ready to pay off, Pa. You said our money's getting low. If I hit the jackpot, I'll win us a thousand nickels."

He dropped a new coin into the slot. It went the way of its predecessors.

They were eating supper a few hours later, when Ula suddenly arose from the table. Going to the back of the trailer, she wrote a letter, though she did not tell the others its contents. Soon after, whenever they halted, she would hurry downtown, and ask eagerly if there was any mail.

They stopped one afternoon along a bayou, and went inside the frame post office leaning perilously on the bank. Captain Asa picked up a pen and began addressing a printed post card to the company that sold the statuettes. Ula went off to make her usual inquiry at the window, where the fine-lined head of a Cajun grandmother showed like an old-fashioned portrait.

The woman searched for some moments, then extracted a letter from a pile and passed it through the window.

Ula took it with a trembling hand. Quickly she tore open the envelope. For the first time in many days her dark face glowed again.

She turned to Captain Asa, still busy with his addressing. "Pretty Boy don't have to hide no more, Pa," she said.

The scratching of the rusty pen continued a moment. Captain Asa laid the holder on the makeshift desk. "How come he don't have to?"

She read the letter again. "It's from Dodie Johnson at Spanish. Her people and Pretty Boy was friends, and I figured maybe she'd know where he was staying. She says Pop Masters has got out of the hospital. And Pop's telling everybody it was like Pretty Boy said—he didn't have nothing to do with the shooting. Dodie's done wrote to a man knows where Pretty Boy's been hiding somewhere in Alabama. . . . He can come back any time now, Pa."

Captain Asa licked a penny stamp and fixed it to the card. "Looks like stamps are the same as everything else nowadays. Glue on 'em won't stick at all. And tastes like putting your tongue on a raw potato. . . . You mighty want him to come back . . . don't you?"

She nodded. She studied her father's bronzed face, marked since her marriage with tiny, ever-deepening lines. Her voice grew tender. "Things are going to be different with Pretty Boy this time, Pa. I know something about a husband now. You ain't going to have no more trouble."

As suddenly as the fogs of the Gulf rolled away, leaving the green marshes shining in the sun, so Ula's dejection faded. Next day as the trailer rattled along, she sat watching the ever-changing panorama of the road, chattering like a merry child.

"Maybe he'll be coming tomorrow," she declared.

Her light-heartedness affected the others as well. The twinkle returned to Captain Asa's blue eyes. Life in the trailer recovered its leisurely charm. Only the dog continued unchanged, watching them out of its grave brown eyes.

The improvement in their spirits, however, had little effect on their finances. Their funds continued to shrink with rapidity.

They were rattling along one morning when Captain Asa heard the loud honking of a horn behind him. Turning, he saw the rickety automobile belonging to the wiry little man in the green suit he had met at the trailer camp months before. The chairs which had been his cargo were absent. Instead there was only a bulky machine outlined under a canvas tarpaulin.

The little man drove up alongside, and called out genially. They halted at the edge of the road for a chat.

The green-suited man spat a sunflower seed into the distance. "How's business?" he demanded.

Captain Asa's blue eyes were touched with momentary worry. "Ain't so good, I reckon. Don't look like people want pretty things. Sell one of the statues or a spread once in a while, but ain't often. And them Home Knowledge Books I was trying ain't getting nowhere. They told me if I bought the ten sets, wouldn't be but a couple of days before they'd all be gone. But it ain't come out like they said."

The green-suited man shot a seed at a brown lizard crawling over the running board of the car. He nodded philosophically. "I figured it'd be that way."

Captain Asa offered the other a stogie. "I studied the little directions book they sent me, and done everything it said. How to do what they call 'Make Talk,' so you can get the people interested, and then you can sell 'em anything you want. If you go into a house and you see it's a farmer, you start talking about the best times for planting cotton or peanuts, that's Volume Two, Science and Discovery. If you see they got a cat, you tell 'em how some people says a cat can't count to more than two, so when they take away a mother cat's kittens, if they leave her a couple she won't miss none—that's in Science and Discovery, the same way. But it ain't done no good. I been a-going five months since I left home pretty near. And I ain't sold but one set."

The little man lit the stogie. "Trouble is, it's like I said when I seen you before. You ain't in the right business." He took a few solemn puffs. "People don't want no statues or they don't want to learn nothing. That's old-fashioned. You don't see no people drawing pictures or no preachers or teachers riding in these fancy big cars that's passing all the time. Or if they are, you know they've stole 'em. You ought to get in an up-to-date business. Maybe the show business, like I'm a-doing now."

He looked off at the bulky object in the car, hidden under the tarpaulin. "There's three ways of making money in the show business. Get people hungry and feed 'em. Make 'em laugh. Or get 'em thinking about women. Right now I'm feeding 'em. That there I got in the car's a machine for making cotton candy. I take it around to carnivals and fairs and things. People see me making the candy, and then their mouths gets to watering and they buy it. I'm doing all right. When I had the chairs, I was starving pretty near. Until one day I painted some naked girls on the seats. And next morning wasn't one of them left. 'Cause fellows'll just laugh themselves sick at sitting down on a naked girl. That way you got two of the three things I figured, the laughing and the women both."

Captain Asa invited his companion to share their noonday dinner. The green-suited man accepted with alacrity. He sat down at the table with the others. They listened with fascination to his tales of pitchmen and barkers.

The visitor ate a hearty meal of pork and beans, then remained with his host smoking the stogie, engaged in a profound discussion of life and philosophy.

Soon after he walked with Captain Asa to the car. He looked off at the trailer where the girls were visible through the doorway, washing the dishes. "It's like I was saying last time," he declared with emphasis. "You got a mighty fine family. But the way you been telling me and the way I seen today, you ain't going to keep none of 'em home selling statues or bedspreads. Young people like them wants excitement. Something like the show business. Then you got a chance of holding 'em maybe. 'Cause all young people likes show business. But if they make up their minds, won't nothing stop 'em from leaving you. Any more than you can stop the sun from coming up over them bayous tomorrow. 'Cause things is always changing. It's nature. And, way I told you, nature's trouble. Just with a different name."

He climbed inside the automobile, and taking a bottle from a pocket in the dashboard, applied the contents to his rumpled black hair until it was plastered flat again.

"If you see anybody wants to sell a big bull cheap, write me about it, will you? My name's Chick Waters, care Billboard, Cincinnati. That's where all the big show people get their mail. Or if it's Spring, I'm always around Natchez. I'm going to start the photographing again, soon as I get a good bull."

He pressed his foot on the starting pedal. The car chugged into the distance.

The travelers set on their way once more.

A bridge over a river showed ahead, where a sign proclaimed a state boundary. They rattled onto the approaches.

Captain Asa halted the trailer some distance from the farther shore.

He gazed out happily. "Always wanted to be in Texas. Biggest state there is anywhere. There's sure somewhere here'll be a fine place to settle down."

They turned inland.

The country changed again. The bayous had ended. The marshes gave way to a flat prairie, covered with tall-waving grass. Occasionally the green had been cut away and there appeared a naked patch of clay, with a steel oil derrick towering into the sky. The derricks grew more and more frequent. Often they were in thick clusters, the arms of the pumps within rising and falling in rhythm, like monstrous metronomes. Nearby was a great refinery, with rows of odd-shaped tanks. The odor of oil lay over the travelers like a mist, so heavy it seemed it must leave a greasy mark on their faces. At night the sky would be bright with gas flares, like giants carrying torches. At times a reddish glow would leap and dance under a black volcanic cloud, marking a well on fire. The smoke, spreading low over the earth, stung their eyes and choked their nostrils.

At the post office in each little settlement, Ula continued to ask for mail. At times she would gaze hopefully as a figure wearing embroidered cowboy boots came walking toward her, only to turn away in disappointment as she saw it was a fancily garbed oilworker, on the search for a sportive evening.

"Guess something's kept him from coming," she would remark. "But he'll be getting here mighty quick."

Their money was almost at the vanishing point. They passed a sign late one afternoon declaring that two miles away was New City, where the Cozy Trailer Camp would accommodate all comers for fifty cents a night.

Captain Asa counted the few bills in his purse, and totaled the change in his pocket. "Sure ain't much left," he remarked cheerfully. "But long as I got my family and my health, I ain't complaining."

Vergil looked off toward the clouds of smoke billowing up from a refinery in the distance. "Maybe I can get some kind of work here, Pa. It's a mighty good town now, with all them new oil wells they been drilling. They says it's just rolling in money."

They stopped to water the horse at a crossroads grocery.

The elderly proprietor spoke to them with enthusiasm. "She's a wonderful town now, New City. Growed from five thousand people to pretty near twenty in just a year. You're sure lucky having the trailer. There ain't no bed to sleep in for sixty miles."

A mass of oil derricks rose out of the brown plain before them, unpainted, rusty, like dismal trees growing in some forest of the damned.

Captain Asa saw them with misgiving. "I kind of don't like stopping here with the girls. It's a terrible rough town, people says. Gambling and shooting and full of bad women. Them oil boom towns are the worst there is."

The derricks increased. From them arose a dull moaning, like condemned souls murmuring in pain. Immense tank trucks roared down the road, with steel chains dangling at the rear that clanked against the concrete, like uneasy ghosts rattling their fetters. The smell of oil was overpowering.

The derricks ended. Buildings began to appear, hastily erected roadhouses and hamburger stands, before which booted men were loitering. From every doorway there came the blare of a juke box, all joining in ear-shattering discord. They seemed like orchestras of mad musicians, become drunk on the whisky inside, and bent on deafening the world with their frenzied melodies.

Captain Asa frowned. "That's what's the trouble with the world, is them juke boxes. When people stopped playing fiddles to play them boxes, it was sure a mighty bad day."

Often the men standing before the roadhouses would see the two girls riding on the seat and give a shrill whistle.

Captain Asa would drive on faster.

They reached the edge of the town and saw the trailer camp, crowded with vehicles and tents of every description. A short distance down the road was a huge squat building made of newly cut pine boards, and roofed over with tar paper. From one corner of the structure came the crash of wooden balls and the noise of falling pins that marked a bowling alley. Stretched across the highway before it were two long strips of canvas, each bearing the same legend "Dance Marathon Tonight. Three Hundred Dollars in Prizes."

They found a place in the camp with some difficulty, and established themselves near the restaurant shack. Their neighbors were the usual varied collection of residents characteristic of the boom towns of the area: weather-beaten oilworkers, with or without their families, unable to find lodgings and driven to live in a broken-down trailer or a derelict streetcar; shrewd-eyed pitchmen, come to sell impossible can openers or watches whose hands would move only when turned by the purchaser's fingers; frowzy but good-natured women of all shapes and sizes, who considered themselves as vital a part of any new oil strike as the giant construction machines lumbering everywhere over the highway.

Ula went off on her usual trip to the post office. When she returned her face was drawn and pale.

She halted before her father, who was outside the trailer hammering some nails to reinforce the door. She stood hesitant. "I got a letter from Pretty Boy, Pa."

The hammering came to a sudden stop. Captain Asa stiffened. "Something's the matter again . . . ain't it?"

She answered with reluctance. "You ain't got forty dollars . . . have you, Pa?"

The tapping of the hammer recommenced. "Why's . . . he wanting . . . forty dollars?"

She avoided his eyes and stared fixedly at the lines scrawled on the sheet of paper she was holding, the rough edges showing where it had been torn from a school tablet. "He's got into some kind of trouble . . . over in Alabama. . . . A policeman done him wrong . . . and Pretty Boy kind of started arguing. . . . He's a-coming home soon as he gets the forty and pays 'em. . . . If he don't get it . . . he's going to jail."

The hammer beat a final tattoo.

The father and daughter grew silent. Down the road where the signs announced the marathon, an orchestra began to play in discordant rehearsal, punctuated at regular intervals by the wooden crashes in the bowling alley.

Captain Asa took out his shabby purse and once more counted its contents. "I'd give it to you if I had it. . . . But you know I ain't got forty dollars. . . . I ain't got more than enough to last us a few days."

Ula watched the huge red sun dropping toward the smoky horizon. Its rays touched the gloomy forest of derricks in the distance till they seemed to be on fire.

Her drawn face grew resolute. "I'll get it for him some way. . . . I got to get it for him."

Soon after she put on her most stylish costume, acquired after her marriage and forwarded with some other belongings by her friend at Spanish Lake—a shiny black dress decorated with large golden butterflies and gilt hoop earrings set with green stones.

She hurried away.

Captain Asa watched her go with foreboding. He returned to his repairing of the door, then took a file and began to smooth a jagged hinge that was a constant peril to the clothes of the passerby. The tool grated harshly over the iron. The ears of the dog, stretched out near the step, twitched in uneasy accompaniment.

The sun began to set, gilding the banners that hung before the squat frame building as though they were pennants of gold leaf. The music of the rehearsing players came in feverish bursts now, as though the moment for their performance was almost at hand. A trap drum beat loudly, punctuated now and then by the clang of cymbals.

Captain Asa was finishing his labor in the afterglow when Ula returned. She was breathless with fast walking and excitement. "I'm going in the dance, Pa," she announced.

The file in Captain's Asa's hand gave a painful metallic whine, then resumed its steady scraping. He did not raise his eyes. "You can't go in no dance, Ula. . . . You know you ain't been strong ever since that winter I worked at the sawmill in town, and you caught pneumonia. . . . There was a fellow died dancing one of them marathons in Chicago."

Her excitement, her tensity were increasing. "I just got to get Pretty Boy the forty dollars, Pa." She extended a slender leg, clad in a sheer stocking. "I can keep dancing and dancing. And they're giving wonderful prizes. First prize is seventy-five dollars for the man and seventy-five for the woman. And the second's fifty. If you come in third they give you each twenty-five. I'm going to try and win first prize. I couldn't make the money no other way, Pa. . . . I got to hurry and get ready."

She put some rouge on her lips and a new flower in her hair, then sat down to join the others in a hasty supper.

Captain Asa's protests had given way to resignation. "What you going to do about a partner? You got to have a partner, don't you?"

She bolted down the turnip greens and hominy grits Fernie set before her. "I'll find a partner."

Captain Asa poured her a glass of milk. "You drink that and give yourself some strength. . . . Maybe Vergil could be your partner."

The son put down his fork in horror. "I can't do no dancing, Pa."

Fernie looked up from the pan of biscuits she was taking out of the stove. She spoke with her usual quietness. "I'd go dancing with you, Ula. But I guess it's got to be a man, don't it?"

Ula nodded. She glanced with pride at her small feet encased in black, gold-buckled slippers. "I'll get somebody. I ain't seen the time yet I couldn't get a partner."

They finished the meal. Ula walked with the others hurriedly down the road. It was dark now, and the windows of the squat building were blazing with light. A crowd was moving through a wide doorway. Ula spoke to a pudgy, shrewd-faced man smoking a cigar who stood near the ticket window. He signaled the collector at the turnstile. Captain Asa and the others went inside.

A moment later the elder girl moved off toward a door reserved for the contestants.

Captain Asa called after her. "You watch out, Ula. And you pick a nice fellow."

She waved a hand and disappeared in the crowd.

Captain Asa and the others walked into the noisy hall beyond.

CHAPTER SIX

It was a bleak interior they entered, an immense assembly room, with walls of rough pine boards like the exterior, badly joined and full of knotholes. Between the planks that formed the ceiling the tar-paper roof showed in wide black patches. Sputtering arc lamps hung everywhere, surrounded by wavering clouds of insects. The dazzling glare lighted up a vast dance floor, white here and there with freshly scattered wax. At the edge of the polished area were rows of wooden benches, rising in pyramids toward the walls like those of a circus. They were packed with noisy spectators.

A long table stood at one corner of the hall, heaped high with meats and sandwiches and marked, "Contestants Only." Not far away was the band, a collection of bored young men in their shirt sleeves, sitting around a bass drum painted in bold letters, "Swing It Sam and His New City Slickers." Beside the drum was an eager youth with crinkly red hair, wearing a white dress shirt and black trousers. From his air of proprietorship, it was obvious that he was the leader of the musical assembly. He sat impatiently tapping a drumstick.

Captain Asa found places with Fernie and Vergil on one of the front benches.

Two sporty young men were sitting at their rear, one a brawny individual resembling a football player, with a loud-checked sport shirt hanging far below his waist, the other a jaded youth in a Palm Beach suit, his insipid face decorated with an embryo mustache.

They surveyed the floor with cynicism.

The insipid one with the mustache lit a cigarette. "Hope there's going to be something happen. Seen them auto races last week over in Louisiana, and wasn't anybody hurt or nothing. Wasn't even one car turned over."

His brawny companion with the sport shirt nodded in agreement. "Ought to be something doing. Ain't going to be like them marathons they used to have where they danced three quarters of an hour and let 'em rest fifteen minutes. Here they're just going to rest ten minutes every two hours. That way people ought to be passing out pretty quick."

There was a confused shuffling of feet at one end of the hall. The contestants began to file inside, like ancient martyrs entering the arena to be fed to the lions. They were a motley collection. An elderly white-haired man, well past sixty, was first, leading a blond-haired girl of twenty. Behind them came a couple who at first sight appeared to be a bearded farmer and his sunbonneted bride, but on closer inspection proved a laughing young man and a girl, disguised with whiskers and false hair. Following these was a portly middle-aged housewife in a spotted breakfast dress, towing in her wake a nervous little man who resembled a worried chipmunk looking for the nearest hole. A tall lanky Texan wearing a wide sombrero shambled behind them, escorting a giggling young woman in a short plaid skirt. Half-a-dozen couples of boys and girls just past high-school age followed in quick succession. Obviously sweethearts, they held each other's hands, and called out greetings to their friends eating popcorn and potato chips on the benches.

Captain Asa surveyed them as they passed. "Wish that white-haired man didn't have a girl with him. He looks like a fine fellow. He'd make a mighty fine partner for Ula."

The solitary figures entered last. A short, overalled young oilman with two flashing gold teeth sauntered along, grinning in embarrassment at a group of his fellow workers sitting nearby, as though his appearance were the result of a dare. Behind him came a stout middle-aged individual in a striped brown suit who appeared to be a traveling salesman temporarily off the road. There followed a large blond girl with dangling pigtails and a pink dress with a blue bow at the back, making her resemble a doll fashioned by some clumsy designer.

Captain Asa grew tense as Ula appeared, her black gown and the hoop earrings doubly accenting the Spanish cast of her face. She seemed calm, confident. Slowly she came forward, with the grace of a professional dancer.

The two sporty young men studied her with interest.

The insipid youth with the embryo mustache struck a match to a new cigarette. "There's a jake number. But mighty skinny. Bet she ain't going to last no time."

His brawny companion with the dangling shirt leaned over for a light. "She's plenty jake, ain't she? Sometimes them delicate ones'll fool you. I seen a marathon a while ago up near St. Louis, and a girl that looked pretty near like her won first prize."

The mustached one returned the cigarettes to his pocket. "Maybe that girl did it, but this one ain't. A dollar says she ain't going to last more than tomorrow. Jake?"

"Make it two dollars and it's a jake bet."

"O K for two bucks. Jake."

Ula passed close to the bench where her father and the others were sitting. She waved her hand.

Captain Asa could see that despite her apparent calm, her face was strained, uneasy.

She stood a moment, studying the single men on the floor. The little oilworker in overalls spoke to her with hesitation, his gold teeth flashing. She smiled, and nodded. He moved sheepishly to her side.

Fernie gazed at him out of her long-lashed gray eyes. "Them oilworkers are awful strong, ain't they, Pa? He's little, but looks like he can keep going for a long time."

Captain Asa's voice was unhappy. "I don't like her dancing with them oilworkers. They're terrible rough, people says."

The contestants wandered about the floor, waiting for the signal.

The night was warm. The air in the hall was close, already thick with tobacco smoke that fought for supremacy with the pungent odors of the pine and tar-paper of which the building was constructed. Occasionally, when the wind swept in from the derricks, all the other odors were lost in the overpowering smell of oil.

A flashy young man wearing a purple jacket and natty white trousers appeared from somewhere in the bowels of the building, and walking to the microphone before the orchestra, began to exchange a barrage of heavy banter with the redheaded drummer. He raised a hand. The drummer tossed a stick high into the air, and catching it with a flourish, shook it at the other members of the band, at the same time stamping his foot on the pedal fixed to the bass drum. There was a noise like a clap of thunder, and a simultaneous crash of cymbals. An instant later there came a blast of trumpets that set the flimsy walls to quivering.

The contest had begun.

Most of the rival couples advanced over the floor with exuberance, in dizzy leaps and whirls. Ula danced in slow, even steps, as though aware of the long struggle ahead and seeking to conserve her energies. The grinning little oil-worker stumbled at her side, trying to follow the movements of her feet.

Round and round the dancers circled. The redheaded drummer pounded wildly at his instruments, tossing one drumstick and sometimes two into the air, constantly exhorting the band to new frenzies. The natty young man remained at the microphone, characterizing each dancer with heavy humorous detail, and with pleas and insults urging any laggards to more violent activity.

The drummer mopped his streaming head and shirt with his handkerchief, and at last slackened his pace. The music subsided to a tuneless droning, rising now and then to a new brief crescendo as a trumpeter or a violinist who had halted for a rest resumed his perspiring place. The natty master of ceremonies settled down to an endless description of the scene before him, punctuating his narration with ancient jokes and stories that exuded from him as the grease oozed from the back of the tall electric fan whirling in the corner. The feet of the dancers shuffled steadily over the floor.

Two hours passed and a loud bell clanged, sounding a period of ten minutes rest. The dancers hurried off to the long tables bearing the refreshments. The spectators rose as with a single movement to stretch their cramped limbs.

Captain Asa watched as Ula and her partner halted near a mound of sandwiches and began to eat. "How you think she's doing, Fernie?"

The younger daughter's silvery hair flashed in the light of the glaring lamps overhead. "Ain't nobody on the floor like her, Pa."

"Hope she's going to be all right. . . . Wish she'd come on over and talk to us. I was sure hoping she'd be coming over."

The bell clanged again, and the band began to play. Ula snatched up another sandwich, and ate as she danced.

On and on the music played, in drowsy monotony. It changed to a country tune. The couple dressed as a farmer and his bride began a solo exhibition now, hopping back and forth in the jaunty rhythm of a square dance. The natty master of ceremonies began calling the steps in a voice heavy with artificial rusticity. The housewife in the breakfast dress took a firm grip on the chipmunk-like man who was her partner and flung him in giddy circles. Nickels and dimes and quarters fell upon them from the benches in a gleaming shower. Some of the other couples caught the contagion. Ula continued to move across the floor in even-measured rhythm.

The gyrations of the dancers subsided.

A clock somewhere in the distance struck midnight. There was a new interval of rest. Ula came over to the bench where her father was sitting, and introduced her sheepish, gold-toothed partner. Captain Asa and Vergil shook hands with him stiffly.

Captain Asa studied his daughter in anxiety. "How you feeling, Ula?"

"I'm feeling fine. . . . Maybe Fernie'll rub my legs a little. They say you ought to rub your legs."

She went off with her sister to a room where through the doorway some of the other feminine contestants were visible, lying on cots, while a companion kneaded their calves.

The little oilworker turned to Captain Asa with a friendly grin. "They got good eats," he remarked, his gold teeth flashing. "The hot dogs is special fine."

He went off to the table and brought back some steaming frankfurters. They had scarcely begun eating, when the bell rang once more.

Ula reappeared in the doorway, and took her partner's arm again. They swung away.

Most of the crowd departed now. The orchestra ceased its playing. The fat drummer and the others put on their coats, and went off to their homes. In their stead a phonograph began to blare out a swing tune. The natty master of ceremonies made a last appearance at the microphone, and with a final humorous sally, took his departure. Quiet fell over the empty benches. The dancers continued to circle slowly, like dervishes performing some strange ritual.

Two o'clock struck in the distance, bringing a new respite. Captain Asa and the others hurried over to join Ula and her partner at the refreshment table.

She was showing traces of fatigue. Dark circles were beginning to appear under her eyes. But she smiled as they arrived, and when she spoke did not let her voice show weariness.

"I got a fine chance of winning, Pa," she remarked, picking up a sandwich and dropping into a chair. "I been watching the others. If it was straight dancing, I know I'd win. But most of 'em ain't dancers at all. They just walk around the floor. . . . You take some of the sandwiches, Vergil. Won't anybody care."

Vergil made two sandwiches into one, and ate with appetite. "They says some of the people dancing do it just to get the eats."

The little oilworker was tiring markedly. His grin had disappeared. He made a hasty attempt at politeness, then sat with his shoeless feet propped up on a bench, massaging the soles with his hands.

Ula glanced at the cheap watch on her partner's wrist. She took a comb from her handbag, and smoothed her lustrous hair. "Be starting again in a minute, Pa. You go on home and get some sleep."

Captain Asa shook his head. They returned to the vacant benches.

Until dawn they remained, Captain Asa dozing at frequent intervals. They went off to the trailer for breakfast.

They returned at noon with the phonograph still grinding raucously. The benches were still deserted, standing like bleak skeletons. The number of couples on the floor had sharply diminished. Ula was dancing as when they had left, her shiny-buckled slippers advancing the same careful distance with each beat of the music. The feet of her overalled partner were scarcely moving. His head hung wearily.

Ula sat beside her father for the brief intermission. Her gold-toothed partner slumped onto a bench nearby.

When the bell rang once more, he rose with limbs so stiff it seemed their creaking must be audible. He faced her in feeble apology.

"Lady, I got to quit," he said.

He staggered off the floor.

Ula looked about the hall. The stout, middle-aged individual who seemed to be a traveling salesman had lost the partner he had found in the audience and was alone again, gazing forlornly at the dancers. He saw Ula and hurried to her as the phonograph resumed its merciless droning.

They moved off together.

By late afternoon the contesting couples had dropped to thirteen.

Ula stopped to introduce her new partner. "This here's Mr. Colker, Pa. He sells for a big shoe company out of New Orleans. He's just a-doing this for fun."

Eight o'clock came again, and the walls were once more lined with spectators. The redheaded youth took his place at the drums. The natty master of ceremonies stepped to the microphone, laughing self-consciously at the new humorous sallies he had prepared for the evening, and often clapping his hands to encourage the audience to join in his appreciation. Once he made a dramatic pause, and pointed to his bow tie that lit up suddenly with two tiny electric bulbs concealed inside the cloth. A moment later the drummer arose, with his tie blinking in the same startling fashion.

The dancers continued their endless circling. The master of ceremonies tried to urge them on to fancy steps again, his voice at times wheedling, at times hurling new insults. There was little response to his pleas.

Ula was becoming a favorite of the crowd. Often as she passed a group of rough-clad figures a rain of silver and an occasional bill would scatter onto the floor. Her stout escort would stoop gallantly and place them in her hand. Her fatigue was growing, being visible to Captain Asa even from the benches. The blackish rings about her eyes had deepened. Her dark skin was beginning to acquire an unnatural whiteness.

Captain Asa's dog, stretched out at his feet, raised its head whenever Ula came near.

The two sporty young men were in their old seats behind Captain Asa. They surveyed the dancers with cynical eyes.

The brawny youth with the dangling shirt bought a bag of potato chips from a boy circulating among the crowd, and stuffed a handful into his mouth. "Them short rests wears 'em out fast," he remarked. "Fellow runs the show was telling me tonight it won't be anything like them other marathons they used to have, sixty days and things like that. He says way they're dropping out it won't last more than a week hardly."

His companion with the embryo mustache puffed a cigarette lazily. "Wish something'd happen. A good fight maybe. . . . Double the two dollars you won on the girl. Four dollars says she won't finish in the money. . . . Jake?"

"Jake. . . . Got a good horse at Lexington tomorrow?"

"Battle Royal in the fifth. Sure winner."

"Sounds jake."

With a sudden impulse Captain Asa's dog arose, and wandered off among the dancers.

"Come back here, Ruby!" Captain Asa shouted.

The dog paid no attention, and advancing until it reached Ula and her stout partner, began gravely following her about the floor. A murmur of laughter drifted up from the spectators. Ula smiled, and petting the animal a moment, ordered it back to the benches. It obeyed with reluctance, its course marked by a tinkling shower.

The dancers halted for the midnight rest. The pallor in Ula's face had heightened. Her breathing was troubled, irregular. Her pulse was beating feverishly.

Captain Asa looked at her with alarm. "You're going to get sick sure, Ula. Quit a-dancing and come on home."

She struggled for breath before answering. "I got to get Pretty Boy the forty dollars."

Her breathing grew normal. She moved onto the floor again.

Hour after hour she continued, finding somewhere a new reserve of strength. To Captain Asa she seemed to be circling like a sleepwalker, in a never-ending dream.

Another night passed, and another and another, while more and more couples succumbed to exhaustion. The contestants remaining had long since ceased to dance. They were no longer human beings. They were captives in some ancient hell, condemned to everlasting torture. At times they moved in a dreary shuffle, their shoes, coated with dancing wax from the floor, advancing by fractions of inches. At times they stood motionless for a long interval, until the natty master of ceremonies who acted as judge came ominously toward them. They would rouse themselves and stagger on.

When Ula stopped for the rests, she had hardly the strength to speak to her family. She would sink into a chair a moment, then limp off with her sister to the rubbing room.

She had acquired a new partner, the stout salesman having gone the way of the oilman. She was dancing now with the tall, lanky Texan, who had lost his plaid-skirted companion. His wide sombrero, coupled with his slow walk and his lazy drawl, marked him as a visitor from some ranch farther to the West.

The sixth morning dawned, hot, stifling, intensifying the trials of the dancers. The temperature increased during the day. By night the flimsy building was a furnace, with the heat rising in visible waves from the walls. The odor of oil sweeping from the derricks beyond was overpowering. The close-packed spectators sat in their shirt sleeves, wiping their streaming faces with their handkerchiefs. Palm-leaf fans and newspapers waved drowsily.

The master of ceremonies walked to the microphone and signaled the band. As the first blaring note of the trumpets sounded the last of the high-school girls remaining crumpled and fell in a faint to the floor. Attendants hurried forward, and with the pale youth who was her partner, carried her away.

Only three couples were left besides Ula and her lanky companion: the bearded young man and the sunbonneted girl masquerading as farmers; the portly housewife who now had as partner a seedy individual who bore on his back a poster advertising the virtues of a nearby restaurant; the blond pigtailed girl with the pink dress who resembled an awkward doll, dancing with a dark, long-haired youth who seemed not many months out of short trousers. Round and round the dancers continued, in merciless torment. An old Negro followed at their heels, scattering wax on the rough floor. The shoes of the rivals pressed it into the boards. Here and there a patch caught the light of the glaring lamps above, causing it to shine like a broken mirror.

The blond, pigtailed girl was wavering visibly. Often she would stop and lean against a pole. Her long-haired companion picked up a glass as they passed near the refreshment table and splashed her face with water.

Vergil watched the scene with intentness. "If she quits, Ula sure gets third prize."

Fernie drew a sharp breath as the pigtailed girl wavered again. "I hope it ain't a sin. But I'm praying the Lord to make her go down before Ula."

The doll-like figure staggered on.

Ula shuffled past, her steps so slow she seemed to be almost stationary. Her eyes were half-closed. Her head was drooping. Only her partner's supporting arm seemed to keep her erect. Once as she reached one of the glistening patches on the floor, she slipped and fell. A murmur of disappointment arose from the audience.

Her lanky partner quickly pulled her to her feet. She went on in a daze.

The two sporty youths had taken their usual places behind Captain Asa, and were eating popcorn.

The young man of the embryo mustache made a fan of a racing sheet, and followed Ula's course with a jaded air. "She ain't going to last an hour," he remarked. "You might as well come across with them four dollars."

His brawny companion with the dangling shirt made a gesture of derision. "When she hits the floor and stays there you'll get it. But you ain't won it yet."

The hall grew hotter with the close-packed bodies of the audience. Sweat streamed in rivulets down the faces of the dancers. Ula roused herself to dab her cheeks with a powder puff.

The bell rang for the first rest of the evening. Ula slumped onto the nearest bench. Captain Asa and the others hurried forward. Her face was drawn with pain; her breath was coming in gasps, as on the night she had run through the swamp. She started toward the rubbing room, then dropped to the bench again, too weak to make the effort. Fernie pulled off her shoes and massaged the calves. They were stiff as iron.

It was time for the bell again. Her breathing showed no improvement. She staggered to her feet, remaining upright only by holding to the back of her chair.

Captain Asa rose in fright. "You got to stop, Ula. . . . You'll kill yourself sure. . . . Like the fellow done up in Chicago."

She shook her head in a feeble negative. "I'll be all right. . . . I just got to keep it up . . . a little while longer. . . . The girl with the pigtails is pretty near gone. . . . And so is the big lady in the house-dress."

A wave of unnatural color swept her face. She swayed with dizziness. "If one of them goes, I'll get third prize anyway. . . . It's twenty-five dollars and a aluminum kitchen set. . . . The people on the floor throwed me over seventeen dollars. . . . That'd be more than the forty I need. . . . I ain't going to let Pretty Boy . . . go to jail."

Her eyes closed tightly.

The bell clanged, like a demon gong in an inferno summoning sinners to new torment.

Ula's lanky, slow-spoken partner came over from the food table. He gazed at her with tenderness. "I'll carry you on my feet so you can sleep," he said.

He set her feet on his own, and with his arm tight about her waist, shuffled over the polished boards. Her head drooped in peaceful slumber.

She awakened, refreshed for a moment, then put her feet to the floor again.

The air in the crowded hall grew stifling. A swarm of tiny midges, attracted by the arc lights overhead, descended upon dancers and spectators alike, their bites burning like the points of fiery needles. There followed a constant tattoo of slapping hands.

The spectators grew restless, irritable. Only the natty master of ceremonies continued his labored humor at the microphone, halting now and then to slap at a burning ankle.

The pigtailed girl seemed to have recovered again, and was moving at a slow but even pace past the benches.

Ula watched her drearily.

A drunken oilman sitting with some noisy companions hurled a whisky bottle. It struck near Ula, shattering into a myriad fragments. The audience booed in anger.

Ula made her way with painful steps past the glass, and stumbled on.

The pigtailed girl was following close behind, while her long-haired young partner spoke constant words of encouragement. Round and round the rivals shuffled, the blond girl watching Ula like a hungry jackal stalking a stricken animal in the desert, waiting for it to die.

Suddenly the blond girl crumpled to the floor. She remained there a moment, prostrate, with her pink dress and pigtails appearing like a worn-out doll thrown upon an ash heap.

The long-haired youth and an attendant raised her with difficulty, and helped her to the exit.

Ula glanced at the two remaining couples, and went on unsteadily. She had circled the hall, and was starting on a new erratic round, when Vergil saw her suddenly shiver.

"She's going," he said quietly.

They darted forward as she started to fall. The lanky Texan caught her, and held her erect until their arrival. Gently they carried her to the drab restroom and stretched her on a couch. She lay rigid. But her eyes were bright.

"I got him the money," she murmured.

Captain Asa and Vergil aided her into the street, carrying her much of the way so that her burning feet would not touch the ground.

They reached the trailer, and placed her in a bunk.

She lay rigid again, but happy.

From down the road came the voice of the natty master of ceremonies blaring over the loud-speaker, and the music of the band playing in monotony.

She raised herself to listen. "If Pretty Boy'd have been here we'd have won first prize."

She dropped back to the pillow.

The glib voice of the master of ceremonies sounded again, raucous in the stillness of the camp. "Pretty soon we're starting a new show, folks. A Kissathon. To see who can kiss the longest without breaking. You ain't seen nothing, folks, if you ain't seen a Kissathon."

All night and the next morning Ula lay without moving.

At her request Captain Asa collected the prize, and prepared to send it off with the other money to her husband.

He was leaving the trailer on his way to the post office when he turned sharply to gaze at a figure walking up the path, a pasty young man clad in a broad cowboy hat, with a red handkerchief tucked into the collar of his shirt, and tight-fitting riding pants thrust into embroidered cowboy boots.

It was Pretty Boy.

The newcomer halted before his father-in-law, and stood irresolute.

"They let me off paying the forty," he said. "I hopped a freight and come."

CHAPTER SEVEN

PRETTY BOY went into the trailer. Ula sat up in the bunk where she was lying, and held him in a long embrace. Pretty Boy sat down at her side.

Captain Asa went off with Fernie to the camp grocery for supplies. They returned, and deposited their purchases in the tiny kitchen.

Pretty Boy turned to his father-in-law. His pasty face grew solemn under its fringe of unshaven blond hair. "I been a lot of trouble to you and Ula, Pa. But that's all ended. I'm going out tomorrow and get me a job."

His arrival was a tonic that brought Ula out of her bed a few hours after. Toward sunset she dressed with her former carefulness and joined the others at the table for supper.

Pretty Boy seemed changed, subdued. When he spoke, his voice lacked its former boastfulness.

Captain Asa watched the transformation with delight.

Pretty Boy went with Vergil into the town next morning to look for work. Captain Asa accompanied them to survey its possibilities as a market for the statuettes and the spreads.

It was his first visit to the business section of the settlement. It proved merely a continuation of the drab and noisy outskirts. At the center was a wide barren square that seemed intended to contain cattle instead of the muddy automobiles parked in a solid mass. Along the streets bordering the plaza were rows of shabby buildings, a weather-beaten hotel with a dingy Greek restaurant attached and several chili parlors from which came the odor of steaming tamales, a dime store whose windows were filled with cheap costume jewelry and overalls, an old-fashioned drugstore displaying two colored bottles, and another, dazzling with its newness, offering everything for sale except medicine. Automobiles squawked noisily, impatient of any pedestrian. Here and there a group of young men stood loitering on a corner, saluting each girl who approached with an ear-splitting crescendo of whistles.

Leading out to the railroad depot, visible a few blocks away, was a street which seemed almost a duplicate of the highway approaching the town, a close-packed line of bars with glaring neon lights and roaring juke boxes. Within, rough-clad men were playing slot machines or were gathered round a table where a roulette ball clicked faintly. On a narrow lane running off from this thoroughfare was a row of frame cottages in whose doorways blowzy women were sitting, calling out invitations to every male passerby.

There was no work to be found in the town that day, and

no one to buy the statuettes. Captain Asa and the others continued their quest in the days following with little success, earning a few dollars now and then by odd jobs for some local citizen. The prize money was quickly spent for necessities. Their funds sank to the vanishing point once more.

The trailer camp reflected the rough mood of the town. All night in the wheeled dwellings stationed along the dim-lit paths there sounded the drunken voices of quarreling men and women, and the crashing of whisky bottles.

It was autumn in the North, but here the weather continued warm. The heavy smell of oil was ever in the nostrils of the residents, as though an invisible oily rag was hidden somewhere about their clothing. A well nearby caught fire, and resisting all efforts to extinguish it, covered the town with a gloomy pall. At night it flamed like a volcano.

The fighting and drunkenness in the camp increased. The atmosphere began to weigh on Captain Asa's spirits.

He stood outside with the others early one morning, watching the burly proprietor of the camp lead off a tall figure screaming in an alcoholic delirium.

"Getting terrible around here," he declared. "I'm going away mighty quick. I want to be where people's living right."

A bony, sunbonneted woman, with gaunt face and piercing eyes who lived in a trailer adjoining, stared at the oil well smoking in the distance. "Lord's going to destroy the people if they keep on shaming Him. That's why He set that well to burning. He's coming down with a flaming sword and end their sinful ways."

Another neighbor, a bent, gnome-like old man carrying a heavy stick, nodded in gloomy agreement. "Ain't going to do no good their trying to put that fire out. 'Cause them flames is coming straight from Hell. When people gets to acting way they are nowadays, Lord's getting ready for the Judgment."

Several times Captain Asa started to set out for some other locality. Each time Vergil and Pretty Boy argued the potential riches of the town, and persuaded him to remain a little longer.

He returned one afternoon with Fernie from a new fruitless attempt to sell the statuettes, when he noticed that the long-empty shelves of the kitchen cupboard were filled to overflowing. From the stove where Ula was occupied there came the fragrant odor of frying ham.

The elder girl looked up oddly as her father entered. "Pretty Boy's got a job," she announced. But she added no further details.

Since her marriage there was often a reticence in her voice that prevented Captain Asa from asking questions. He made no comment.

Pretty Boy failed to appear for supper. Captain Asa ate in deep reflection. When the meal ended, he put on his hat, and went off to the town again. Slowly he walked down the street of the bars and gambling houses, peering into each glaring doorway.

He halted before a smoky interior crowded with the usual high-booted oilmen. He remained a long time, then returned to the camp.

He entered the trailer, where the girls were busy sewing, Fernie hemming a pillow slip, Ula making a collar for a new dress.

Captain Asa gazed at the elder daughter with unhappy eyes. "I figured that's what he'd be a doing. . . . I sure never thought I'd have a son-in-law . . . working in a gambling house."

Ula went on with her stitching. "He tried and tried and couldn't get no work, Pa. And he was walking down the street today, and he seen a man he used to know in New Orleans. It's him that gave Pretty Boy the job."

"He's going to get in trouble again. . . . Like he done at Spanish. . . . I'd make you come away. . . . But he's your husband. . . . I guess I can't do nothing. . . . When you met him it was sure a mighty sad day."

A week passed. Each afternoon Pretty Boy went off to his employment, returning at two or three in the morning. Several times unpleasant-looking characters came to call for him at the trailer.

Captain Asa watched with new foreboding.

A group of oilworkers arrived from another field, more drunken and more violent than any of their predecessors. The camp after dark became bedlam.

Pretty Boy was still at work one night when Captain Asa was awakened by the sounds of a wild orgy, suddenly interrupted by a fusillade of shots. A few moments later the wail of a police car sounded down the road.

Captain Asa pulled on his clothes, and hurried with Vergil out the door. The girls put on their cheap wrappers and followed.

In a broken-down streetcar occupied by some of the newcomers, eight or ten rough-looking men were battling furiously across an upset card table, striking at each other with chairs and beer bottles. Two brandished smoking revolvers.

The struggle was at its height when the police car approached with a dying wail of its siren, and came to a stop at the edge of the camp. Several officers rushed into the derelict trolley, and began laying about with their clubs. The turmoil subsided. One by one the officers dragged out the combatants, and packed them into a patrol that had drawn up in the road.

The two cars with a new wailing of their sirens sped away.

Captain Asa and his family had joined their neighbors gathered in a crowd before the scene of the battle.

"Judge'll give 'em all ten days and ten dollars," mumbled a sleepy oilworker in bare feet and overalls.

The bent, gnome-like old man, clad in a flapping raincoat at whose bottom the edge of his long underwear was showing, shook his heavy stick in warning. "The Judgment's sure a-coming. Fires and wars and flying machines. And the beasts rising out of the sea."

A honey-haired young woman gave a bottle to the tiny baby she was carrying. "They won't be fighting and carrying on much longer. Oklahoma Jack's a-coming. He'll make this town right before the Lord."

Captain Asa turned to her quickly. "I've heard a-plenty about Oklahoma Jack. But I never seen him. When's he coming to New City?"

The young mother grew eager. "In a few weeks, I reckon. I heard 'em talking about it over at the Holiness folks' church today. He's out by Amarillo now. He's mowing down the people for the Lord in Texas just like they was ears of corn."

A statuesque, friendly matron with a mass of auburn hair done up in curlers, adjusted her red kimono to hide a nightgown. "Oklahoma Jack can save this town all right. He's the finest preacher ever was in the country, they says. Lord sent that preacher used to play baseball, and then he sent the Gypsy and the Gypsy's son. Now he's sent Oklahoma Jack. And he's the best of all."

As the days passed, more and more rumors drifted about

of the evangelist's coming. There were stories everywhere of his spectacular conversions, sweeping men's souls like the grass fires which often ravaged the countryside. Then one morning, as though by magic, huge yellow streamers appeared on the walls of the squat building which had housed the marathon, announcing the visit within two weeks of the preacher who would save the sinners of New City from eternal damnation, and proclaiming that this edifice would be his tabernacle. Similar banners appeared on every vacant fence and door.

Captain Asa stood with Ula and some of the neighbors while a billposter tacked up an enormous photograph of the evangelist on the side of the trailer-camp grocery.

The eyes of the bony woman who lived nearby were glazing. Her gaunt face was touched with a feverish light. "I want to hear him. I want to touch his mantle. They says he's a wearing the mantle of the Lord."

Captain Asa turned to his daughter. "He's sure a fine-looking man, ain't he, Ula? Maybe when he comes you can get Pretty Boy to hear him. Maybe he can show Pretty Boy the right way of living."

Ula's dark face was thoughtful. "I'm sure going to try. Maybe he can get Pretty Boy back to going to church regular, like he did when he lived with his uncle that was the preacher."

The honey-haired young woman rocked her wan infant lovingly. "Ain't nobody can hold against him. They says that even little babies like this one I'm carrying stands up and praises the Lord when he passes. He'll save your husband and all the sinners. He'll lead him on to Jesus."

The morning for the arrival came at last. The camp hummed with activity. From most of the tents and trailers women dressed in their Sunday clothes emerged with stiff-clad children, and began walking down the road to the railroad station.

Vergil hurried off for some temporary work he had secured at the refinery.

Captain Asa and the girls prepared to join the procession.

Ula went over to her husband who had risen late, and still sleepy-eyed, was eating breakfast. "Ain't you coming, Pretty Boy?"

He shrugged his shoulders. "I told you I had enough churching up in Arkansas. I used to jump around like a chicken with its head cut off at them Holiness meetings. I don't want to do it any more."

Captain Asa set off with his daughters down the road.

They arrived at the shabby depot where a crowd composed mostly of the poorer inhabitants of the town was already gathered. Along the platform some portly, self-conscious individuals were waiting, wearing badges marked "Committee." Behind them was the choir, a group of thin-faced, worried-looking men and women, with lilies pinned to their coats and dresses. Nearby was a double line of children dressed all in white, some giggling, some with grave expressions, as though they felt the solemnity of the occasion. At their head stood a score of little girls in long, snowy robes, each with a pair of cheesecloth wings attached to her shoulders.

For some time they waited in the warm sun. The white-clad children began to fidget. The starched wings of some of the angels wilted, and drooped over the snowy backs. The nervous mothers hurried forward, and tried with needles and safety pins to mold the gauzy fabric into shape again.

At times a booted man, in whose hip-pocket a pistol was clearly outlined, would come over from the street of the bars and gambling houses opposite the station; he would stand with a frowzy female companion, watching in curiosity.

A floridly-dressed, beefy individual whom Captain Asa recognized as Pretty Boy's employer, stopped for a moment with several hard-visaged men, and made some loud, humorous remarks.

Captain Asa shook his head. "Them's the ones that ought to be here, instead of all the good people. There's going to be plenty of trouble in this town, way people are saying. And Pretty Boy'll sure be in it if he don't quit them fellows. Maybe if I talk to him, he'll come to the meeting tonight."

The crowd continued its patient waiting.

Suddenly a hoarse whistle sounded in the distance. The onlookers grew tense with expectation. The whistle sounded again, nearer. A locomotive appeared down the track and came speeding toward the depot, with two long coaches rattling in the rear.

The choir began to sing in jubilation.

With a shrill grinding of brakes the locomotive slowed down almost to a halt, and pushed the cars onto a siding.

A trainman opened the doors of the first coach, a structure of unusual design, half being built to carry passengers, the other half apparently for baggage. From it there descended a score of genial, well-fed individuals, all clad in immaculate white uniforms, and carrying musical instruments of various shapes and sizes. A moment later the baggage-like side of the car opened to form a ramp. A large automobile truck, spotlessly white like the uniforms, appeared in the aperture and rolled slowly to the ground. In the center was a platform surrounded by camp chairs. On the sides were huge banners demanding, "Where Will You Spend Eternity?"

The statuesque matron of the auburn hair stood nearby with some of the other camp dwellers. "He used to be a terrible man," she told Captain Asa. "He was drinking and fighting all the time, a-driving a truck for a brewery in Oklahoma City. And one day he was taking a load of beer, when the Lord come to him in a vision. And he throwed all the barrels out on the prairie, and took up preaching the Word. That there's the beer truck he run before he was saved."

The bandsmen mounted the decorated vehicle, and took places on the chairs.

There was a stir aboard the other coach now. The band began to play a lively hymn. A murmur arose from the crowd as a figure appeared in the train vestibule, an enormous, heavy-set man dressed in loose-hanging black clothes, and carrying a wide-brimmed black sombrero. His head, like his body, was huge, and was covered with a great mane of shaggy black hair. Slung low on his massive neck, it gave him the air of a charging buffalo. It was Oklahoma Jack.

He stood a moment, smiling, and waving a heavy hand at the spectators. At first glance his size, his professional geniality, made him seem more of a carnival promoter than a churchman. Yet on closer inspection there was an arresting quality about his great black eyes that approached the hypnotic. When he spoke his voice boomed like a deep-toned cathedral bell.

He descended the train with slow, ponderous steps, all the while continuing his cheery greeting to his audience. Several black-coated figures followed at his heels, then an energetic young man carrying a camera. The playing of the band became a joyous frenzy. The choir began to sing the refrain, joined by the snowy-robed little girls with the wings. The childish voices quavered sweetly.

The evangelist walked toward the truck in majesty. He halted an instant before the chanting angels to let the cameraman take a picture.

The band and choir joined in a mighty hallelujah.

The evangelist resumed his march, and climbed up among the musicians. The worshipers fell in line behind. The odd parade wound through the town.

Captain Asa and the girls followed till the procession arrived at the building that had housed the marathon, its yellow streamers shining like a golden halo.

The evangelist entered with the choir and the committee. Some of the children began to distribute bills announcing the program for the coming week.

The crowd drifted away.

Captain Asa and the girls went off to the trailer.

The excitement of the camp increased.

All day the newborn tabernacle seethed with feverish preparations for the evening service that would open the revival. Trucks drove back and forth bringing chairs and mountainous piles of hymn books. Carpenters sawed and hammered, putting the final touches on platforms and runways.

Darkness fell. Vergil sent word by one of the neighbors that he was remaining downtown to put in some extra hours at the refinery. Soon after Pretty Boy came in for supper.

When the meal was finished, Captain Asa turned to his son-in-law hopefully. "You coming to the meeting tonight, Pretty Boy? Looks like it's going to be mighty fine."

Pretty Boy looked up from the sport pages of the newspaper he was reading. "I got to be working, Pa."

"Do anybody good to hear fine preaching like Oklahoma Jack. Lots of places closing in town so people can come."

Pretty Boy's lips set with stubbornness. "I ain't going, Pa."

Captain Asa and the girls departed.

The tabernacle was a blaze of light now, with a dense mass of men and women milling before it that spread far beyond the narrow pavement. They made their way inside.

The pine-boarded hall where the marathon dancers made their tottering rounds had undergone a considerable transformation. The once-polished floor was now covered with endless rows of chairs, already crowded with spectators. A large platform stood at one end, on which were seated the portly committee, looking out in dignity, and the good-natured bandsmen, eating ice-cream bars.

At the front of the platform, instead of a pulpit, was a table bearing a huge Bible, with a microphone suspended overhead. Near it the white-painted truck was stationed, covered with banners like a decorated altar.

Captain Asa and his daughters managed to find seats on a wooden step near the entrance.

A hush fell over the assembly. A pompous individual arose from among the badge wearers, and walking to the microphone, began to intone a prayer. He ended. Suddenly the hall was plunged into darkness. From a narrow balcony there came the loud sputtering of electricity. A spotlight swung over the heads of the spectators. As the band and choir burst into a hymn of triumph, its dazzling rays revealed the childish angels standing in a double line before Oklahoma Jack. The spotlight rested on the evangelist, vividly illuminating his huge body and his head of a charging buffalo.

Slowly the winged children came down the aisle. The evangelist followed in benevolent majesty.

He climbed the platform, and smiling at the sea of faces before him, waved his massive hand in blessing.

He spoke in a voice low, caressing, as a mother in a sick-room might speak to a beloved child. "Let's get at peace with God, folks. Let's sing Sixty-Nine."

He nodded to the choir. Through the hall there came the shrill chanting of *Clean Train:*

> *This train's a clean train,*
> *Come on and ride.*
> *This train's the Lord's train,*
> *Come on and hide.*
> *Ain't no tobacco smokers or ain't no gamblers,*
> *Ain't no drunkards or midnight ramblers.*
> *This train's the Lord's train,*
> *Come on inside.*

Captain Asa and Ula joined lustily in the chorus. Fernie sang in her usual gentle voice, her silvery-framed face touched with serene light as she bent over the hymn book.

She laid the volume at her side. "It's wonderful singing, ain't it, Pa?"

Captain Asa nodded with enthusiasm. "Never heard nothing like it. There's three thousand people here if there's half a dozen. Bet it sure makes the Lord feel good to hear three thousand people a-singing."

The massive face of the evangelist grew solemn. He turned the pages of the great Bible on the table as though for inspiration, then began to preach a sermon. Quietly he talked at first, as though he were a teacher, discussing the day's lessons with some favorite pupils. Then almost imperceptibly, his voice began to alter. His words grew louder, faster. The hypnotic quality in his eyes accentuated. His breathing grew fevered. He began pacing up and down, shaking his huge fists, pleading, exhorting, his voice booming like approaching thunder.

Wilder and wilder he grew. His head sunk lower and lower on his shoulders. His speech became an unintelligible roaring. As he rushed back and forth across the platform, it was as though the charging buffalo he resembled had broken through the corral confining him and was bellowing his fury at the world.

Often there would come an answering shout from the worshipers. At times a stiff-clad woman would cry out as in agony, and leaping to her feet, start dancing madly. The playing, the singing of the hymns grew frenzied. There came the curious, frightening sound of row on row of booted feet stamping as though they were one.

Suddenly the evangelist bounded to the white truck alongside. With a fierce, accusing finger he pointed to a huge streamer at the end of the hall that bore in immense letters the question, "Are You Driving On The Highway Of The Lord?"

He lifted his shaggy head toward heaven. He seemed almost on the verge of apoplexy. "Oh, I was a terrible sinner, Lord! I wasn't driving on Your highway! I was driving with the Devil sitting beside me! But you saved me, Lord! You kept me from going over the cliff to eternal damnation! Help me show these sinners the right road, Lord! Help me save these poor sinners from driving down to Hell!"

Cries of joy and hallelujahs arose from the worshipers as he leaped into the truck, and taking the steering wheel, pressed his foot on the starting pedal. The motor roared. The truck wheels, raised from the floor by wooden blocks under the axles, spun giddily.

"Clear the road, Jesus!" he shouted. "Straighten them curves and fill them holes! I'm coming to salvation!"

For several minutes he sat in the car, pressing pedals and shifting levers, all the while making his preaching follow his actions.

Captain Asa turned to Ula. His face was rapt. "It's the way they says. Ain't never been a preacher like him before. If we can get Pretty Boy to come he'll sure be won for the Lord."

The evangelist bounded back to the table and took a glass of water, then whipped himself into a frenzy more violent than before. More figures leaped from their chairs, and began dancing crazily.

A bulky woman in a red-buttoned dress and blondined hair full of cheap-jeweled combs, who was sitting on the steps next to Captain Asa, began whirling in giddy circles, as she spun pointing first with the right hand and then with the left in an odd machine-like motion. Buttons and combs shot out everywhere from her, and rattled to the floor.

The bodies of Captain Asa and the girls were swaying a little. Their feet tapped out the strident rhythm.

The evangelist gave a new leap to the edge of the platform. With one hand on his forehead, as a sailor might gaze at some vague object floating on the distant waves, he looked across the ocean of upturned faces toward the entrance of the tabernacle. His hypnotic eyes dilated until they seemed enormous, possessing some quality beyond humanity.

"I see him, Lord!" he shouted. "It's the Devil standing yonder! It's Satan that you cast out of Heaven and throwed into Hell! He's come here from the Hot Place to spy on us, Lord! He's come here to keep these poor sinners from kneeling before You! Help me catch that Devil, Lord!"

Breathless, he dashed down the steps of the platform, and

ran furiously along the hall, as though in pursuit of some desperate fugitive. Hysteria seized the assembly. Women shouted and wept and laughed and sang. The walls and roof of the flimsy structure quivered as in an earthquake with their leaping bodies.

The evangelist reached the doorway. He stood a moment looking about with wild, fierce eyes, then retraced his steps, panting heavily.

He mounted to the platform again, and shook his head in sorrow. "He got away, Lord. I let him get away."

He wiped his streaming brow, then put a hand to an ear, as though listening, and looked up at the sky. "What you say, Lord? I can't hear you, Lord."

He continued to listen for an answer, then smiled as with understanding, and put his ear to the great Bible. "I hear You now, Lord. Amen. If that's the way You want it. We'll catch him next time, Lord."

An hour and a half passed. Still he went on, while more and more penitents rushed out from their seats and dropped to their knees in the sawdust-covered aisles. Sobbing, they confessed their sins, and called on Heaven for forgiveness.

The evangelist reached a final booming crescendo, and ended. A great calm came over his face. He smiled and stretched out his massive arms in benediction. "Let all them that wants to walk the Lord's way follow the angels," he said.

The white-robed children with the wings began to march up the aisle. The penitents and the spectators crowded behind. Captain Asa and the girls joined the others waiting in line to shake the evangelist's hand.

Their turn came at last. Captain Asa pressed the great hand in reverence.

They made their way out the door and walked toward the trailer.

Captain Asa glanced back at the tabernacle where the band was playing a final rousing hymn.

His bronzed face glowed with happiness. "Ain't we all had a nice time?" he said.

Night after night the revival continued. The excitement in the town spread to the surrounding country. Special trains and busses began to bring worshipers from the nearby settlements. Broken-down automobiles and rickety wagons filled with ranchworkers and their families were visible everywhere in the streets. The tabernacle was no longer large enough to accommodate those who sought admission. Loud-speakers were set up outside, surrounded at each service by surging crowds. The voice of the preacher boomed across to the trailer camp in new terrifying exhortations.

The hysteria spread out from the meetings and seized the poorer inhabitants of the town everywhere. Business in many of the little shops was suspended. Whenever men and women met they would stop to discuss the evangelist's latest triumphs.

"He's saving 'em, Hallelujah!" the bony neighbor declared, as Captain Asa waited at the counter of the camp grocery. The feverish light in her eyes was heightening. "He's saving everybody, excepting the gamblers and the bad women. He'll save them, too. Hallelujah! Lord's put the power in his hands."

The hysteria of the community intensified. Only the street of the glaring bars and the narrow lane beyond were still unaffected. There began to be talk of a miracle.

On several occasions as they sat in the trailer, Ula and Captain Asa made new attempts to take Pretty Boy off to the services. Each time he refused. But as the chanting of the hymns and the steady booming of the preacher's voice drifted out from the loud-speakers down the road, they could see that he was growing tense, nervous.

The unpleasant-looking men came to call for him once more.

Captain Asa watched with his old anxiety.

CHAPTER EIGHT

The first day of the new week of the revival came, bringing with it heavy clouds that threatened imminent rain. The smoke from the oil fire lay like a fog over the town, often blotting out the derricks on the horizon. The oppressiveness of the air increased as the day advanced. The smoky pall thickened as night descended. The air grew difficult to breathe.

The services began soon after sunset. The voice of the evangelist rolled out again like thunder.

Captain Asa was in the trailer with his immediate family, Pretty Boy having gone off to work some hours before, when there came a sudden change in the revivalist's tone, followed by a vague murmuring from the shadowy crowd before the tabernacle.

Vergil went to the door. "Something's a-going on," he announced.

Captain Asa and the girls hurried with him down the road. They arrived at the squat building, and saw that the dense-packed mass of men and women before it was electric with excitement. They halted as the crowd parted to clear a path. A moment later the white truck bearing the banners rolled out the entrance, with Oklahoma Jack standing in the middle, staring grimly into the night. About him the band was circled, playing a strident tune.

Captain Asa questioned a black-haired figure in a faded dress nearby.

She answered almost in a chant. "He's going to save the gamblers and the bad women. Amen. They wouldn't come to the preaching. Hallelujah! They wouldn't come to the Lord's temple. So the Lord done told him to go down to 'em. The Lord done told him to show 'em the way. Bless the Lamb. Amen."

Through the town the truck lumbered, while the worshipers fell in line behind, singing in a swelling chorus. The procession halted where the street of the bars joined the narrow lane with the cottages. The devotees swept forward, swarming over the sidewalks.

Booted men came hurrying out from behind the swinging doors that marked the saloons and the neon-lit gambling houses. Other men and frowzy women emerged from the drab shadows beyond.

They collected in groups, discussing the invasion, some angry, some laughing, some shrugging their shoulders.

Captain Asa thought he saw Pretty Boy in the street for a moment, talking to his beefy employer. But both disappeared in the crowd.

Oklahoma Jack continued to stand on the truck in silence, his arms folded on his massive chest, his fierce black eyes staring down the gaudy thoroughfare.

Suddenly he dropped to his knees, and began an impassioned prayer. "O Lord, these here's Satan's Children," he intoned. "These here's the sons of the Tempter. The daughters of Jezebel. They wouldn't come to hear Your word. They wouldn't come to kneel before You. Help me save 'em, Lord."

He continued for some time, his words more accusing than suppliant, then rose to his feet. The band descended from the truck, and re-formed in the road. As he gave a signal, the musicians struck up the stirring tones of *Washed In The Blood Of The Lamb*. The choir and a small picked group of worshipers fell in behind and burst into song. Back and forth they paraded in military formation, chanting the hymn in hypnotic rhythm. Their voices and the booming drums drowned out the juke boxes echoing through the doorways.

The evangelist began to preach, calmly at first as was his custom, then in a fury surpassing any of his previous outbursts. Like a maddened giant he swept up and down the platform, conjuring up fantastic visions of death and destruction to come.

The well burning on the horizon afforded a fitting background for his grisly prophecies.

A drunken figure went reeling past.

The evangelist pointed toward him in reckless denunciation. "Look at him, Lord! Look at him! Walking straight down the pathway to Hell, Lord! Walking straight down to eternal damnation! You hear the Devil hollering, Lord? You hear the Devil laughing and screaming? It's because he's going to get another soul, Lord! It's because he sees what's going to happen to this blind sinner! He sees him laying in the street with the whisky bottle in his hand, Lord! He sees the police taking him off to the morgue, and laying him on the cold stones! He sees the medical students cutting him open, like he was a chicken! Do you feel them knives in your stomach now, brother? Do you feel them knives slicing in your liver? Maybe you're too full of rum and gin and whisky to feel 'em now! But someday you'll feel 'em! Someday when it's too late you'll feel 'em, brother! And them knives'll be hot and burning! 'Cause they'll be the knives of the Devil a-cutting you up in Hell!"

He fell to his knees, and began to pray again.

The drunkard reeled away.

The evangelist arose, and tossing his buffalo-like head, went on with a new oration.

Up and down he stormed, his massive body dissolving in perspiration once more, his eyes flashing till they seemed to be a reflection of the sullen fire in the distance. About him the worshipers began to moan and sway.

Often he would pause to let the band repeat its playing. The worshipers along the sidewalk would clap their hands. The choir would recommence the hymn, and parading up and down with the others, call on all sinners to come to salvation.

The preaching, combined with the singing and the booming of the drums, was beginning to affect the onlookers. The juke boxes ceased their clamor. The faces of some of the spectators were growing taut.

On and on the evangelist continued.

The tensity of the audience heightened. Still no one came forward to answer his impassioned pleas.

His anger mounted. Suddenly he bent over a box set near

the front of the truck, and thrusting in a hand, lifted out a huge blacksnake. Wildly he brandished the struggling reptile over his head. The spectators gasped with horror.

He gave a sardonic laugh, and held the neck tight in one hand so the figures in the street could see the frightening head, with its wicked eyes and forked tongue.

He lashed the spectators with his words, as though he were laying whips on their naked bodies. "It's the Evil Thing the Lord drove out of Eden!" he thundered. "It's the black soul of every sinner that won't come and confess the Lord."

With an unexpected movement, he drew back his arm and hurled the reptile into the midst of his audience. The nearest spectators bolted in panic. The blowzy women screamed. The men on the sidewalks darted back into the doorways, then halted and looked about uneasily at their feet.

The snake disappeared.

The evangelist taunted the spectators in bitter tones. "I seen you running!" he shouted. "I seen you big men with your pistols hollering and yelling! But it ain't the blacksnake that scares you! It's your black souls a-hiding down in Hell!"

He went on in a new frenzy.

His audience neared the breaking point.

A slim, overdressed young woman with a pretty but dissipated face came closer to the truck, trembling a little.

He concentrated upon her the full intensity of his holy wrath. "Look at her, Lord! Look at her! Once she was a beautiful girl, Lord! But she's shamed that beauty, Lord! Every night she takes her pay from the Devil! Every night she takes Satan to her breast! She's got the wickedness of

Jezebel on her, Lord! The evil of Delilah! Amen! But she wants to be saved! Hallelujah! Make her come to you, before it's too late, Lord!"

The band and the marchers halted and formed about her in a wide half-circle. Their chanting rose with redoubled fervor.

Suddenly with a cry the young woman darted forward and flung herself in the road at the evangelist's feet. "I'm a evil woman, Lord! Take me and cleanse me, Jesus!"

She lay there sobbing.

A cry of joy arose from the worshipers. The singers closed about her in a protective shield, joined in a moment by the white-winged angels. They burst into a hymn of glory.

The resistance was ended. As ice breaks in a pack, another thickly-rouged girl and another darted forward and flung herself to the pavement. Soon a score of the tawdry-dressed figures were on their knees near the truck, their made-up faces streaming with tears, their bodies shaking convulsively. Men began to come forward now, some with a feverish light in their faces like the gaunt woman at the trailer camp, some quiet, with a far-off look in their eyes as though they were walking in a trance. At the hoarse urging of the preacher, they began carrying out dice tables and slot machines and gambling wheels from the doorways alongside, and collected them in a great pile at the center of the road. Tossing knives and pistols on the top, they emptied a can of kerosene, and waited while the evangelist struck a match. The mound burned luridly, lighting up the women kneeling in the road, and the dancing worshipers lining the sidewalks. At times there would come a loud pop as the heat exploded a cartridge in a pistol. The worshipers would leap into the air as the bullet whistled past.

The evangelist preached with unabated fury.

One after another the bars closed; their interiors darkened. Here and there, where a light still showed, the marchers, followed by some of the brawnier converts, would push their way inside. Occasionally there was argument, and at times resistance. The brawny men would crowd forward. The lights would go out.

The last doorway blackened.

The frenzy of the preacher suddenly ceased.

With stern eyes he gazed down the row of shadowy buildings, then off toward the lane of the cottages, now gloomy, deserted.

He dropped to his knees, and looked up at the heavens. His face shone with sweat and triumph.

"New City's safe for God," he said.

He murmured a prayer of thanksgiving.

The services concluded. The worshipers drifted off to their homes.

Captain Asa and the others looked around for Pretty Boy, but could see him nowhere. They returned to the trailer, wondering at his whereabouts.

They had been indoors a little while when the long-threatening rainstorm descended, sweeping in opaque sheets down the road. The camp became a lake, full of strange-shaped islands. A fine layer of moisture covered the windows. Captain Asa arose and wiped them with a cloth.

The deluge slackened to a gentle patter. The branches of the nearby trees began to drip musically. The offensive odor of oil vanished. There came instead the pleasant smell of dampened leaves and grass. A mist arose from the ground, blotting out the walks, and draping each tent and trailer with a mysterious veil. The camp seemed a spectral village, lost in the clouds.

There was a noise in the path outside. Captain Asa hurried to the doorway. To his surprise he saw Pretty Boy standing beneath a tree, staring off into the rainy mist.

Captain Asa called through the darkness. Pretty Boy roused himself, and came inside. Water was dripping from his cowboy hat; his shirt, his riding pants were sodden sponges.

He stood in silence. About his lips was a curious tightness; in his eyes was the far-off look which had marked many of the penitents, as though he were a dweller in some distant world.

He spoke at last. His voice was hushed. "I seen the light tonight, Pa. I'm through working in the gambling house. I'm through with any kind of sinning. I'm going to take care of you and Ula. Way a good son ought to do."

He changed into the dry clothes that his wife brought him and sat staring into the mist again.

The dog went outside, and returned, its shaggy hair glistening. It shook itself luxuriously, spraying great drops of water on the floor.

Some latecomers from the services moved in a ghostly group through the fog, chanting softly. Down the road there came the muted sound of the bandsmen, returning to their quarters in the tabernacle for the night. Their playing was no longer fevered but casual, relaxed.

The last of the rain ceased. The mist lifted. The moon broke through the gloomy sky, flooding the earth with a calm radiance. It transformed the oil derricks in the distance till they seemed like silvery ladders mounting to paradise.

Pretty Boy watched them a long time in silence. "I'm going to be a preacher, like my uncle and Oklahoma Jack," he murmured. "I'm going to take the Lord's word to all the sinners like me."

The faces of Captain Asa and the girls grew bright. Ula arose and took his hand.

In the morning Captain Asa went with Vergil to the town. A deep stillness lay over the square, as though it were under some strange enchantment. The voices of the people in the street and the shops seemed softer, their manners gentler. The loungers who had stood on the sidewalks, whistling at every girl, were no longer visible. Even the passing automobiles seemed affected, their tooting horns silent.

The street of the bars was empty, the doors of the buildings boarded up, as though some dread epidemic had passed and destroyed all the inhabitants. In the road lay the charred remains of the dice tables and the gambling wheels, still smoking faintly, like a funeral pyre. The narrow lane beyond was bleak, untenanted. Only from one of the drab cottages there came the voice of a woman, singing a hymn.

Captain Asa surveyed the scene with satisfaction. "Now it's changed, looks like New City's going to be a mighty fine town for all of us to stay. I kind of figured we'd find a place if we came to Texas."

The alteration in Pretty Boy was marked as that of the community. Hour after hour he sat turning the worn pages of his father-in-law's Bible, stopping only at mealtime for a little food. Whenever he roused himself to speak, his sentences were crowded with phrases from the Scriptures.

Next day the evangelist made ready for his departure. Pretty Boy went with Captain Asa and the others to the depot, where the choir and the white-winged angels were waiting. The ramp was lowered from the baggage-like car still standing with the second coach on the siding. The bannered truck rumbled aboard. A locomotive appeared, and coupling itself to the foremost car, puffed impatiently.

The evangelist mounted to the rear platform, and smiled

upon the crowd with massive benevolence. Pretty Boy followed the other penitents up the train steps, and shook his hand.

The bell of the locomotive clanged, and the great wheels began to turn.

Oklahoma Jack raised his arms in blessing.

The faraway look in Pretty Boy's eyes heightened.

The cars moved slowly down the track.

For perhaps a week the spell the evangelist had wrought continued to grip the inhabitants. Then little by little it began to lessen. The square grew noisy again with the squawking of innumerable auto horns. The whistling loungers gathered once more on the sidewalks. The voices of the citizens hardened. One by one the gambling houses reopened, with new tables and wheels to replace those destroyed in the conflagration. The blowzy women sat once more before their drab cottages, calling out invitations to every passerby.

The far-off look in Pretty Boy's eyes faded. The worn Bible lay unopened on the shelf. The Scriptural phrases in his language ceased. Often he would pace the floor, as though trying to make a decision. Occasionally he went off to town early in the morning and was away all day. Several times he took Ula on these expeditions. When they returned she would gaze at her father with deep concern.

Captain Asa's joy vanished.

He was in the trailer alone late one afternoon, lost in reflection as he sat listening to the phonograph, when Ula returned from one of her journeys with Pretty Boy, and began to prepare supper. Her dark face seemed more and more worried as she took a knife, and peeled some potatoes. Several times she looked up, as though about to speak.

She dropped the final potato into a pan filled with water, and watched him rewind the phonograph. "Pretty Boy's going away, Pa," she said.

The turning handle in Captain Asa's fingers halted for an instant, then resumed its steady circling. "Where's he a-going?"

"Over to Dallas. . . . The fellow he worked for here's opening up a big pool hall and bowling alley. . . . He wants Pretty Boy to help him."

Captain Asa pressed the starting lever. The record began to grind out the melancholy strains of *Sparrow On The Mountain.*

He walked back to his chair. "When's . . . he starting?"

"He's leaving . . . tomorrow. . . . Your hair's mighty long again. I'm going to cut it for you while I'm waiting for these potatoes to cook."

She took a towel from the bureau, and tucking it about his lean neck, began to ply the scissors.

Her dark eyes grew tender. "It's the last time I'll be cutting it for a while, Pa."

The colorless patches appeared in Captain Asa's cheeks and spread farther and farther. His bronzed face seemed to be absorbing the whiteness of the towel beneath his chin. "You . . . going . . . with . . . him?"

She nodded. "He's my husband, Pa. . . . I can't do no other way."

Captain Asa made no answer.

The phonograph continued its scratchy playing.

There came a sudden shifting of the record. The nasal voice of the singer broke into a quavering, unintelligible tremolo, like that of the hero in a Chinese opera.

With halting steps Captain Asa made his way to the instrument, while clumps of hair fell from the towel round his neck in a grayish trail to the floor. He looked at the irregular hole in the center of the record, then shifted the disk on the worn turntable. The ballad singer resumed his usual doleful lamenting.

Captain Asa returned to his seat. "It ain't played right . . . since that night he done the cutting on it. . . . But you tell him I don't hold it against him. . . . Get them scissors back of my ears, will you? . . . You always misses them hairs behind the ears."

The music played on in sad monotony. The scissors clicked in accompaniment.

At noon next day Ula hurried off with Pretty Boy to the town, their possessions packed in several cardboard dress boxes and a shabby suitcase tied with twine. Captain Asa and the others walked behind. They reached the bus station, a dilapidated building with a lunch counter outside where several young gallants were lounging, flirting with the blond, gum-chewing waitress. A score of tired-faced men and women were visible through the windows, sitting on long wooden benches beside bundles of fruit and clothing. Children sat near them, fidgeting restlessly, or munching the popcorn and stale cheese sandwiches they had purchased at the counter. A single bluish fly buzzed about drowsily as it eluded the sooty strings of flypaper left over from midsummer that swung from the ceiling. On one of the benches a baby was stretched out sleeping, whimpering a little whenever a skinny dog belonging to one of the travelers moved past and brushed its dangling arm.

An old Negro with a few tufts of snowy hair on his chin was sitting on the sidewalk near the doorway, holding a burlap sack. At times he peered through the half-open top, and spoke to some object hidden within.

Pretty Boy looked inside and saw a fat white rabbit with blinking pink eyes.

"He's my luck," the old Negro explained. "He's done been in two states. Soon as I get the bus fare I'm taking him across the line, so he'll be in three. Rabbit that's been in three states is finest luck there is. . . . You ain't got a nickel for me, has you, Boss? Be mighty good luck to give an old nigger with a rabbit a nickel. There's a heap of accidents these times when you're a-traveling."

Pretty Boy put a coin in the outstretched palm.

The old man tucked it into his pocket. "You can't make it no dime, can you, Boss? Good people's getting mighty scarce."

Captain Asa accompanied Pretty Boy to the ticket window where the bald-headed, loquacious agent was chatting with one of the bus drivers. "It's like you said, Joe. You sure see life in a bus station. . . . There's your two tickets to Dallas, friend. It's a mighty good town. They had a mighty fine Exposition."

Pretty Boy led the way outside to the lunch counter. A bright-eyed little man was eating off a dish where strips of banana and chunks of pineapple lay at the foot of some rainbow mountains of ice cream, all partially hidden under snowy glaciers of marshmallow.

Pretty Boy questioned the bright-eyed man, then turned to Fernie standing next her sister. "You and Pa and Vergil take one of them Paradise Dreams, Fernie. It's the special."

She studied in awe the price list painted on the smudgy wall. "The Paradise is thirty-five cents. That's a terrible lot of money to pay for a sundae, ain't it?"

Pretty Boy's face was touched for a moment with its old bravado. "It's O K, Fernie. You go on and get it. I'm going to do mighty good in Dallas."

They took places on the stools.

The gum-chewing waitress put the confections on the counter. They ate in leisurely fashion.

The bright-eyed little man finished, and wiped his lips with a handkerchief. "Them Paradises sets good on your stomach," he declared.

He went into the station.

Some leaflets from the revival were tucked into a rack at the end of the counter. Captain Asa took one, and read the large-printed phrases, "The Lord Will Comfort You. Come Unto The Lord." He placed it carefully in his coat.

There came the hoarse honking of a horn somewhere in the distance. A moment later a huge blue bus roared up the road, and halted at the curb. Pretty Boy and Ula walked toward it, and stood waiting.

Captain Asa pressed close to his daughter. "Get a seat near the front, Ula. They rides easier in the front. And the driver can tell you what you're passing."

A young Negro porter began piling in baggage. The driver descended, and collected the tickets.

Ula vanished inside, then reappeared in a seat at a window. She reached down and tenderly pressed her father's hand.

The transfer of the baggage was finished. The driver mounted again and blew a long blast of the horn. Two men sitting at the lunch counter came running. The motor sputtered in final warning.

Ula leaned far out of the window. "I'll send you all kinds of souvenirs, Pa. . . . They got wonderful souvenirs in Dallas, they says."

Tightly Captain Asa clutched her hand, as though by some curious magnetism he might hold the great vehicle immovable. "It's a fine place, like the ticket fellow was saying. But the Exposition wasn't nothing like the one in St. Louis. That was the best Exposition there ever was. . . . You be careful crossing them streets. . . . It's a mighty big town."

The motor emitted a deafening roar. The bus sped away.

Captain Asa watched it become a bluish haze on the horizon. His face grew desolate.

Fernie and Vergil went off to the lunch-stand for a moment to spend some change Pretty Boy had given them in parting.

The old Negro with the snowy tufts of beard sitting at the entrance studied Captain Asa with a quizzical air. "That's the way it is with children. They comes and they goes. I raised four fine children. And they've done forgot me. Even the one that died didn't send me no insurance money."

There was a stirring in the sack at his feet. He took a half-eaten carrot, and held it inside. "Maybe it'd be better if people was like rabbits. Tells their young ones good-by before they even names 'em. Way it is with humans, children ain't nothing but sorrow. . . . You ain't got no nickel, has you, Boss? A nickel'll make fifteen cents. When it's a quarter, I can git him across the line."

Vergil and Fernie returned. Captain Asa did not seem to notice their presence, his eyes still fixed on the hazy distance.

Fernie touched his arm. He walked slowly up the road.

They reached the trailer.

Vergil brought the horse from a little farm at the edge of town where they had put it to graze, and harnessed it in the shafts. Captain Asa took the reins.

Back in the direction they had come they traveled, past the roadhouses and hamburger stands with their frenzied juke boxes that fringed the highway. They reached the oil derricks rising like a gloomy forest from the brownish plain. The pumping arms creaked and whined in mournful harmony.

Captain Asa took from his pocket the leaflet he had found at the counter. Over and over he read the words, "The Lord Will Comfort You."

His lips moved sadly. "I guess I ain't a good man. 'Cause if I was a good man, I'd know how to find the comfort of the Lord. And seems like I can't find it no way."

CHAPTER NINE

THROUGH the grassy plains and the wide marshes they made their way again, back toward the delta of the great river.

The warm days faded into the cool of autumn, drifting imperceptibly into the brief but gloomy winter. The skies grew gray, with chilling rains that beat dismally upon the plodding horse and the roof of the trailer. At times a Norther would sweep across the countryside, or a sleet storm that transformed the roads into icy mirrors. When the travelers stopped at night they would huddle close about the tiny stove in the kitchen.

As the trailer lumbered from hamlet to hamlet, they tried again to peddle the statuettes and the spreads. Their sales were so few, Fernie soon ceased her painting and sewing. They managed to exist only by stopping for short periods, while Captain Asa and Vergil took any odd job they could find.

Ula's departure was a shock from which it took Captain Asa a long time to recover. His affections centered with new intensity on Vergil and Fernie. Often in the middle of the night he would arise from his bunk to glance at the delicate face of the sleeping girl, or the lanky body of his son, wrapped like an Indian in a blanket, and reassure himself of their presence. Little by little the pain of Ula's absence lessened.

Vergil continued to read his books and magazines, occasionally plucking at his ukulele or poring over his collection of souvenir matches. The dreaminess of his face was heightening.

The days became weeks, the weeks became months. The gray winter began to drift into spring. They were in the Cajun country once more. The sky was a brilliant blue again, with spectacular clouds, transformed by the setting sun into turreted castles of gold and ivory. Cranes and pelicans and huge man-of-war birds circled lazily across the flat landscape. Along the sides of the highway delicate-leaved plants were springing into life, with tough-stemmed weeds beside them, like the children of the rich and the poor in the cities where the road was leading. Everywhere there came the rich fragrance of hidden flowers. When the travelers crossed a bayou, often they could not see the surface, only a mass of purple water lilies.

Vergil continued to grow more and more abstracted. At times when a train swept over the tracks that paralleled the highway he would follow its course until it vanished, and gaze for a long time at the green horizon.

A streamliner raced one afternoon along the shore of a flower-covered bayou, like a silver serpent. The whistle blew a mournful warning.

Vergil spoke absently. "It'd sure be nice a-working on one of them new trains."

Captain Asa grew uneasy. He pulled the horse beyond the edge of the concrete to make way for a huge moving van rumbling down the road. "You ain't figuring on going off somewheres, are you, Vergil?"

The youth drew in his long legs, dangling over the side of the vehicle. The suggestion of a stammer in his voice was growing more noticeable. "I ain't figuring on it, Pa. But I been thinking plenty I ought to be working at something. This ain't no kind of life for a young fellow, way I'm doing now. Just a-sitting all day, maybe getting a job a couple of times a week. It ain't right, Pa."

The van rumbled past. Captain Asa drove the horse back onto the concrete. His blue eyes were worried. "What you want to be doing, Vergil?"

The youth relieved his father of the reins. He guided the horse down the winding road a long time without answering. "I don't kind of know exactly, Pa. Sometimes I figure I want to work on one of the trains. And sometimes I want to work on one of them big airplanes. And once in a while when I start to playing the ukulele I'd like to be one of them band leaders. That'd be a mighty fine life, if a fellow knowed something about music. Or maybe I'd like to play with one of them big baseball teams." He gave a dreamy flick of the reins to drive away a fly on the horse's back. "Then sometimes I want to go to college and study about engines. I ain't had no schooling hardly. And I guess I ain't so smart, 'cause I failed in spelling and geography. But I know a-plenty about engines."

Captain Asa held the brake as they descended the steep incline of a bridge spanning a railroad track. "I'd mighty like to send you to college. And then me and Fernie could come and live with you while you was studying. Ain't nobody in our family been nothing since your grandpa was a preacher. But we're mighty poor, and them colleges takes a-plenty of money."

That night Captain Asa lay awake until almost dawn, in troubled reflection.

Spring was in its full glory now. Yellow-hammers tapped gaily in the trees, and bluejays screamed insults at every traveler. Squirrels chattered furiously in the branches overhead when the trailer lumbered near, as though it were some ungainly, crawling monster seeking to attack their nests. In the yards before the little cabins along the road cocks crowed with boastful voices, and hens scratched for worms to bestow upon their downy offspring. Even the automobiles seemed to have become suddenly endowed with reproductive powers like the animals, hatching out limitless progeny on the concrete pavement.

The carnivals were on the road again, moving to the North. A little caravan passed with a few scarlet-and-gilt vehicles where bold-eyed girls sat smoking cigarettes.

Vergil watched in a deep reverie. "The fellow I knew up in Clay Creek that hit the jackpot on the slot machines traveled with a carnival once. He's railroaded and towboated and pretty near everything. He said a carnival was the best of all."

Captain Asa made no comment. His anxiety increased.

The ancient horse began to limp a little. Captain Asa investigated and found a slight swelling about one of its knees. He treated it with his simple medical lore acquired in the mountains. The swelling subsided.

They crossed the Mississippi over the great bridge at Baton Rouge, and turned northward.

"Ought to be seeing that little fellow had the chairs pretty soon," declared Captain Asa. "He said he'd sure be around Natchez in the Spring."

He began to keep a sharp lookout along the road.

The trees were thickly festooned with Spanish moss once more. Occasionally through a leafy tunnel they caught sight of some stately, white-pillared mansion that had escaped the torches of the ravaging Yankees a century before. Horsemen galloped past, booted, broad-hatted white men and barefooted Negroes, on their way to some plantation. High-wheeled wagons creaked along, loaded with cotton bales on which weary pickaninnies were sleeping.

Natchez came into view, perched high on a bluff overlooking the river, haughty with the memory of its ancient grandeur. They reached the outskirts of the town, and submitting to the gaze of a stern-eyed policeman who watched with deep suspicion, moved toward the business district, between rows of wide-balconied buildings where slaves had once come to do their masters' errands.

Past the Eola Hotel they drove, where two well-fed politicians were arguing over the merits of several local brands of moonshine whisky. A women's club convention was in progress. The streets were crowded with smartly dressed matrons, chattering in vivacious voices.

Fernie looked in admiration. "I never seen so many pretty dresses, Pa."

Captain Asa glanced at her own homemade, awkward-fitting garments, and nodded. "Someday we'll make a-plenty of money. And then I'll get you all the pretty dresses you want."

A small photographer's booth was erected in the window of a vacant storeroom, where some rows of empty shelves and a sign advertising canned tomatoes were all that remained of a departed grocery. At the back of the booth was a curtain painted to represent the deck of an ocean liner, with an actual life preserver on which was printed in bold letters "S. S. Lover." At the front, to attract the attention of the passersby, was one of those flickering mercury lamps that instantly invest the freshest skin with the greenness of death, and touch the gentlest countenance with the mood of murder. Under it was a canvas of the type popular in summer resorts, painted to represent the naked bodies of twin babies, and cut off at the neck so that the heads would be supplied by any persons who stepped behind. Nearby was a canvas portraying a male and female South Sea Islander wearing real grass skirts, and decapitated in similar fashion. Beyond it was another of two headless monkeys holding hands, their hairy bodies clad in bathing suits. At the moment there showed above the guillotined Islanders the actual heads of a sheepish sailor and a giggling red-haired girl. Before these stood the jaunty Chick Waters, manipulating a battered camera.

The travelers halted, and waiting until the photographer had finished with his clients, went inside.

Mr. Waters greeted them cordially. "Ain't bought the bull yet," he declared. "Instead of that, getting people to make fools of themselves, and then paying me for it. Good thing monkeys don't know about pistols. If they did, and seen some of the heads that gets put above them monkey bodies, they'd sure start a-shooting."

It was almost dark. With alacrity Mr. Waters accepted Captain Asa's invitation to a meal. Climbing into his rickety car, he led them off to an open stretch of ground overlooking the river where they could park the trailer. The travelers pitched camp for the night.

Mr. Waters ate a hearty meal. He sat outside with Captain Asa in the starlight, smoking one of his host's handmade stogies.

Far beneath them the river lights twinkled. In the Government fleet anchored up the shore a towboat was moving back and forth, shunting some barges. It whistled sharply, summoning a galley-boy to bring coffee to the pilot-house. On the bluff there showed a gloomy factory building with dimlit windows. From it there came the rumble of machinery.

Inside the trailer Fernie was busy with the dishes.

Captain Asa watched as she moved back and forth past the window. He told of Ula's departure. His face grew bleak. "Looks like Vergil's getting ready to go, too," he said.

He talked of his son for a moment, then fell silent.

Mr. Waters' face was touched with rare sympathy. "It's bad when they start acting that way," he said.

On the road far below them a motor truck sputtered, struggling up the steep hill. From some shacks along the water's edge, all that remained of the rows of dives which had once been Natchez Under the Hill, there came the blaring of a radio and the harsh playing of a mechanical piano. On the Government fleet a shadow holding a flashlight began gliding over the long line of barges. There came a loud halloo. The flashlight went out.

Captain Asa spoke again, sadly. "I been thinking plenty what you told me about the tame fox they locked up, and then he run away. Maybe I ain't been doing right with them children. I guess things'd be different if I could find a wife to help me make a home for 'em. But getting a good wife ain't easy."

He patted the dog, who had stretched out in the grass

and laid its head on his shoe. "I ain't worried about Fernie. She's the quiet kind. She ain't never going to leave me. But selling these statues and these spreads sure ain't no good for Vergil. I was thinking maybe I ought to try to get more up-to-date and find something more lively for a living, like you said. Then maybe he wouldn't want to go away."

Mr. Waters nodded in the darkness. "Them young fellows eighteen are always a pile of trouble. I knew a policeman when I was working New Orleans was mighty smart, and he said he'd rather handle a eighteen-foot alligator than a eighteen-year-old boy. You can tell which way they're going to jump easier. He said eighteen was what they called the danger time, when them young fellows want to try everything, and go everywhere. They got kind of St. Vitus dance of the brain. If you can keep a boy home that year and the next couple of years maybe, he said you generally wouldn't have no trouble keeping him afterwards."

The towboat in the Government fleet whistled again, a long mournful blast warning a misty phantom that was sweeping down the river. The phantom blew in melancholy answer.

Captain Asa waited till the echoes died in the distance. "I been thinking what you told me about the show business. Every time you been here and start telling show stories, Vergil and Fernie sit like statues a-listening. And when the carnivals go past, Vergil watches till their automobiles ain't nothing but a little dust in the sky. Must be that young people's always craving for a show. Ula was always talking about going with a carnival. If I'd done what she wanted, maybe she'd still be staying home."

Mr. Waters struck a match to relight his extinct stogie. He blinked like a startled cat to avoid the glare. "Never seen a young fellow or a girl yet that didn't like a show."

Captain Asa looked out over the dark water. "My people in the hills never held with a show, 'cause Grandpa was a preacher. But I never figured that way. Me and my wife that bore them children never could find anything in the Bible against it. We always liked a show, long as it was the right kind. A fellow came up Clay Creek last year with a moving-picture machine in a truck giving shows, and stayed in my cabin for a night. He was as fine a fellow as you ever seen. Kept us sitting up all night, pretty near, talking. Maybe if we could get some kind of show like that for a while, Vergil'd be settled in his mind."

The whistle on the Government towboat blew a new muted blast. Its searchlight flashed blindingly over a long row of barges, piled high with lumber for use in some construction against the marauding river. In the dazzling circle two men picked their way across the timber, carrying heavy coils of rope. The searchlight darkened.

Mr. Waters smoked in silence again. The glowing end of the stogie pulsed in steady rhythm, at times illuminating his reflective face. "More I figure more it looks to me like maybe you ought to try it. You don't fit no place the way things are going today. You're a little fellow, and these times the big fellows are eating up the little ones everywhere. Looks like show business and tramping's about the only things left for a little fellow. In show business, as long as you can catch a flea on a dog and train him to jump over the comb, a little fellow can keep going."

There came the thud of barges bumping below, then the labored puffs of a donkey engine tightening some chains.

Captain Asa shifted on his stool. "Trouble is you got to have some money to get started, don't you? And I ain't got no money left for beginning something new."

Mr. Waters' face, visible in the glow of the stogie, had

recovered its old cynicism. "You don't need nothing. Show business is like getting somebody to hold a lot of money in front of a mirror and then you use the money that's showing in the glass. It's just doing good thinking."

A shower of sparks fell onto his green striped trousers. He brushed them away. "Now you take them statues—I seen how many you got in the trailer. You can't sell 'em no ways. But you listen to me, and I'll show you how to make 'em go so fast you'll think somebody stole 'em."

"How you figure on doing it?"

Mr. Waters grew a trifle didactic. "Ain't no trouble at all hardly. Just build yourself a little board with wooden pegs and numbers on it, and some kind of little hoops to throw over the pegs. You charge a dime for five hoops. And if they ring the right peg, they get one of the statues. You'll see. Instead of getting fifty cents like you're doing now, they'll pay you five dollars. . . . If you want to, I'll show you how to make the board tonight."

A little later Captain Asa went inside the trailer. He talked some time with Vergil and Fernie, explaining the other's proposal.

Their faces glowed with pleasure.

Early in the morning they all set to work under Mr. Waters' expert direction. The board was quickly finished. Fernie tacked some cheap green cloth about the legs which formed its support to afford an air of solidity. Captain Asa bought some wooden embroidery hoops at the ten-cent store, and proceeded to set up the apparatus in a vacant lot next the photograph booth. Over it Mr. Waters erected a sign he had lettered in vivid scarlet "Ringo. Win a Beautiful Statue. Fun For Old and Young."

Darkness fell. Mr. Waters was compelled to be off in a

nearby hamlet photographing a wedding, thus depriving the others of the assistance on which they had counted. Captain Asa brought an acetylene lamp from the trailer and hung it on the brick wall of the building alongside, as Mr. Waters had directed. Nervously Fernie took a place at the counter to receive the money they hoped would drop into the cigar box that served as a temporary cash register. Captain Asa and Vergil moved to the rear where the statuettes with numbers fixed beneath stood on a row of shelves, and waited tensely for the customers.

The night was warm, with a full moon overhead. Promenaders were constant along the tree-girded sidewalks. Some high-school boys searching for adventure came over from the drugstore across the street, and halting before the booth, stood examining the statuettes, keeping up a constant crossfire of labored, youthful humor.

Captain Asa's blue eyes lighted. His face fell as the boys moved away.

A heavy-set man smoking a cigar and carrying a suitcase, who had wandered over from the neighboring bus station, approached the shy cashier and jingled some keys on the end of his watch chain, as though debating whether to idle away a few moments in the competition for the prizes. He put his hand in his pocket, then suddenly shrugged his shoulders and turned down the road.

More passersby halted for a similar tantalizing moment, only to drift off like the others. Then there moved to the booth a pale, undernourished young woman clad in a faded dress and carrying a baby, accompanied by her young husband whose shabby overalls were covered with bits of cotton. They were sharecroppers from one of the plantations beyond the town.

With longing eyes the young mother gazed at the grotesque figures on the shelf, as though they were jewels beyond all price.

She spoke to her husband in a gentle voice. "Maybe you could win me one of them Cherry Boys. We ain't got nothing pretty in the house. I'd mighty like something pretty for the baby."

With solicitude her husband counted the sparse change in his overalls, and took out a ten-cent piece which represented a third of the total. He smiled at her tenderly. "I'll git it for you, Essie."

He put down the coin, and taking the wooden hoops which Captain Asa gave him, tossed each one with painstaking care, as though he were a surgeon, performing a delicate operation on which the life of a patient depended.

The hoops rolled and bounced over the board. The pale young wife stood breathless.

She grew taut as the final spinning hoop circled a peg that bore a bold-printed 22.

The husband looked at the winning numbers painted beneath the prizes.

He shook his head. "I didn't get nothing, Essie."

The young wife turned away forlornly. They started down the road.

Captain Asa hurried out to the sidewalk. He thrust the Cherry Boy into the husband's arms. "It's opening night," he declared. "This here's a souvenir for opening night."

The face of the young woman shone with ecstasy.

The spell seemed broken now. More of the passing figures halted, and put down their coins: tired parents, taking their noisy children home from a visit to a relative, hoping for a moment's respite; fishermen still reeking of their catch, their overalls shiny with scales; youthful factory workers with their giggling girls, full of the pride of their masculinity.

Midnight came, and Captain Asa counted the receipts.

His blue eyes shone with delight. "It's four dollars and twenty cents," he announced. "I didn't figure nothing like that for just the first night. We're a-starting mighty good."

For two weeks they remained, with new crowds each evening. The lid of the cigar box opened and shut without ceasing. Their pride in the new enterprise grew rapidly. The days, spiced with Mr. Waters' drolleries, passed once more in gay procession.

Mr. Waters at length decided that the possibilities of the town had been exhausted. They prepared to move on to new territory.

They tied the playing table on top of the trailer. With care Captain Asa tacked the scarlet-lettered streamer along the front and sides of the vehicle, adding some red stars of tin for decoration.

They set out at dawn, Mr. Waters quickly disappearing in the distance. The horse jogged down the highway. Past cotton fields the trailer lumbered, past desolate swamps where white cranes circled like graceful-floating flowers.

The horse was limping a little again. Captain Asa descended and saw that the swelling had reappeared in its knees. He drove slower.

They passed a mat plant along the river where black men were laboring, weaving willow branches into carpets to protect the banks from the water's ravages.

Their chanting rose melodiously above the creaking of the trailer:

Shake, Mattie
Lawd, Lawd,
Quake, Mattie
Lawd, Lawd.

Step it, fetch it
Lawd, Lawd,
Shake it, break it
Lawd, Lawd.

A cabin showed down the road, where a wrinkled old white woman and a sad-eyed girl with plaits of dark hair trailing down her back were hoeing in a garden overgrown with weeds and hollyhocks.

Captain Asa went over with Fernie to purchase some vegetables.

The sad-eyed girl looked off at the scarlet sign fixed to the trailer. "You show people?"

Captain Asa helped her pull up some turnips. "You throw the hoops and win a statue. If we was stopping, I'd let you play free. It's a mighty fine game."

The girl shook her head in fright. "We're Holiness folks. I can't play them games or listen to them funny jokes and singing. I've done put all that life behind me."

She dug some potatoes, and put them in the basket Captain Asa was carrying.

The old woman gazed with stern eyes at Fernie, who stood near the cabin petting a scraggly kitten. "That there girl of yours got her hair bobbed?" she demanded.

Captain Asa shook his head. "No'm. She wears it long. It's my other girl out in Dallas that's got it bobbed."

The old woman nodded gloomily. "It's the other one that's going to die then. It's the bobbed hair that's the trouble with the world today. A girl baby was born last night up at Coldspring, with hair growing all the way down to her feet. And first thing when they laid it on the bed by its mother it stood up and said, 'Everybody that's got bobbed hair ain't going to be living when I've drunk my mother's milk a year.' You'd better tell that there girl of yours to let her hair grow quick as she can."

The limping of the horse increased as the sun rose higher. The animal was walking in obvious pain.

They neared a hamlet, surrounded by cotton fields. Captain Asa descended again and examined the horse anxiously. "Can't get no further with his leg like that," he said to Vergil. "Going to get somebody to look at it."

He unhitched the animal from the traces, and with his son went off to a white-painted cottage where the sign of a veterinarian showed down the road.

They returned to the trailer, to find Mr. Waters, who had been far ahead, waiting with his car at the edge of the highway.

Captain Asa's worry had deepened. "Veterinarian says he's got to rest two or three months maybe before he'll be all right. Have to find a place for him to stay and get a new horse someways, I guess. Don't know where we're going to get one neither."

Mr. Waters gazed at the ancient animal in expert appraisal. "If you listen to me you won't buy a other horse. You ain't going to get nowhere in show business with a horse. Everybody'll see right away you got something old-fashioned. These here's modern times. You got to be up-to-date and get a automobile."

Captain Asa paled a little. "I ain't got no money for a automobile."

Mr. Waters shrugged his shoulders. "There's plenty of people has automobiles today don't know how they done it."

Vergil's dreamy face lighted with extraordinary enthusiasm. "Way feed is a horse costs twice as much as a automobile, Pa. I know plenty about engines. And I drove a car whenever I could that winter when we was living in town and I was doing odd jobs around them garages. Let me ask in the filling stations here, and see if maybe I can't find something."

Captain Asa agreed with reluctance. Vergil and Mr. Waters hurried off in the direction of the village.

A half-hour later there was a terrific clattering down the road. There came rattling toward the trailer a derelict automobile in the last stages of dissolution. Its battered wheels wobbled until the eyes of the beholder grew dizzy. From its exhaust a trail of smoke was issuing, at times so thick it seemed like the cloudy tail of a comet, blotting out all that lay in its path. From the motor there came a mad clamor of rods and pistons, as though a thousand metal arms had broken free and were striking against the rusty hood. Long black strips hung from the sides of the vehicle, at first sight appearing to be pieces of torn cloth. On closer inspection they were seen to be ragged sections of the fenders, torn into shreds by time and accident.

In the front Vergil sat proudly, holding tight to the bouncing steering wheel, while Mr. Waters jolted perilously at his side. The youth brought the car to a halt in a burst of smoke that seemed to obliterate the sun.

"It's thirty dollars, Pa," he called out, his usually slow voice electric with excitement. "And she's got a radio. It's a wonderful bargain with the high prices they're getting for used cars nowadays."

Captain Asa stood in silence a moment, torn between fascination and worry. "Golly, I never thought of getting no car. . . . And it'd take every nickel we got."

Vergil and his companion climbed out of the car.

Mr. Waters kicked at a tire with his toe. "Car'll get you around twice as many places, so you can make twice as much money. You'll get the price back in no time. And you can't tell what'll happen. Maybe you'll be getting another kind of show pretty soon, and then you got to have a car."

Captain Asa hesitated. "You like to have it, too, Fernie?"

She caught her breath with incredulity. "I ain't hardly ever got to ride in a car, Pa."

Captain Asa's lips set with resolution. "We'll buy it."

Vergil lost the last vestige of his usual gravity. In a frenzy of joy, he hooked the car onto the trailer, and with Fernie and Mr. Waters as passengers, hurried off to a crossroads store and filling station visible in the distance where he had found the new treasure. Captain Asa followed with the horse. The amiable proprietor of the establishment agreed to graze the animal on his farm adjoining until the travelers' return. Captain Asa paid the money, and went into the courtyard where Vergil was already flat on his back beneath the automobile, tightening loosened bolts and springs. The youth emerged soon after, his overalls covered with oil and clay, his face almost hidden under a thick layer of grease. A long time he bent over the engine, adjusting the timer and the spark plugs and the rusty carburetor. Fernie took soap and a bucket of water and began scrubbing the derelict sides. Captain Asa attached a hose to the feeble pump nearby, and joined in the labor.

The work was finished at last. They bade an affectionate farewell to the horse, grazing contentedly now behind a fence, and made ready for their departure. Some freckled-faced boys and a few muddy-booted men had come over from the store, attracted by the decorated trailer.

Mr. Waters prepared to resume his travels. "Now you bought the car you can go places," he remarked to Captain Asa. "You drive out in the back country around here where they ain't got any picture shows. The people there don't know nothing. And if you can play a show where people don't know nothing, that's the finest kind of show business there is. I'm going to run up the Vicksburg road a little ways to see a fellow owes me some money and meet you over at Hoxie tomorrow. There's a lot of men pulling lumber out of them swamps, and they ought to be good pickings."

Captain Asa and the others climbed into the car. The dog followed with its usual solemnity.

Vergil pressed the starting pedal. A new wave of volcanic smoke spread across the countryside. The car rocked forward, and rattled onto the road.

Across the holes and broken stones they bounded. Fat sows with half-a-dozen baby pigs waddled in panic before them, and hens clucked wildly. From a frame school building some children came running, with a pack of yelping dogs at their heels. The children raced after the car, shouting, panting, till a call and a loud ringing of the school bell ended their breathless chase.

Vergil swung the wheel. His dreamy face glowed with a brightness that its black coating of grease could not hide. "All my life I been wanting a automobile, Pa. . . . I ain't asking for nothing more."

Captain Asa smiled happily.

The car rattled over the highway.

CHAPTER TEN

THEY had proceeded a short distance when there came a sudden hissing at the back of the car, then the sound of an irregular bumping. The wheel in Vergil's hand began to jiggle violently. With a shrill screeching of brakes he brought the car to a stop.

He dismounted with the others, and looked at one of the worn tires at the rear, spreading wider and wider over the concrete.

"It's a flat," he announced.

Removing the casing, he quickly patched a split in the rotted inner tube, and resumed the journey. Several other times that day their progress was halted by similar collapses. They bought two secondhand tires for a few dollars at a wayside filling station, and substituted their purchases for the worn-out rubber.

They drove on gaily again.

For several weeks they wandered over the countryside, stopping frequently to repair some new defect in the rickety vehicle. At times the road wound through the piny forests that covered the Mississippi Highlands, at times it skirted the tangled swamps that lay along the great river. By arrangement they followed the same route as Mr. Waters. Their meetings were frequent.

Vicksburg appeared before them, with its stately houses of another day and its hilly streets crowded with picturesque Negroes. The rickety car chugged past a row of cafés exhaling the rich odor of frying catfish, and crossing the great river again, rattled northward. Each night when the travelers halted at some drowsy settlement, they would set up the green-draped table in an empty store or a vacant lot, and wait hopefully for customers. Their good luck, however, seemed ended.

The brightness in Vergil's face faded. Long spells of abstraction seized him once more.

Captain Asa's anxiety returned.

They met a little carnival, on the way to some nearby town.

Vergil watched dreamily as he held the wheel. "Wish we could get a show like one of them, Pa. Maybe if we had a real show, we could make some money."

Captain Asa wiped a spot from the cracked windshield with his handkerchief. "Takes money to get money, the way they says. A show like that costs a pile."

The dreaminess in Vergil's eyes heightened. With a sudden impulse he pressed the accelerator, and drove the car close behind the red-painted caravan. The trailer rattled crazily. A blond girl, clad in a dressing gown, was sitting at the rear of the last scarlet vehicle, drying her hair in the sun. She saw Vergil and waved a jeweled hand.

He drove the car faster.

The road became a long rise. The motor began to sputter feebly. The pace of the automobile slackened to a crawl. Vergil stamped on the accelerator as in a fever. It had no effect. The distance between the car and the carnival grew ever wider.

The caravan neared the top of the hill. One by one the ornate vehicles vanished over the crest. With a deafening roar of its motor the final car reached the summit. The nymph-like rider waved again in farewell. She, too, vanished.

The road was empty, desolate.

Vergil's foot on the pedal relaxed. He leaned back from the wheel and drove on quietly.

Captain Asa gazed at him in wonder.

The days passed in even succession. Spring was advancing. The air grew warmer. Often the sky would cloud with suddenness, and a heavy shower would sweep down the flat valley where they were driving. The roof of the car would become a sieve through which poured innumerable rivulets of rusty water. The travelers covered themselves with carpets or tarpaulins, trying to avoid the deluge. The shower would end, leaving the earth pungent, refreshed.

They crossed a river late one afternoon, and neared a little settlement lost in a swamp, a collection of bare frame shacks clustered about a sawmill. Everywhere there arose the fragrance of new-cut lumber mingling with the smoke of an immense fire beyond the mill where the waste wood burned in a continuous flame. The travelers began watching for a camping place. They were about to come to a stop in a strip of ground between the grocery and the filling station that formed the community's business district when they saw that they had been preceded. A weather-beaten tent stood near the roadway, with a crudely lettered sign fixed over the entrance, "Animal Show." Before it was standing a plump, middle-aged woman with bright-hennaed hair and a red-spotted dress hung loosely over her ample form. She was chatting with the oil-smeared attendant of the filling station.

The travelers hesitated. The henna-haired woman saw them, and called out a cordial greeting. They halted with relief.

"Glad you come," the henna-haired one declared cheerfully. "Ain't seen no show people for a couple of weeks. These here swamps sure get you to feeling blue."

The voyagers made their preparations for the night, and set up the table for the hoops. Fernie began to cook their supper.

The sun set through the flaming waste beyond the mill, like a golden ingot dropped into a furnace. Darkness settled over the swamp. Bats wheeled and dived mysteriously. Mosquitoes rose up in trailing clouds, like long strips of gauze waving in the wind. At the mill lights still burned faintly. There came the whine of the saws, shriller than in the noisy daylight hours, as though the captive wood were protesting this continued torment when elsewhere the world was at rest.

The travelers ate. Captain Asa lit the acetylene lamp, and hung it over the playing table.

The henna-haired woman brought half a creamy lemon

pie, and presented it to Captain Asa. "Getting kind of tired of show business," she remarked. "It's nice. But ain't my real business. Me and my husband had a restaurant in Memphis. 'Joe's Coffee Pot—A Clean Place to Eat.' Over near the L & N Station. I guess you seen it. All them L & N conductors says we had the best lemon pie in Tennessee. And ain't nobody knows pie like a train conductor. Then Joe died and I was lonesome and I thought I'd get a change. And somebody told me I ought to go into show business. A fellow that come in the restaurant one day had this animal show over near the depot and said he wanted to sell it. So I bought it. . . . I'm glad you like the pie."

She took the empty dish in her plump hand. "Wish I didn't have nothing to do but bake 'em. This here going around in a tent ain't no life for me. I like cooking, and looking after a lot of men, and feeding them, and joshing with them, way you do in a restaurant. Once you done it, you ain't good for nothing else. There's a fellow in Memphis that's been wanting to marry me ever since Joe died, and open up a wagon diner. I'm sure going to do it, quick as I can."

She walked away.

Captain Asa and his family took their accustomed places.

Booted figures began to come down the road, millworkers, their overalls still heavily coated with sawdust, lumbermen fresh from the woods, their faces brown as the dry leaves clinging to their clothing, in their hip pockets a bottle of whisky and an occasional revolver. Often they halted before the tent to exchange a running fire of banter with the henna-haired proprietress who stood at the entrance. But only rarely a lone individual stopped before the statuettes.

The plump lady waited until the number of ticket purchasers was sufficient, then disappeared inside to give her show. Her voice came through the canvas walls in a cheerful monologue.

The patrons began to file out, and she reappeared again. Captain Asa looked with envy at the departing visitors.

The henna-haired proprietress caught his glance. "Ain't the statues going good?" Her voice was sympathetic.

He shook his head. "Did mighty fine in Natchez. But seems like we can't get started nowhere else some way."

She tugged at her dress to adjust a strap beneath that was cramping one of her stout shoulders, and grew thoughtful. "How'd you like to take over this show of mine?" she asked unexpectedly. "Ain't much, but you can make a living from it. And then I can go back to my restaurant."

Captain Asa was too startled to answer.

The plump lady turned to make change for a customer. "Wouldn't cost you nothing hardly. All you'd have to do is pay a few dollars down, and send me a little each week out of what you made. Why don't you come on over when you get through, and then you can see if you want it?"

Captain Asa spoke slowly. "We been kind of thinking about a show."

They closed their booth when the last lumberman had started homeward, then hurried to the tent of their neighbor. It was one of those shabby little exhibitions so often encountered in a village square, or at the edge of the humbler section of some metropolis. A single large electric bulb swung to and fro from the ceiling, surrounded by a halo of insects. Beneath it, set at irregular intervals about the sawdust-covered floor, were a half-dozen glass cases, their wooden frames scratched with the initials of patrons who had taken this means of leaving their mark for posterity.

The proprietress took the guests on a tour of inspection. She halted before a case where a large yellowish lizard lay torpidly on some sand, its ugly head near a baking powder top filled with water. She began to talk in an amiable attempt at the curious mechanical singsong of the professional showman, without doubt taught her by the previous proprietor. "This here's what they call a Gila monster," she intoned. "Most poisonous thing that's alive in the world anywhere, they says. Puts its teeth in you and then blows its breath over where it's bit. Its breath's so bad, when it hits the bites, you get blood poisoning."

Next it was a small stuffed bat suspiciously like those flying outside. Beyond this a small king snake crawled about, with a curious design resembling a woman's face tattooed on its back that roughly followed the mottled markings of its skin.

The proprietress advanced toward these with the visitors. "This here's a genuine vampire bat. He's dead. If them South American people don't like you, they get a hold of a drop of your blood and give it to the vampire. Then when you're asleep the bat puts its beak in your throat and drinks up all your blood, just like it was taking water out of a tap. . . . That picture of a lady on the back of the king snake looks kind of like it's tattooed, but it growed there natural. It's what they call a snake photograph. The fellow that caught the snake seen the lady's picture on it, and started looking for her. He found her, and they got married. They're a-living down in Gulfport, Mississippi."

She walked about the tent, explaining the other exhibits: a baby alligator perhaps ten inches long, gazing as though hypnotized at a great moth fluttering outside the glass; a preserved tarantula and a scorpion, standing in dusty menace near a frayed bit of cactus; a live rattlesnake, following the newcomers with evil eyes, and rattling viciously as they came near.

Captain Asa and the others were fascinated.

"They ain't no bother to take care of," the henna-haired hostess continued. "Just a little chopped meat for the lizard and the alligator, and a egg once in a while for the snakes. I got a bird act goes with it. It's the big act of the show."

She took from behind the screen a cage where a dilapidated parrot with half its crest feathers missing stood on a perch, chattering pleasantly but unintelligibly to itself, its distinct utterances being confined to a shrill "Scramble Two!" and a long-drawn-out "My O My!" With care she lifted out the bird, put a tiny American flag in its beak, and set it down before two toy ladders placed together to form a triangle. The parrot raised a hesitant claw. Rung by rung, urged on by some sunflower seeds in the hand of its mistress, it climbed the nearest ladder, muttering as though in self-encouragement and almost dropping the flag, then quickly descended.

The plump woman set the flag in a wooden holder. The parrot began to sing in a ludicrous squawking voice a few bars of what was intended to be "Yankee Doodle." It concluded its performance by lifting tiny cards out of a box, and telling the fortunes of the visitors.

The henna-haired lady moved off to let her visitors make their decision.

They stood talking a few moments.

Captain Asa hurried forward to where the proprietress was feeding the dilapidated bird.

His face glowed with simple rustic pleasure. "We're just hill people, don't know nothing about a show. But we got to get some way of making a living, and this here looks fine to me and my children. . . . We'd mighty like to try it for a while, and see what we can do."

The transfer was effected in the morning. The henna-haired woman spent the day teaching them her lecture, and showing them how to water and feed the inhabitants of the glass cases, then hurried off after supper on the night bus to Memphis.

Captain Asa and the others went about investigating their new property with curiosity and enthusiasm. In a few hours each creature had become a personality, the baby alligator freezing into a new trance each time a fly or bee buzzed about the glass, the Gila monster coming crossly forward to be fed whenever Captain Asa tapped on the wooden frame, like a sleepy old man in a boardinghouse, angry at being awakened for the meal that is his only goal.

The rattlesnake became the focus of Vergil's attentions. The youth found a book the henna-haired woman had left behind, full of lurid natural history. He would study the section on reptiles, then would sit for a long time before the rattler, observing each twisting of the lithe body, each sinister dart of its forked tongue. The parrot, accustomed to a woman, had adopted Fernie as its mistress and protector, for whom alone it would climb the tiny barrier and sing its grotesque solo. It would dance back and forth on its perch, blinking and clucking with impatience, until the gentle girl would come forward and scratch its battered crest.

Fernie's eyes would glow with tenderness.

Only the dog did not share the common pleasure. Again and again it would walk about the tent, sniffing the cases in suspicion; whenever it neared the rattlesnake stiffening and growling faintly.

They were still at work the second day, when the car of the jaunty Mr. Waters came chugging down the road.

He gave a pessimistic approval of the enterprise. "I seen plenty better but I can't remember no worse," he declared, as he walked about the tent with Captain Asa. "If you paid more than five dollars for it, they sure robbed you. That painted snake and the Vampire, Noah throwed off the Ark, 'cause people was tired of them acts already. But any kind of animal show's pretty good, I guess. They been having animal shows since Lord trained the snake to give Eve the apple. That's the first show business there ever was."

He pointed a stick at the rattler to make it sound a vicious warning, and sauntered outside. "Anyhow your children likes it, the way you says. Everybody likes animals. Kids and old people both. A man looks at you sad and you say, 'Go away. I'm broke.' But if a dog or cat does it, you give 'em all you got."

He gazed at the exterior of the tent a moment. "I better paint you up a good sign. A good sign's the biggest thing in show business."

He found a wide strip of cloth and set to work with a paintbrush. The design was finished by midnight. He exhibited it to the others with an artist's pride.

On the crudely painted canvas a helmeted explorer was standing with two kinky-haired natives carrying spears. Beyond them were arranged a startling collection of wonders: a trio of elephants smoking cigars and a half-dozen parrots playing banjoes; an enormous bat carrying off a baby and an alligator drinking beer through a straw; a giant dragon attacking a hunter and a troop of seals in catchers' masks playing baseball. Beneath was the scarlet legend, "Stanley's Combined African Bird And Animal Shows. World's Biggest Show Bargain—Ten Cents."

Captain Asa was torn between doubt and admiration. "She's a beautiful sign all right. But we ain't got all them things in the show."

Mr. Waters was unimpressed. He applied a little more red to the dragon's eyes to increase their sullen, bloodshot appearance. "You're figuring on getting 'em, ain't you? That's the way all them big shows started—Ringling and Barnum and all of 'em. Didn't have nothing but the sign at first. Then they built up to it. That's the up-to-date way of doing."

They tacked the sign to one side of the trailer, and made ready to set out in the morning. Abandoning the playing table, they lashed the folded tent in the place the other had occupied on the roof, and crowded the cases bearing the exhibits into the trailer and the back of the car.

"Remember what I told you and you'll get along," Mr. Waters, who was remaining behind for some photographs, called to Captain Asa with solemnity. "These here's advertising times. Just figure out some way of getting your name in the paper and you won't have to do any worrying. If you don't get any advertising, you ain't going to get nowhere."

He was hidden from their sight by a smoky blast as Vergil pressed the starting pedal. The car rattled over the deserted road. Along the swamp they rocked gaily, leaving behind them a trail of whirling blackness, like a gathering tornado.

Fernie pinned down her worn hat decorated with a single frayed feather. "It'd be mighty nice if Ula was here, now we got the show."

Captain Asa saddened for a moment. "If I'd have known how things'd be, looks to me I could have kept her from going away. Maybe when she finds out what we're doing, she'll want to come back."

He watched the speeding landscape. "I guess you got to live and learn, the way they says. I didn't do so good a-living at Spanish, but I learned something. And I didn't do so good a-traveling with the hoops, but I learned a-plenty more. Now maybe I'm through a-learning. 'Cause this time it looks like we're really started right."

His glance fell on the banner tacked to the trailer. His blue eyes lighted.

A long curve showed ahead. The road began to wind through a forest of lofty pines. Somewhere overhead a mockingbird chanted sweetly, and a distant woodpecker hammered as though drumming an accompaniment. A flock of blackbirds rose up, darkening the sky like a coming storm. Above them drifted a gray eagle, flying in solitary majesty.

The car was running better now, after numerous repairs. Vergil sat at the wheel in dreamy content.

They stopped that night at a little town and set up the tent in the drowsy square. As Mr. Waters had suggested, the parrot was stationed at the entrance beside Captain Asa to attract customers. Constantly the bird shifted its position, at times hanging by the beak from its wooden perch or clutching the bar in its claws and swinging upside down, at times swaying with dignity from side to side, uttering in varying intonations the two phrases that formed its vocabulary. Now and then it would make an unexpected dart at the grave dog, and laugh raucously at the animal's fright, ending its jest with a startling, "My O My!"

Vergil remained waiting in the tent until a little group of spectators had gathered, then ushered them about the cases, explaining each exhibit with quiet earnestness. Fernie resumed her old place at the cigar box, quitting it when the time neared for the parrot's exhibition. She would stroke its head, and carrying it inside, urge it with soothing words and sunflower seeds through its brief performance.

They halted at new towns many nights thereafter. But the crowds they had expected failed to materialize. To send off the weekly payments to the henna-haired woman in Memphis was a task more difficult than they had anticipated.

With painful regularity they could see laughing groups of young men and women hurrying off to dance halls and picture shows, or an occasional carnival, glaring with neon lights and roaring with loud-speakers. The path before their own tent would remain deserted.

It grew more and more difficult to send the installments. Their funds sank lower and lower. Mr. Waters was in another section of the valley now, and his advice was not available. They reduced the price of admission from ten cents to five, in the hope of attracting new customers; raised it again when the change accomplished nothing.

Captain Asa began to grow discouraged.

They arrived late one morning in a little cotton town, its buildings touched here and there with a grayish film drifted out from the whirring gins and spindles. Moving to the drowsy square, they set up their tent in an empty lot next a building covered with signs proclaiming extraordinary bargains in ladies' and gentlemen's sample shoes, six months credit, free souvenirs for the children.

Vergil went off to distribute some bills. He returned soon after, full of enthusiasm. "Looks like we ought to do mighty good today, Pa. Picture show's been closed down a month for remodeling. And there ain't no dances going on in ten miles. Fellow up in the drugstore was telling me they're just dying for a show."

His optimistic report affected the others.

"Sure looks like we ought to do extra fine," remarked Captain Asa. "Got a wonderful location right next to a big shoe store. A place like that's mighty hard to get."

They made ready to receive a crowd.

They were eating lunch in high spirits when there came a roar of motors off toward the edge of the town. Looking out, they saw a score of rainbow-colored trucks coming down the road, piled high with baggage and machinery. On the vehicles odd-appearing men and jaded girls were sitting, gazing with appraising eyes at the passing citizenry. It was a carnival.

The trucks drove past, and coming to a halt a block away beside a cotton warehouse, began to unload their cargo.

A hush fell over the trio at the table. They went outside. Silently they looked on as the practiced roustabouts began to erect a merry-go-round and a Ferris wheel and a great scarlet bowl contrived to shake its riders to a jelly. Sadly they saw the laborers set up a score of smaller structures to house giant fortune wheels and luscious Oriental dancers. They returned to their meal, and ate the cold food in silence.

The day dragged on. Night fell at last. A spectacular glow appeared in the sky as the lights of the carnival blazed into sudden life. There arose a shrill clamor of loud-speakers, and juke boxes in penny museums, and the musical din of the merry-go-round.

Men and women began to stroll along the sidewalk. Captain Asa and the others took their accustomed places. Even at a distance the noise from the carnival forced them when speaking to raise their voices to a shout. At times some passerby would stop for a moment, thinking the tent was part of the larger exhibition, then would realize his mistake, and hurry on. Only a single visitor put down his coin and went through the entrance, a glum, silent boy of fourteen, his pockets bulging with lurid-printed magazines.

"They got a animal show in the comic books," he announced in a stern voice to Captain Asa. "It's about a fellow trains lions and tigers without a gun or nothing. Just 'cause he's got the magic eye."

He waited moodily for the show to begin.

A long time Captain Asa stood outside, hoping for more visitors, until he saw he could delay no longer. Vergil made the round of the exhibits for the single spectator, omitting no word of his usual accompanying lecture. Fernie took the parrot inside and started it on its nightly climb up the laddery barrier.

The performance ended.

The glum boy moved to the doorway. He fixed Captain Asa with a stony stare. "It ain't like the show in the comic books," he said.

He walked toward the dazzling lights down the road.

The carnival was at its height now. The noise grew deafening. No more promenaders stopped before the tent even by mistake.

With bleak eyes Captain Asa watched them wander on their way.

Round and round the Ferris wheel turned in slow neon-lighted circles, while the Virginia Reel and the Laugh Barrel whirled madly. The great metal arm of the Loop The Loop hung for a tantalizing moment in midair. From it there came the piercing screams of the upside-down occupants, who had paid dearly for this delightful terror.

Captain Asa's sadness deepened. "Ain't no place for a little fellow in the world no more. It's the big fellows gets all the crowds and all the money. You got to make a lot of noise, just like them loud-speakers and them juke boxes."

He extinguished the acetylene lamp flickering overhead, and raised the tent flap. "Ain't no use staying open no longer. If we don't do no better pretty soon we're going to have to quit."

They set out in the morning again, leaving the business of the town to their giant rival. They were driving through the swamps once more when an automobile with two broad-hatted men wearing badges began to follow at a little distance. A moment later the strangers drove alongside, and motioned Vergil to pull off the road.

The youth's Indian-like face quivered with unexpected defiance. At a word from his father, he obeyed reluctantly.

The officers' car halted. The taller of the two, a heavy individual with a pock-marked face, confronted Captain Asa. "Got a license for your show in this county?" he demanded in harsh tones.

Captain Asa spoke a worried negative.

The officer's heavy lips tightened. "I figured that-a-way. We don't want no tramps a-running around this county. You're under arrest for operating without a license. You come on down and tell it to the judge."

He climbed back into the car beside his companion, and motioned the others to follow.

Captain Asa turned pale.

They neared a settlement, and came to a halt before a dilapidated frame courthouse, where a score of muddy automobiles and wagons were gathered. Quickly they went into the sheriff's office, and giving their names to the grim deputy behind the desk, took chairs in a tobacco-reeking room to wait. Beyond, through the open door, they could see a courtroom filled with overalled farmers, firing irregular barrages of tobacco at the distant cuspidors. On the bench a bald-headed little man was sitting, turning the pages of a battered law book.

"You people's going to be the Grand Jury of Jackson County when we get started tomorrow," he pronounced with solemnity to his rhythmic-munching audience. "But before I swear you in, I want to ask you: Is there anybody sitting here that's under indictment for anything? I don't want nobody on my jury that's under indictment."

There was a long silence. Then a bearded figure arose, and shifted uneasily. "They got me up in Federal Court over at Moundsville for moonshining, Judge."

The jurist shook his bald head in regret. "You got to get off the Grand Jury then, Jeff. I ain't going to have nobody serving on my jury that's under indictment."

The bearded rustic strode out the door.

The jury was sworn in, and the courtroom emptied. The pock-marked officer led Captain Asa and his family before the scarred wooden bench.

The judge questioned them closely, studying their faces.

He turned in reproach to their captor. "You oughtn't have arrested these here people, Luke. These here's good people. They don't need no license."

The officer murmured an apology. "You said to pick up all these funny kind of Okies and gypsies was going around, Judge. You know we been having plenty of trouble."

The judge's shiny head crimsoned with sudden impatience. "You ain't got no brains, Jeff. If your brother wasn't county clerk, I'd tell the sheriff to get rid of you in a minute. You let these people go."

He relaxed again, and gazed at Captain Asa a moment. "You say business ain't been so good?"

Captain Asa murmured a reply.

The judge took up the rusty pen lying on the desk. "I'll tell you where you can make a few dollars anyway. Tomorrow's a big day over at Kingsfork, where they got the big penitentiary. It's the day they let the penitentiary fellows out to play the Kingsfork people baseball. They always have some shows and things at the Fair Grounds where they play the game, and there's a big crowd. You go over there and you ought to do all right. You got a good clean show and we like clean shows in this county. I'll give you a letter so they won't pick you up no more."

Eagerly Captain Asa took the note. With light footsteps he hurried with the others from the courtroom.

They asked directions of some figures sitting on the paintless wooden steps leading down to the square. "You're a-going somewhere when you're heading for Kingsfork," declared a brawny villager munching a banana. "She's pretty near the biggest penitentiary in the state, they says. Got more than five hundred people."

An overalled individual beside him nodded. "That's where they got the fellow they calls Red River Johnny, held up all them banks in Texas and Arkansas. Him and Dillinger's biggest bandits there's been for a long time. He's got Billy the Kid's pistols, they says."

Vergil's face was touched with awe. "I read a-plenty about Red River Johnny. I seen about him just last week in one of them true detective magazines."

The brawny villager tossed the banana skin into a distant trash box. "Ain't a magazine or paper where he ain't been wrote up. Sure funny about them detectives arresting him. Long as he had the pistols they never could catch him. But one day a woman in a restaurant got him to put 'em on the counter. And they caught him right away."

The dreaminess in Vergil's eyes heightened. "It'd sure be something to see Red River Johnny."

They climbed into the car, and sped off.

Soon after the settlement of Kingsfork came into view. They drove through it, and a little way beyond saw the high barbed fence of a prison farm, stretching across a desolate swamp toward the horizon. Here and there rose a wooden tower where a guard stood holding a rifle. Nearby buzzards roosted on the wire, in grim caricature of the sentries, as though waiting for some luckless prisoner to venture into the wilderness and provide them with a melancholy feast. Behind the fence showed the prison buildings, ugly, barrack-like structures covered with tar-paper.

On the opposite side of the road lay the fair grounds, a shabby oval with a whitewashed row of stables, and a high arched gateway. The travelers drove inside. A few automobiles had already arrived, with their owners busy erecting tents and making preparations for the following day. Vergil brought the car to a halt.

Some prisoners with shaven heads and black-striped uniforms had come from the camp across the road, and were working idly under a guard, pulling up weeds from the cinder paths.

Fernie's voice trembled. "Won't them people bother us none, Pa?"

Captain Asa aided Vergil in blocking the trailer wheels. "Sometimes they got good people in them penitentiaries. That's where Leef Brothers lived up at Clay Creek studied preaching, was in the penitentiary. And that's where Ab Johnson learned carpentering. There's plenty of big people got their education in a penitentiary. They says when you get to know them jail people right, some of the toughest ones are gentle as kittens. Don't you go to worrying."

They erected the tent, and began to feed their charges. A new group of convicts appeared and joined the others clearing the paths. One of the arrivals stood up to light a cigarette, a tall, sleepy-eyed figure with face half hidden by unshaven red hair so that he somewhat resembled a drowsy possum.

The tin of water which Vergil was carrying to the alligator shook a little. "That's Red River Johnny," he whispered.

They watched spellbound.

A deputy wearing a badge sauntered toward the trailer. He read the judge's note and nodded. "O K," he pronounced. "Just so long as you ain't one of them girlie shows. Going to be a big day for 'em tomorrow. They do plenty of celebrating. Guess you can celebrate plenty when you only got one day out of the year to be a human."

The afternoon advanced. The prisoners assembled in military formation, and marched off to the penitentiary.

Some local youths, inspired by the coming contest, began to play baseball with a few of the carnival followers. Vergil brought his glove and joined in the game. Captain Asa and Fernie chatted with a friendly, white-haired couple who presided over an ice-cream stand. Across the highway they could see the massive steel gate of the prison, with two guards pacing up and down carrying rifles, like mechanical figures set atop a clock.

They sat up late with their neighbors, then went to bed, too excited by their strange surroundings to sleep. All night they could hear the weird sounds of the great swamp beyond. Occasionally there came the tread of tramping feet, as the guard changed somewhere in the darkness. At times they could see the flash of a searchlight sweeping the gloomy wilderness.

The booming of a deep-throated whistle waked them with a start. A bugle sounded. Arising, Captain Asa and the others could see the convicts in the prison enclosure, carrying their mess-kits as they marched off to breakfast. One of the dismal, tar-papered buildings was now draped with a single pathetic strip of bunting.

The prisoners who had been clearing the fair grounds the

day before returned to finish their casual labor. Among them was Red River Johnny.

Fernie brought the parrot outside, so that it could preen its feathers in the sun. She was rearranging the cards that served for its prophecies, when Red River Johnny sauntered near, and gazed at her in deep reflection.

He spoke with a pronounced drawl, in harmony with his drowsy, possum-like face. "That there one of them fortune-telling birds, sister?"

Fernie nodded in fright.

Captain Asa hastened to answer. "Tells a fortune like a gypsy."

The convict's sleepy eyes grew wistful. "Let him tell my fortune, will you?"

Captain Asa assented with pleasure. Timidly Fernie set the box with the predictions on the ground. The parrot hesitated an instant, then picked up one of the minute pasteboards with its beak, and dropped the card into the other's palm.

The prisoner held out the pasteboard to Captain Asa with the air of a troubled child. "I ain't got no reading. Tell me what it says, will you?"

Captain Asa scanned the close-typed lines, one of those stilted glimpses into the future printed by the thousands to be dispensed by mechanical soothsayers for the dropping of a penny. "It says your omen for today is a arch—that's a symbol of good fortune. It says a important letter's on the way to you. It says good luck you ain't expecting'll let you travel and take a pleasant journey mighty quick."

The convict's face lighted with childlike pleasure. "It's got all that wrote on the card?"

Captain Asa nodded in affirmation.

The convict grew meditative again. "I guess it sure means that pardon's a-coming then. I done give it up, 'cause I thought that lawyer I've got just took the money I sent him and wasn't doing nothing to change the life sentence they put on me. But I guess he's doing all right after all. Or it wouldn't say all them things on the card."

He noticed Vergil beside the tent, batting a ball with one of his companions of the previous day. "That there your boy?" he demanded.

Captain Asa assented with pride. "Fine-looking young fellow, ain't he?"

Red River Johnny murmured agreement. "Looks like he plays a good game of baseball, too. The Warden done picked me to run the team in the Walls. If your boy was in 'em I'd sure let him play."

The guard with the rifle came closer. The convict shambled off to his work again.

More automobiles gathered in the enclosure, and more amusement devices were hastily erected at the edge of the grandstand: roulette wheels for winning groceries and rolling boards for winning clocks or cushion covers; popguns fitted with corks for shooting cigarettes and darts to burst rainbow-colored balloons.

Noon sounded on the whistle of the prison. The spectators began to arrive now, and the town baseball team, lanky rustics clad in ill-fitting blue-and-white uniforms. The players spread out over the field, and started to practice. Their movements were awkward, amateurish.

A bugle blew once more on the other side of the highway. The convicts filed through the grim steel gate, and marching across the fair grounds, took seats in a special section of the grandstand. A moment later the prison team appeared, with their shaven heads and their striped uniforms appearing like puppets in some curious Punch-and-Judy show. Red River Johnny shambled to the pitcher's box. They began to play.

The result was never in doubt. The awkward townsmen were hopelessly outclassed by the disciplined prisoners. Like a perfect-geared machine, Red River Johnny hurled ball after ball toward the batter, each toss bringing the enemy nearer to annihilation. The convict spectators, with a rhythm perfected in their confinement, shouted encouragement of their champion in roars like hungry lions, stamping their feet with a thunder that threatened to bring the flimsy grandstand toppling about their heads. Some cameramen went about taking photographs.

The game ended. The convicts, shouting their triumph, marched off to the prison, to remain until another year.

The baseball team, with a guard carrying a rifle, came down the path alongside the grandstand where the entertainment booths were centered. The drowsy-eyed pitcher saw Captain Asa standing in front of the tent with the parrot and halted. Carefully he took the card with its glimpse into the future from a pocket of his striped uniform. "Read it to me again, will you?"

Captain Asa repeated the prophecy.

Red River Johnny's sleepy face grew bright. "That's what I figured you said. I been a-thinking about it all day. That there letter that's coming and the traveling and everything can't be nothing but a pardon. I sure been doing that lawyer wrong."

A photographer snapped his picture. He shuffled down the field. The players crossed the highway. The massive gate clanged shut.

Soon after the guard came up the path again. He thrust into Captain Asa's hands a pearl-handled revolver.

"This here's one of Red River Johnny's pistols," he declared. "He wants you to have it. He says he ain't going to have no use for neither of 'em when he gets out of jail the way the bird said."

Captain Asa took the pistol in awe.

His glance rested with pride on Vergil waiting inside the tent.

"He told me my boy could have played on the baseball team," Captain Asa said.

CHAPTER ELEVEN

THEY remained at the fair grounds until late that night, then set out again in the morning. They stopped after a few miles at a filling station for gas. An overalled boy came out from the dwelling nearby to man the pump. He saw Captain Asa and gave a start of astonishment, then hurried into the house, emerging again with an aproned woman whose hands were still covered with the dough she had been kneading. They stood staring at the travelers, talking mysteriously. The boy came forward after a moment, and putting a few gallons of gasoline into the tank, rejoined the woman at the door. They stared in silence as the car drove away.

Vergil glanced back at the motionless figures in wonder. "Them people's sure acting funny, ain't they, Pa?"

Captain Asa nodded. "They're a-acting mighty queer."

They halted again at a country grocery, where some farmers sat on boxes exchanging comments with the blue-shirted proprietor. A hush fell over the store as the travelers entered. The farmers stared like the boy in the filling station. When Captain Asa took the tobacco he had purchased and walked outside, the proprietor followed. He stood on the steps, watching until the car was far up the road.

Vergil turned from the wheel. "Something funny's sure going on, Pa. I'm getting worried the way them people's looking."

Captain Asa echoed his concern. "It sure ain't right, the way they're behaving. Hope we ain't going to get arrested again. I'm trying to figure out what we done that's wrong."

They went on anxiously.

They reached a drowsy little settlement at noon, and began setting up the tent in an empty lot next a drab little dry-goods store. In the window some vacant-eyed wax ladies, clad in printed dresses, were grouped about an electric sign that announced in ever-changing colors a sale of indestructible stockings. Near the doorway a sporty young man wearing a yellow straw hat sat on a packing crate, dangling his loud-socked feet as he whistled at the passing girls. He stared at Captain Asa a moment like the others, then arose, and swaggered forward.

"Ain't you the fellow Red River Johnny give the pistol to?" he demanded.

Captain Asa looked up in surprise from the tent rope he was tying. "That's right, friend. But I didn't figure nobody way over here knew about it."

The sporty youth whistled piercingly at a girl in a tight-fitting green sweater who was emerging from the drugstore across the road. He set his hat at a conquering angle and prepared to go in pursuit. "Don't take no brains to know what you seen in the paper," he grunted.

He pulled a folded newssheet from his pocket, and tossing it to Captain Asa, swaggered after the green-sweatered siren.

Captain Asa turned the pages. Suddenly he gave a muffled gasp. Trembling with excitement, he darted into the tent where Vergil and Fernie were arranging the cases. "Look at that!" he exclaimed. "In the Little Rock paper!"

They gazed spellbound. On an inside page was a story of Red River Johnny, the hero of the baseball game at Kingsfork, with a long account of his life and adventures and his many encounters with the law. Leading off the narrative was a picture taken as the prisoner stood talking to Captain Asa before the tent, with the dilapidated parrot hanging by the beak from its perch.

They looked in silence a moment, too overwhelmed for speech, then examined the photograph in detail, talking in hushed phrases.

Captain Asa's face glowed with childish pleasure. "It's the biggest picture you ever seen, ain't it? Pretty near half the page, looks like. We'll send one to Ula and one up to Clay Creek. They'll sure be glad to get it. Ain't nobody in our family ever had their picture in the paper before."

He went down the street soon after with Fernie, looking for a piece of canvas to repair a hole in the tent. The news of his arrival had already spread through the community. Everywhere he walked, curious glances and whispered comments followed. When he returned and set about applying the patch, a group of villagers gathered to watch.

The day wore on. More passersby halted outside, looking on idly. At times a spectator came forward and asked a question.

Captain Asa replied with enthusiasm.

A white-haired old man clad in torn overalls descended from a rickety wagon, with a gentle-faced old woman carrying a child in her arms.

The snowy-haired figure spoke to Captain Asa with hesitation. "You don't reckon we could see that there pistol Red River Johnny give you, do you, brother? We'd mighty like to show it to this boy belongs to my daughter. Me and my old woman knowed Johnny mighty good."

Captain Asa hastened inside, and brought out the weapon.

The snowy-haired visitor regarded it with reverence. "He was sure a wonderful man. Robbed the bank in this town of thirty thousand dollars, and didn't hurt nobody. And then give away all of it to the poor people around here. He'd walk into some poor woman's home, and put down a hundred dollars on the table and say, 'Hear you need a doctor for that stomach misery, Ma.' Or he'd go to where a old man was out in the barn trying to get some milk from his cow that'd gone dry so he could give it to his children needed it bad and say to him, 'Don't you waste your time a-trying to milk that cow no more, Tom. You go on over to Will Stack's place and get yourself one of them new cows he's just got in from Memphis. It's done paid for.' "

His wife nodded in gentle affirmation. "Never spent a nickel on himself with fancy living or women or nothing. Just ate turnip greens and grits, and sometimes when he'd come around, I'd fix him a pork chop and some corn bread. I tell you things sure ain't been the same around here since they put Johnny behind the Walls."

The old man let the child touch the pistol.

They went on their way.

The proprietor of the drugstore across the road, a seedy individual exhaling a faint odor of moth balls and soap, who was standing nearby, walked over to Captain Asa. "Ought to put that pistol outside where people can see it. If you want to, you can put it in my window. Be good advertising for you and the store both."

Soon after the weapon with a suitable card attached was on display behind the glass, next a half-shaved cardboard gentleman brandishing a gold safety razor. Captain Asa looked on happily.

They prepared to open the show at sunset. For the first time since they had acquired the property, a crowd was gathered outside, waiting to enter. All evening visitors continued to arrive. Occasionally a patron carried a newspaper, and compared the photograph with the originals.

Captain Asa was in ecstasy. As he stood outside the tent, the sleepy little town seemed transformed, magical. The flashing, many-colored sign in the window of the dry-goods store next door seemed a gorgeous rainbow; the vacant-eyed wax ladies grouped around it were angelic creatures floating in the sky above, smiling upon the world as in blessing.

Eleven o'clock came, and the last coin dropped into the cigar box.

Fernie helped her father arrange the money in gleaming piles.

A soft light touched her silvery-framed face. "It's thirteen dollars and sixty cents, Pa. That's more than we took in a whole week before."

Captain Asa counted the money again, with incredulity.

"That's sure right, ain't it? I thought maybe you made a mistake, but it comes out the same way every time. I sure never figured on no thirteen dollars."

Quickly he made some calculations. "Get that every night it'd be a hundred dollars a week, pretty near. That's pretty fine for hill people like us, don't know nothing about a show. And I guess it's like Chick Waters was saying, once you get something started it keeps on going more and more."

They remained another night, with the crowds even larger. Captain Asa's joy was unbounded.

For several days they went on, with no lessening of their attendance.

They were passing through a little town, and had halted for lunch in a roadside restaurant, when a large mud-stained automobile drew up along the curb. From it there emerged a squat figure with a derby hat set over the blur of fat that formed his head, and wearing shiny blue coat and trousers that made no attempt to conceal the enormous balloon of a stomach which was the focal point of his body. His red-checked shirt, topped with a string tie, was slightly open at his throat in a studied attempt at carelessness; his wide red suspenders showed prominently and were buckled in uneven fashion so that his enormous trousers pulled higher on one side than the other. He paused outside the car a moment, and took off his hat to wipe his sweating bald head with a handkerchief. As he turned, the movement revealed his face, extending in pendulous layers beyond his chin, like quaking ranges of mountains.

After him came a tall, thin individual clad in a tan Palm Beach suit, with sharp beady eyes set close together that gave him something of the appearance of a ferret.

The two men came into the restaurant and took places at

a table. A murmur arose from the scattered diners on the stools at the counter.

"That's Judge Thrasher," whispered a bearded farmer next to Captain Asa, pointing to the fat man. "Big Slick, they calls him. It's him went around with the hillbilly band last year when he was a-running for Road Commissioner. That's his brother, Little Slick, the skinny one sitting with him. They're the two smartest fellows in the State."

"Judge is a-running for State Senator this year," added a crescent-mustached rustic on the stool beyond. "He'll get it easy. 'Cause he's always way ahead of anybody a-figuring things. This year he ain't got the band. Instead of the playing he's giving out hotcakes."

"Mighty good hotcakes, too," declared the bearded one. "Makes 'em himself, right in front of you, and passes 'em out, as many as you can swallow. He was talking over at Deep Spring yesterday, and I done eat twelve."

The fat newcomer gave his order in a voice that rumbled through the restaurant, and began to attack a great platter of meat and potatoes. His slight companion ate sparingly.

One by one the other diners departed.

The politician's fat eyes wandered to the bannered trailer parked before the window, then settled on Captain Asa and his family, who were now the only patrons left at the counter. The oily smile that seemed a permanent feature of his face vanished for a moment. His expression became cold, calculating. He leaned over to his ferret-like companion.

A moment later the thin man came hurrying to Captain Asa's stool. "Seen about your show in the paper," he declared with effusive cordiality. "Judge's got to make a speech to some school children and their people up at White's Creek this afternoon, and he don't like to talk to no children without giving them some kind of entertaining.

What you say you come along and let 'em see your animals? Pay you a nice clean ten-dollar bill."

In astonishment Captain Asa put down the watery cup of coffee he was drinking. "Golly. I ain't ever give a show for a school."

The other waved a hand in deprecation. "Ain't no different than anywheres else. You come on and do it."

They finished their lunches, and went outside. At the tall man's invitation, Captain Asa climbed in beside the mountainous figure at the back of the large automobile, letting Vergil and Fernie follow with their own car and the trailer.

The politician adjusted his bulging rear uncomfortably on the cushions. He looked at the somewhat shabby interior of the vehicle and shook his head. "Politics sure ain't what they used to be. Look at this car. Just falling to pieces. Been wanting to get a new one for three years, but can't do it or they say you stole the money."

Though his voice was deep, sonorous, he spoke with a sort of pant, as though the excessive weight he was carrying made him breathless. He took out a banded cigar, and offering one to his companion, slumped back in the seat. "Ain't nothing the way it was. Used to be all you had to do was see a few of the right people before election and maybe buy a little whisky. Nowadays you got to keep jumping every minute. And any money you do get, you have to pay right back to talk over the radio. I'm getting wore out. You hire a hillbilly band, and then turns out the fellow running against you writes songs and sings 'em, like that fellow a while ago they made Governor of Louisiana. You start making hotcakes, and first thing you know the fellow against you'll be giving out waffles with a brick of ice cream on 'em."

He relaxed into a moody silence. Then his swollen head

slumped onto his breast. He dozed, with his mouth half open, breathing heavily.

They reached the outskirts of a drowsy village, and drew up before a two-story brick schoolhouse, with patches of red paint scaling from the walls.

The politician wakened with a start. He arose, and prepared to squeeze himself through the door of the car. "One thing they ain't spoiled. That's the school children. I talk to the school kids every time I can. I got plenty of people voting for me today just 'cause I give 'em a good show and a peppermint cane twenty years ago."

A small platform had been erected near the entrance of the school building, draped at the rear with a huge American flag. In the center was a portable griddle, gleaming like silver, with a Negro man and woman standing beside it, wearing high chefs' hats. A crowd was already gathered at the foot of the structure, boys and girls clad in their Sunday clothes, accompanied by a worried mother wearing a cheap store hat, or a gaunt farmer whose scarred chin gave evidence of an unaccustomed shave. Here and there a woman sat hushing a whimpering baby, or a small boy tried to restrain a too-energetic dog.

The politician and his brother went among the crowd, shaking hands, and talking jovially to all they encountered.

Captain Asa erected the tent a short distance from the platform. In high spirits, he helped his son drive the stakes for the final ropes. "It's mighty fine giving a show for a school and getting mixed up with big people like Judge Thrasher, ain't it?"

Vergil nodded eagerly. "It's going to be on the radio, too. I been watching. That's what they're doing with them boxes and things. It'll sure be something if they put the show on the radio."

They went into the tent and continued their excited preparations. Fernie polished the glass cases until they flashed like mirrors, and smoothed the parrot's battered crest.

They finished and waited tensely at the entrance.

The crowd continued to increase.

The politician abandoned his handshaking at last, and climbing with his brother upon the platform, took a seat on a camp chair near a microphone. The Negro man and woman in the chefs' caps disappeared into the schoolhouse. Quiet descended on the spectators.

The fat man arose and began to speak. On and on he declaimed and ranted, in accents thick with calculated rusticity, sometimes shouting, sometimes pleading, often waving a hand toward the great flag that formed a curtain at the rear. His panting ceased. His vast stomach shook with his emotion.

He neared the end of his oration. In sardonic tones he denounced some local attackers of his character. With a dramatic gesture he whipped a handful of coins from a coat pocket and let them fall to the floor.

"Do you see any money sticking to them fingers?" he bellowed. "Do you see any thousand-dollar bills sticking to that palm? I ain't lived my life like some of them candidates that's running around talking against me. I've lived my life so that when I go to sleep at night I don't have to put a pistol under my pillow. Ain't a man or woman standing out here don't know how I've been living. 'Cause I've lived round here fifty-five years, thirty of 'em with my wife and children. I ain't never had a speck of trouble with my family. I ain't never had trouble with a living human in this county. And that's the way it's going to be with all the people when you go to the polls and elect me State Senator."

He concluded soon after, amid scattered handclapping.

There was a brief pause. The Negro man and woman came out from the schoolhouse and mounted to the platform again, carrying several pails filled with batter. They deposited their burden beside the griddle. The faces of the audience grew expectant.

The politician picked up a pancake turner. "Now we're going to have a party. Guess I don't have to tell you nothing about Judge Thrasher's parties. I'm going to make you all some of my hotcakes. And then I got a fine animal show for the children and anybody else wants to go."

He looked off at a dapper young man in flashy tropicals, who had arrived in a car a few minutes before and was standing near a portable microphone, smoking endless cigarettes. "That there's my friend Jeff Dabney from the radio station in Moundsville came out all this way just to be at the party. In a minute, soon as it's time for us to go on the air again, Jeff's going around asking you some questions so the people that ain't lucky enough to be here can know about the good time you're having. And if any of you old folks wants to say why you're going to vote for me, it ain't going to do no harm."

He poured some batter on the griddle, and raised the turner with a flourish. Beaming, he passed the golden hotcakes out to the waiting crowd. His arm rose and fell like a swollen pendulum.

Vergil gazed in fascination at the dapper announcer who had begun to move toward the tent with the microphone. His voice shook a little. "He's coming over this way, Pa. Maybe he's going to put the show on the radio right now."

Eagerly Captain Asa followed his glance. "Sure looks like he's coming over."

The announcer walked almost to the entrance, then changed his direction abruptly, and moved off among the spectators. His voice, interviewing some of the bystanders in glib phrases, drifted out monotonously from the microphone.

Captain Asa and Vergil saddened.

They went inside and prepared for the exhibition. In a moment the tent was swept by an avalanche of children, their hands and mouths filled with hotcakes. Noisily the young visitors followed Vergil as he moved about the cases. When his back was turned, they rapped on the glass covers, hoping to arouse the torpid inhabitants.

The parrot alternately screamed and laughed in scorn at the invaders, now and then flapping its wings and darting out with its beak as some unruly boy came too near. The grave dog slunk away in distress at the turmoil, and crawled beneath a chair in the corner.

Vergil left his charges a moment, and hurrying to the doorway, looked off again at the announcer, now in a distant part of the school grounds. "Don't look like he's coming at all, does it?"

Captain Asa shook his head with regret. "Guess he's got too many other people."

Vergil returned to his duties. He was escorting a new group of children, when Captain Asa hurried forward. "He's a-coming, Vergil."

The announcer strolled through the doorway. He walked about the tent a moment, smoking cigarettes and describing the exhibits with heavy humor, then saw the rattlesnake, coiled viciously, ready to strike.

The announcer grew interested. He brought the microphone close to the case and turned to Vergil. "Make him rattle, will you, Jack?"

With eager fingers Vergil put a stick through the grill at the top of the case, and little by little moved it forward.

There was a moment of breathless waiting. The snake's bony tail continued immovable.

Vergil's dreamy face grew pale.

He withdrew the stick and renewed the operation, bringing the point nearer and nearer the tight-coiled body.

Still there was no reaction. Then the beady eyes flashed with minute lightning. Almost imperceptibly the jagged tail began to quiver. The rattles made a faint sound like the crackling of dry leaves in the autumn, rising soon to a loud, fierce rhythm, like dueling castanets. The evil head shot forward, its fangs striking the stick with a sinister violence that caused the announcer, bent over the glass, to draw back in fright.

He recovered his poise, and making a labored comic observation, turned to Vergil again. "O K, Jack," he said.

He sauntered outside again.

Vergil watched the other disappear down the path. His voice was exultant. "I sure never figured we'd be on the radio."

Fernie put the parrot through another performance, and joined her father at the entrance. The corpulent politician was still busy at the griddle, making new mountains of hotcakes, while several helpers were pouring coffee from huge boilers mounted on a truck.

The judge's brother passed, and spoke to Fernie. "You want to help pass out the coffee and the hotcakes, Sister? People always likes to get things from a pretty girl."

She blushed and moved shyly into the crowd.

The party ended at last. The children and their elders drifted off to their homes. Captain Asa and Vergil took down the tent, and prepared for their departure.

The politician came over to pay the promised fee. His swollen head was dripping with sweat. He gave Captain Asa a flabby hand. "You got a nice family," he panted. "When I get elected bring your boy to see me. Maybe I can give him some kind of job."

He watched while the Negro in the chef's cap lifted the griddle and the other cooking paraphernalia into the truck with the coffee boilers, then waddled beside his brother to their waiting automobile.

The car sped away.

Captain Asa watched in reverence. He turned to a gaunt farmer standing nearby. "That's sure a wonderful man."

The other nodded sagely. "The finest fellow ever come out of this state. He's sure a-going to be President."

The travelers climbed into their places. The trailer lumbered down the dusty road.

Captain Asa looked back at the schoolhouse growing smaller and smaller in the distance. His eyes were bright. "I was hoping for plenty of things. But I sure never figured a day like today. Getting mixed up with a big fellow like Judge Thrasher, and he says maybe he'll give you a fine job after election. And then on top of everything a-putting us on the radio. When you get on the radio, you don't need anything else, they says. Way it looks to me there ain't no figuring where we're going to stop. 'Cause we're a-climbing mighty high."

For several days they continued their travels, their attendance increasing again as a result of their new advertising. In a little cotton town they encountered Mr. Waters and his headless company.

The photographer listened with pleasant cynicism to Captain Asa's account of their adventures. "Be all right if it keeps up," he remarked pessimistically, as he sat beside his car, adding some new fibers to the grass skirt about the waist of the lady Hawaiian. "But don't go to figuring on it.

Show business is like a ripe banana. You eat the meat and it tastes mighty good. And then if you ain't careful, you slip on the skin and it kills you. Where you figuring on heading now?"

Captain Asa took the worn road map from his pocket. "We're getting pretty close to St. Louis. I figured maybe we'd be starting there. She's the finest town in the country, way everybody's told me. And then I can see where they had the Fair. After that we can go up around Chicago and Pittsburgh and New York and them other places. That's where they got the big money is up North, I guess."

Mr. Waters surveyed the headless beauty a moment, and with a paintbrush retouched a thigh to increase her abandon. His voice hardened with warning. "Don't you go fooling with St. Louis. Don't you go fooling with any of them big towns. The big towns is for big-town people. You're a little fellow, like I told you. You're doing all right now, 'cause the people that's seeing your show don't know any better. But in them other places you got to have neon lights, and loud-speakers, and all kinds of up-to-date things. A old-fashioned fellow like you wouldn't have no more chance than a nickel in a New Orleans slot machine."

Captain Asa was unconvinced. "We been doing mighty good. And I'd mighty like to go to St. Louis. Besides I seen in the paper they're going to have a big convention of some of them fellows that was soldiers, and everybody says they spend a-plenty of money."

Mr. Waters' lips grew grim. "They had one of them soldiers' conventions in Chicago last year, and they pretty near carried off the town and set it in the big lake there, people was telling me. You go to that soldiers' convention in St. Louis and you ain't just fishing for trouble. You're reaching out and pulling it off the hook, the way they says."

Captain Asa set out next day, leaving Mr. Waters to go off in another direction. Past Little River they traveled, and Oran and Cape Girardeau, past Apple Creek and Longtown and quaint St. Genevieve.

A painted hotel suddenly appeared on a billboard at a road junction, with crowds of fashion-plate men and women passing through the gilded doorways. Beside it a large arrow pointed to St. Louis.

Vergil brought the car to a halt. "You want to go, Pa?"

Captain Asa's voice was hesitant. "Chick Waters is mighty smart, but I'd sure like to see St. Louis. How you figure it, Vergil?"

"I'd mighty like to go to a big town. I ain't never seen a town as big as St. Louis."

Captain Asa smoked in reflection. "Looks to me like maybe it's the place we're looking for to settle down. I been hearing about it all my life. And I ain't never heard a bad word against it. And then when we get some money, maybe you can go to college the way you're wanting. I was talking to a fellow a while ago used to work in a big barbershop there, and he said they got the best colleges in St. Louis there is anywhere."

They turned down the road.

A rustic filling station showed ahead. They stopped for gas and confided their plans to the loquacious, tobacco-munching proprietor.

"Wouldn't go there now," he cautioned. "She's a good town. But them big conventions is rough when they get going. Sure is funny about people, ain't it? Live quiet all year a-going to church, and getting mad at their children if they don't study in school. Then they come to these here conventions, and first thing they do is go around breaking up store windows, and talking sassy to a policeman so they can get themselves put in jail."

The travelers drove on. The stretches of forest and the little farms they were passing began to vanish. More and more filling stations came into view, scarlet, ugly, like a sinister crimson rash marking some grim disease that had seized the countryside. Hamburger stands appeared, where truck drivers with stomachs as hard as the steel they drove were bolting down indigestible sandwiches. Here and there a great factory stood at some distance from the road, with vast columns of smoke pouring from its chimneys that spread a rain of soot on the unhappy earth beneath. From behind prison-like fences there came fierce hissings and loud clangings of metal and the dismal reek of boiling drugs, as though some ancient alchemist were practicing his wizardry.

The traffic on the road thickened. Giant trucks roared down upon them, carrying steel and coal and gasoline and all the other vital elements out of which man has built his modernistic fantasy. The drivers, seeking to pass the clumsy trailer, honked and swore in vivid phrases. Freight trains rocked along the tracks paralleling the highway, filling their eyes with cinders.

Suddenly a mass of towering buildings appeared in the distance, surrounded by a smoky halo.

Captain Asa's stogie quivered. "It's St. Louis," he said.

They followed a trolley line toward the center of the town.

Captain Asa looked down the busy thoroughfare. "Stop when you can and find out the way, will you, Vergil? First thing I want to see is where they had the Fair."

They asked the route of a friendly pedestrian, and drove past a maze of glittering shops and apartment houses. The traffic was bewildering, for it was late afternoon. Men and women swarmed like ants from the doorways of office buildings. Horns tooted in a frantic chorus, and policemen waved their arms wildly. Vergil kept his eyes fixed on the roadway.

Captain Asa studied a cheap paper guide he had purchased at a newsstand. He glanced at a street sign.

His body grew taut. "We're getting close," he announced.

They swung round a busy intersection and halted.

Before them lay a wide park, where an automobile road bordered by low shrubbery circled into the distance. The sun had already set, and the sky was graying with the twilight. There was about the landscape a feeling of quietness, of sadness. No building was visible; there were only the trees, spreading out like a great forest. The sidewalks along the highway were ghostly, deserted.

A long time Captain Asa stood, his face glowing as one who beholds a vision.

"It's where they had the Fair," he said.

In the branches of the trees overhead birds chirped sleepily, preparing for the night. Cars moved past in endless shadowy lines, showing no sign of the drivers within, like strange monsters of metal from some distant planet.

Captain Asa consulted the guide again. He pointed off to the horizon. "Past them big trees is where they had the Midway. Where that road turns around was the Cascades, and that open place was the Filipino Village. Over there where I'm pointing was what they called the Tower of Jewels."

He restored the guide to his pocket. He spoke again, slowly. "Those were the best times ever was anywhere. If things now was like it was them days, it'd sure be a wonderful world."

CHAPTER TWELVE

THEY drove back to the business district as night descended, and parking the car, went into a busy restaurant. They took cups of coffee, marveling at the trim waitresses hurrying past with their gleaming trays, and the well-dressed men and women moving up and down the aisles.

They finished and went outside again. Vergil examined a tiny cardboard packet he had picked up at the desk. "They got wonderful matches here. Each stick's made like a little bottle. I never seen any matches as pretty as these before."

They walked along the street, crowded with friendly-spoken men and women, and peered into the shop windows, filled with rich treasures.

"It's sure a wonderful town," Captain Asa declared.

The city was already decorated for the convention, whose preliminaries were to begin the following day. Huge American flags hung over the doorways of the stores and office buildings. Streamers of bunting were looped across the streets at regular intervals, like a series of gorgeous rainbows.

The travelers ended their promenade, and climbing into the car, began driving about, searching for a place to set up their exhibition.

They reached the Eads Bridge, spanning the dark Mississippi. On a drab street that fronted the water were a few penny museums and shooting galleries, trying to lure the workers waiting for the busses that crossed to the Illinois shore. A few patrons showed within, firing an occasional rifle, or playing one of the pinball machines set against the wall.

A vacant lot showed nearby.

Captain Asa surveyed it with satisfaction. "Couldn't get no better place than this for a show."

They erected the tent and prepared to open the next day. Captain Asa slept fitfully, feverish with excitement. Again and again he awakened when a towboat, pushing a great convoy of barges down the river, blew a sonorous whistle. He would arise and look out the door at the dim Illinois shore a moment, then gaze a long time at the lighted windows high up in a shadowy building, where some accountant toiled at an all-night labor.

A wave of delight would sweep over him.

They arose early and went about their tasks with increasing excitement. The delegates were beginning to arrive for the convention. Fattish middle-aged men with graying hair and wearing bright-colored uniforms strolled along the streets beside their placid-faced spouses. Near them walked delegates in civilian clothes, topped by overseas caps. Some were well-fed, genial individuals showing the unmistakable signs of prosperity. Some were thin, tired-looking men with pathetic faces, bookkeepers, clerks, and factory workers, to whom this excursion was the one gay period in a year filled with monotony, and out of which they were determined to lose no possible moment of pleasure. There were women in uniform as well, some smiling, cheerful, motherly, some stern-eyed, with officers' insignia on their shoulders, who gave the instant impression they would make unpleasant wives.

Captain Asa drew back the tent flap. "We better get the show opened up. Them people's sure going to spend money."

Soon after, Captain Asa took his usual post at the entrance. A few local residents waiting for the busses wandered inside, then a stout veteran escorting a squalling little boy decked out in a midget soldier's uniform. Captain Asa greeted the latter visitors with enthusiasm. Hurrying off to a stand on the street corner, he bought a pennant marked "Welcome Delegates", and fastened it above the opening of the tent.

More and more uniformed figures arrived as the day advanced. Crimson-cloaked bands began to march down the street, preceded by statuesque drum majors tossing their batons incredible distances into the air, and bare-kneed drum majorettes prancing like circus ponies. Groups dressed as Indians followed, and men with miners' caps, the lamps at the peaks burning brightly. Others wore overalls covered with lint, to resemble cotton pickers just off a plantation. Occasionally at the head of a delegation there would appear an individual with a heavy, crafty face and displaying half-a-dozen meaningless medals on his breast, one of the group's politicians, who was using the patriotism of his comrades at arms as a means to his own advancement.

With the paraders, individuals carrying water pistols roamed the sidewalks, deluging the passersby. Others carried electric canes, which they thrust at the arms or legs of any tempting pedestrian.

A band of these sportive promenaders passed before the tent, squirting Captain Asa until his face was streaming.

He received the assault with good nature. The pistoleers saluted, and went on to search for new victims.

Captain Asa dried his cheeks with a handkerchief. He turned to a grinning bystander. "Them fellows are sure having a good time."

More pistoleers came down the street, shooting new liquid volleys. Fernie, now outside as cashier, received most of their attention. She was frightened at first, then accepted the barrages with a resigned smile. Many of the promenaders went into the tent. The tinkle of coins in the cigar box was frequent.

All day airplanes roared in the sky and balloons glided above the brown river. Paper bags filled with water came dropping from the windows of buildings everywhere, bursting as they struck the pavement with a report like gunfire.

Darkness descended. The dropping of the coins into the cigar box became a continuous rain. Several times delegates who had been drinking entered, and growing rough, attempted to open the case containing the Gila monster, or threatened to carry off the rattlesnake as a reinforcement for their water pistols and their canes. Each time soberer companions restrained their ardor.

Captain Asa closed the tent as a distant clock was striking one, and waited while Fernie emptied the cigar box on the table. With care he sorted out the coins and the rumpled bills, far surpassing any previous collection. His voice was exultant. "I knew things'd be fine if we came to St. Louis."

He put the money in a worn leather wallet, and lit a stogie. He smoked in deep content.

The flood of visitors swelled enormously during the night. By late morning the streets had become seething rivers of uniforms flowing under bright-colored arches of bunting. Shrewd-faced hawkers appeared like magic along the curbs, selling canes and candy and chameleons. Gay costumes began to appear in preparation for the parade scheduled at twilight. The atmosphere everywhere was one of carnival.

New spectators continued to file into the tent. Captain Asa and the others were so occupied with their duties they had not even time to eat.

The attendance slackened toward sunset, as crowds gathered along the sidewalks nearby to wait for the coming procession. There was no hope of attracting any patrons to the exhibits until this greater spectacle had ended. Captain Asa and the others joined the onlookers at the curb.

There was a distant burst of music, and the procession moved down the road, the police on their roaring motorcycles clearing the way. Behind them a yellow-plumed band came marching, with tasseled drums beating in strident rhythm.

This was a humorous parade, giving vent to the droller instincts of the delegates, as though it might provide a safety valve for their boisterous spirits. There were men dressed as convicts, and men dressed as women, hard-faced harridans with wigs of crimson hair. There were men dressed like babies riding in perambulators, and masculine mothers pushing the vehicles proudly, their vast bosoms heaving with a bellows under their blouses. A wild man came dashing along the sidewalk, gnawing an enormous bone which he offered at intervals to the spectators. Behind him walked a lion tamer cracking a long whip and leading by a huge rope a tiny Pekinese. Pirates with skulls and crossbones on their chests rode trucks transformed into sailing ships, and red-feathered Indians uttered wild war whoops.

The end came at last, with that familiar aftermath of all processions, long rows of jangling streetcars and honking trucks and screeching automobiles.

Captain Asa and the others hurried back to their posts.

The evening advanced. The crowds, still good-natured, were growing rougher. At times a humorous assault with a water pistol would bring an indignant outburst from some woman's escort, and a fight would threaten. Police or uniformed delegates would interfere, until the danger of a conflict passed.

A stoutish promenader went reeling past, and tossed a giant firecracker into the tent, filling it with the fumes of exploded powder. The smoke drifted outside in an acrid cloud. The parrot, beside Captain Asa at the entrance, choked and sputtered with indignation.

Vergil joined his father and looked down the surging street. "Getting kind of wild, Pa. Maybe we ought to be going."

Captain Asa glanced through the tent flap at the visitors clustered about the cases. "I hate to be leaving when we're doing so good."

Vergil went inside again.

A group of young men wearing overalls appeared, with wisps of hay tucked behind their ears, and entered the penny museum adjoining the show. A crash of breaking glass followed. A moment later the counterfeit farmers reeled into the street again, escorted by the burly proprietor.

The museum owner walked over to Captain Asa. "I'm

closing up," he announced. "In a little while them toughs'll be coming across the bridge from East St. Louis, and then there ain't no telling what'll happen. If I had a trailer like you I'd sure get out of here while I was all in one piece."

He walked back to the museum and turned out the light.

Captain Asa grew worried. He called to Vergil, and stood discussing their course of action.

They were still undecided when a pudgy, round-headed man wearing Indian feathers over his bright blond hair, came staggering down the street rolling a beer keg, with a skinny Indian and a black-shirted pirate as his reeling assistants. Every few feet they would come to a stop, and taking a drink, offer a foaming stein to any delegate or civilian who happened to be near.

They halted before the tent a moment. The blond Indian saw the parrot, and ignoring its screams and the wild thrusts of its beak, tried to take the bird in his hand. Only quick action by Vergil prevented its capture.

The tipsy trio disappeared with their barrel into a bar. A sound of riot and battle followed.

Vergil listened. "Things are getting worse, Pa. Looks like we better get going."

"Guess we better while we can."

They took down the tent in haste, and packed up the trailer.

An impromptu parade began to pass, led by a score of wide-paunched, graying men singing *Madelon*, with a band and a ragged line of delegates behind. Some boys came roving in their wake, toppling the boxes and trash cans at the curb into the street. Behind them another group of veterans appeared, pulling a dilapidated buggy discovered in a forgotten stable. On the driver's seat were two lanky soldiers, their passenger a female wax dummy, naked except for a long black glove on one pink-tinted arm.

The ancient vehicle came to a halt near the trailer, completely blocking the already-crowded roadway. One of the drivers dismounted, and offering a bottle of whisky to the lady passenger, began sharing it with his companions. It was obvious they would not be moving for some time.

Captain Asa hurried out with Vergil, and began pushing the trash cans aside to clear a passage for the car. Fernie and a few stalled motorists aided.

As they worked, the two Indians and the pirate emerged from the bar again, rolling the keg as though from force of habit, for by the sound and the open spigot it was empty. They saw the bannered trailer parked at the edge of the lot where the tent had stood and halted, staring at it in maudlin admiration.

The workers in the streets soon cleared away most of the debris. Captain Asa was returning with Vergil and Fernie to the automobile, when to his horror he saw the blond Indian suddenly leap behind the wheel. Almost simultaneously the lean Indian and the pirate tossed the beer keg into the back seat and hopped onto the running board. There was a roar of the motor. The car and the trailer plunged wildly over the sidewalk. As Captain Asa came running, the feathered head of the blond man was thrust in tipsy delight out the window. "S'long, Pop!" he shouted.

The car rattled down the road. As it sped away, other plainer-garbed figures scrambled aboard. They stood on the guards and the rear step of the trailer, clinging to the door handles and shouting jubilantly.

Captain Asa and the others darted in frantic pursuit. The grave dog, who had been nosing through the upset trash, dashed after the speeding vehicles, barking in fury. The kidnaped car turned, and began to disappear up a swarming avenue.

The pursuers raced faster.

Waves of picturesque hats swept past them: the plumed hats of the drum majorettes and the towering busbies of the drum majors; the scarlet or green overseas caps printed with the name of the wearer's town; the painted steel helmets of some crack marching corps. Streams of squirted water stung the runners' faces. Electric canes struck against their legs, like the touch of fiery iron.

They paid no heed.

They lost the trailer behind a slow-moving truck. A moment later there came the shrill screeching of brakes, followed by the sickening sound of rending metal and the crack of shattering glass.

Captain Asa's legs seemed suddenly to turn to ice.

It required some time for the family to reach the scene, fighting their way through the surging sea of uniforms. They saw the car. They stood rigid.

It lay like a dying animal upon the sidewalk, where the driver, in what seemed an attempt to avoid an accident, had swerved and struck a light pole. The front bumper had collapsed, and a great gash appeared in the radiator, with water spouting in rusty streams from half-a-dozen places, like blood from fatal wounds. The fenders at one side were crumpled, and the headlight turned at a grotesque angle, as though it were a great eye gouged out from its socket in some mortal combat.

The trailer lay with its rear end in the entrance of a barbershop, the door of the vehicle smashed and the glass in several of its windows only a gaping void, the whole structure leaning at a curious angle from the perpendicular.

When they looked closer they saw that a wheel was torn away, the hub and the fractured spokes lying grim on the sidewalk, like broken bones. Over all stood the black light pole, bent in melancholy, like a solitary mourner grieving over its dead.

A crowd stood about, discussing the accident. Captain Asa and the others moved past and went inside the trailer, the broken wheel forcing them to stand oddly, as though they were on a ship listing in a gale. The cases bearing the exhibits were thrown about in wild disorder. The reptiles were unharmed, but long cracks showed here and there in some of the glass panels. The cheap china dishes had toppled from the shelves of the minute kitchen and lay in fragments on the floor.

They re-emerged and saw the blond Indian, who had gone into a nearby drugstore to bind up a slight cut in his hand. He was sober now, his pudgy face pale with shock.

"Sorry, Pop. I was drunk," he murmured, and slipped some bills into Captain Asa's hand.

The pirate and the other Indian followed his example.

A cynical bystander without cap or badges watched them move away. "Boys'll be boys," he said.

A towing car came from a neighboring garage in answer to a telephone call. The mechanic fixed a chain to the disabled automobile. They climbed inside and proceeded down the street, the trailer bumping behind with the rhythmic clatter made by a four-wheeled vehicle when it is running on only three.

Vergil sat stunned, silent.

Captain Asa brushed some broken glass from the seat. "We'll get her fixed up all right. Ain't as bad as it looks maybe."

Vergil did not answer.

The car rattled on. The waves of gay-colored uniforms parted to let it pass.

They spent several days in a cheap rooming house, waiting until the repairs were completed, then set out again through the busy streets of the city, strange now with no uniforms and no gay banners hanging from the windows. The automobile seemed little different than when they had first come to the city. The bent bumpers and the dented fenders had been straightened. A secondhand radiator no rustier than its predecessor showed between the headlights. A new wheel supported the rear end of the trailer.

Captain Asa smoked a stogie as they drove through the suburbs. "They done a good job on her, didn't they, Vergil?"

"They done a fine job."

They stopped in a Missouri village that night, and continued their travels in the pleasant little settlements to the North. But the good fortune attending their recent wanderings had ended. Picture shows were everywhere, and only the poorest farmer failed to possess an automobile to take him to the larger towns, where entertainment of every variety fought for the contents of his pocketbook. It became more and more difficult to send off the payments to the henna-haired woman in Memphis. They had not seen Mr. Waters for many days, and could not turn to him for counsel.

They drove into a settlement to find a large carnival standing in the square, clamorous with loud-speakers and the raucous voices of barkers.

Vergil stopped the car, and watched thoughtfully. "Maybe we could join up with that there show, Pa. If we could get in with a big show like that, we could sure make some money."

They drove closer, and in a little office behind the merry-go-round found the manager, a hard, quick-spoken individual smoking a huge cigar. He walked with the travelers to the trailer, his countenance in striking contrast to the innocent faces of the children seated upon the painted horses.

He glanced an instant at the snakes and the Gila monster in their cases, then spat sardonically and turned away.

Captain Asa and Vergil walked back to the trailer.

The summer passed and the first trace of autumn touched the air. The nights grew colder. Long, melancholy rains began to fall, the certain sign of coming winter in the Valley. The visitors to the tent grew fewer and fewer. Vergil's old restlessness returned. He began devoting all his time to his scientific magazines and his books of locomotives. Once more when a train would thunder over a crossing, he would follow it with his eyes until it was only a drifting thread of smoke along the horizon. Often at night, when they sat in the trailer and a lonely whistle would blow in the distance, he would raise his head and listen till the sound grew faint as the cry of a night bird lost in the darkness.

The rains increased. Now and then when they erected the tent they would be surrounded by pools of water.

The weather affected their attendance sharply. Sometimes at night there was not a single customer.

A week came at last when they could not make a payment. Other similar weeks followed in regular procession.

Captain Asa sat up late one night writing a letter to the proprietress.

The answer arrived soon after at a tiny settlement lost in a wooded valley.

Captain Asa read it, then turned to Vergil and Fernie. "She's got a fellow that'll take the show. She says to send it back."

They received the news with the stoicism of the mountains. Carefully they boarded up the cases, and labeling the tent and the other equipment, drove off to the dingy express office adjoining the railroad station. One by one they turned the boxes over to the blue-capped agent behind the counter. They walked slowly back to the car. A high-pitched, plaintive "My O My", followed them through the doorway until they were out of sight.

They drove over the highway once more, winding through low, pine-covered hills.

Vergil looked away from the wheel. "What you figuring on now, Pa?"

Captain Asa waited a long time before replying. "I don't know. We'll find something. We got the car. We can travel around a lot of places. Long as I got you and Fernie with me, I ain't going to be a-worrying."

They went on much as in the days before Ula's departure, Vergil and Captain Asa doing odd jobs in the little towns they visited, Fernie now and then selling one of the statuettes still remaining in the baskets.

Vergil's restlessness continued to heighten.

They parked along the highway one afternoon near a railroad construction camp. A score of Negroes were laying a new track, chanting in rhythm. Across the mounds of newly-sawed ties their rich voices drifted:

Haul up and down this old railroad,
Haul up and down this line.
Haul up and down this old railroad,
A dollar's hard to fin'.

Beyond them showed a half-dozen old boxcars, transformed into rolling houses, at whose windows were visible the wives and daughters of the white crewmen. Nearby lay the mess car, where a sweating Negro cook was bent over a stove.

The chanting track layers finished their toil, and went off on a work train to the neighboring town. Captain Asa and his family walked over to visit the white crew remaining.

They sat in the car of the genial foreman, sipping coffee out of heavy china cups brought by his blue-eyed daughter. As they drank, great passenger trains charged past, like monstrous black panthers just loosed from their cages. Giant switch engines puffed and snorted as they shoved their loads about the adjoining yards, like laboring elephants.

Vergil's glance followed wherever they moved over the shining rails.

The visitors left at nightfall and went off to supper.

Vergil bolted down his food, and hurried back to the construction camp.

When he returned to the trailer at bedtime his dreamy eyes were glowing. He sat looking down the shadowy yards where the signal lights along the ground were blinking, green and red and yellow, like the eyes of giant cats stalking their prey in the darkness. The monstrous switch engines clanked past, dark and full of mystery.

"It's a wonderful life, railroading," he declared.

Next morning as they were driving along the low hills that had become their usual horizon, he turned suddenly to Captain Asa. An odd, troubled expression touched his Indian-like face. "When we get to some flat ground today, I'm going to start learning you to drive the car, Pa."

Captain Asa looked at him in surprise. "I ain't got no call to be a-running a car, Vergil. How come you want me to be a-learning driving?"

"You ought to learn, Pa." He spoke at unusual length,

and with an odd insistence. "Something might happen to me. I might get sick or anything. And then if you couldn't run the car, you'd have to stay wherever we happened to be riding. Out in a swamp, maybe."

He argued with such earnestness, Captain Asa had no escape but in agreement.

The lessons began that afternoon, on a gravel road where passing automobiles were rare. With patience Vergil taught him the intricacies of the clutch and the mysteries of the gearshift, the complexities of a backing turn and starting on a hill. Captain Asa's progress was slow.

The troubled expression in Vergil's face heightened.

His pupil had mastered the difficulties at last, and had been conducting the rattling vehicle several hours each day for perhaps a week without assistance, when as dusk approached they saw a little railroad town ahead, its squat buildings almost obliterated by the black haze arising from the freight yards that stretched along the highway.

They approached a roundhouse, with mountainous volcanoes of smoke rolling from a score of chimneys, like storms collected by some angry god to destroy an offending world. A cindery stretch of ground was visible not far away where several railroad boardinghouses stood gloomily, their once-white paint long since vanished under innumerable layers of soot. Only a pair of stiff-starched white curtains showed in one of the windows, defying the descending blackness, like a freshly bloomed lily in a dismal field of mud.

Vergil brought the car to a halt.

Captain Asa looked at him in wonder. "You ain't a-stopping here, are you, Vergil? Be a lot nicer up there in town."

Vergil descended from the car. There was a tensity about his eyes, a strain about his lips, as though he were trying to make an announcement, but was restrained by some conflicting emotion. "I'd rather stay here, Pa, if I can."

They made the trailer ready for the night, obtaining water at the house with the snowy curtains.

The sun set and a fog arose, drifting in sheets over the blackened waste.

They ate their supper in silence, interrupted at frequent intervals by the deafening rumble of the trains sweeping past. Clouds of yellowish smoke would linger in the locomotives' wake, mingling with the mist, and seeping through the trailer windows. Cinders would rain upon the roof, with a noise like drifting sand.

They went to bed. All night there came the varied sounds of the rails: the painful chugging of a freight engine, like a weary old man, despairing of ever moving its grievous burdens; the nervous puffing of a passenger engine, like a highstrung, worried woman; the angry whistling of an engine in the yards, summoning the brakeman; the unearthly moaning of a streamliner, like a weird trumpet heralding the arrival of some demon king, commanding all in its path to clear the way.

Often Captain Asa was roused by a violent shuddering as some monstrous shadow rocked past, so close the heat from the glowing fireboxes seemed almost to scorch the windows. Each time he saw Vergil sitting up in his bunk, gazing into the foggy night.

Dawn came, at first only a patch of gray in the smoky pall shrouding the earth.

Vergil arose, and lighting the lamp, began packing his belongings.

Captain Asa, clad in a nightshirt, put on his straw slippers and came to where his son was stooping over a blanket roll. He stood in silence a moment, his face showing no sign of his emotion. "You . . . going . . . away . . . Vergil?"

The youth placed his baseball glove and the ukulele in the roll bearing his other possessions. "You can drive the car good now, Pa. . . . I didn't want to leave you before you could drive the car."

"Where . . . you . . . a-going?"

"I'm going to get a job railroading. I was talking to the foreman at that construction camp the other day, and he seen I knew about engines. He said I could start out getting a job as helper in the shops. . . . Soon as I eat I'm going over to the roundhouse."

Captain Asa took down his clothes from a hook on the wall, and began to dress.

Vergil tied his books with a frayed rope. "I been thinking a long time, Pa. I don't want to leave you. But I got to get out and do something. A fellow has to go away sometime. I'll get a fine job, and send back a lot of money for you and Fernie. . . . If the car don't start easy, kick the pedal twice before you turn on the gas."

"I don't want no money. And I can get the car started all right."

Fernie appeared, and preparing coffee, began to set the table. Now and then she turned to gaze with deep misgiving at her father, making his morning toilet near a window.

Captain Asa dried his face. Putting on a clean shirt, he arranged his tie and brushed off his black coat with painstaking care, as though this last meal together, like a funeral or other tragic occurrence, was an occasion demanding unusual formality. "You'll get yourself blowed up on them trains. Them locomotives is always a-bursting. Or you'll get run over by one of them switch engines. That's terrible dangerous, working on a railroad."

They sat down at the table. The fog was lifting. The sky grew brighter. Off in the boardinghouse with the white curtains there came the tinkle of a breakfast bell. From the railroad shops, vaguely visible beyond the roundhouse, there came a long whistle, marking a new day.

Vergil finished his breakfast and put on his hat. He took his box of souvenir matches and placed it in Fernie's hands. "This here's for you, Fernie. It's got the ones from the restaurant in St. Louis, too. I'm going to do a-plenty of traveling now on the railroad, and be eating in all kinds of places. So I'll be getting all kinds of matches."

He started out the door. Captain Asa and Fernie followed.

The roundhouse was smoking like a series of volcanoes again, the squat chimneys bursting into different-colored eruptions, black and yellow and gray and brown, and fleecy white masses like clouds in June.

They walked toward it, and halted at a row of tracks, stretching like strands of polished silver into the distance.

Vergil prepared to cross.

Captain Asa gave his son the bundles he was carrying. He spoke quietly. "You be careful of them slot machines, Vergil. Railroad people's terrible gamblers, they says."

The youth stepped over the rails and began walking alone down a cinder path. The wind was blowing the smoke from the roundhouse in sooty gusts that clung close to the ground. His Indian-like figure began to grow dim as he moved farther and farther into the melancholy haze.

A freight train came speeding down the main line, blocking him from view with its huge cars of coal and lime and gravel and lumber. On and on it thundered. It passed, with a noisy rattling of the red caboose that brought it to a sudden end. Captain Asa strained his eyes to see beyond.

Vergil's figure still showed in the smoke, like a ghostly shadow. A sooty burst, denser than the others, issued from one of the roundhouse chimneys and swept over the bleak landscape. The shadow vanished.

Captain Asa turned away.

III

CHAPTER THIRTEEN

THEY walked to the trailer, halted at the roadside. Captain Asa climbed behind the vacant wheel.

Fernie glanced at him doubtfully. "Can you drive her by yourself, Pa?"

He fumbled with the ignition. "I can drive her."

All day as the car rattled along he sat watching the highway, tense, uneasy, clamping on the brakes when a huge truck shot before him at a crossroads, or swerving with fright to avoid a child or a dog running out from a path between the trees.

They were journeying near the Mississippi. Sometimes the river, flooded with the rains, stretched like a muddy ocean beside them, in low brown swells tipped with blackish driftwood. Here and there a fisherman was out in a rowboat, running his lines. At times a steamboat chugged past, pushing a solitary barge of timber to a sawmill whining on the opposite shore.

Darkness neared. Captain Asa's muscles were growing weary, cramped. He began looking for a halting place.

They rode under an avenue of lofty pines, rising like a vast cathedral in the twilight.

Captain Asa reached down a hand from the wheel, and rubbed his stiffened knees.

Fernie took off her shoes, and rested her feet. "Maybe I can learn to drive and help you, Pa. I heard Vergil a-teaching you."

"I don't need no help. Ain't right for a girl to be driving. People says it's them women drivers causes all the accidents."

They stopped for the night, the river below them once more, rushing ominously. A cabin showed at the edge of a clump of trees. They walked toward it to buy some corn meal. Through the window they could see a little old man sitting before a smoky fire, so frail he seemed about to be blown away by the gusts coming down the chimney. Near him a solemn small boy was moving about, cooking a meal on a rusty stove.

The old man arose with difficulty from his homemade straw chair, and greeted the visitors with the simple cordiality of the poor. At his invitation, they sat down before the crackling blaze.

They talked, while darkness crept over the valley.

The eyes of the frail host were touched with longing. "You ain't got none of them spelling books the children uses in school, have you, brother?"

Captain Asa shook his head. "Ain't got nothing except

them Home Knowledge books I was trying to sell for a while."

The other feebly poked the fire with a piece of railroad iron. "I been trying and trying to get one of them spelling books. I ain't never had no kind of schooling. And I'm getting old. Before I die, I'd mighty like to spell out the three Holy words, God, Heaven, and the Savior, so I could know whenever I came on 'em in the Bible. That way when I died and was talking to the Lord, he'd see I knowed His name."

Captain Asa stared at the leaping flames. "If you want me to, I'll teach you. . . . When you're in trouble . . . them's good words to know."

They stayed for supper, eating the turnip greens and pork the boy set out on the table. The old man brought out a yellowed Testament. Until late Captain Asa sat beside him, pointing out the varying shapes of the letters. He followed with a shaky finger.

They returned to the trailer, and went to bed. Captain Asa tossed restlessly.

Outside a high wind moaned through the pines. The branches swayed with a noise of rushing water, seeming an echo of the river that swept below the road. Often a wave larger than the others would climb far up on the bank. A curtain of spray would dash against the windows.

Captain Asa arose, and lit the lamp. Taking his own tattered Bible from the shelf, he spread it on his knees and began to read.

Hour after hour he sat there, the only sound the movements of the dog at his feet when it shifted position, or desiring attention, thumped its tail sepulchrally against the floor.

A light showed down the stream, and a motorboat sped through the shadows, shattering the night with the noise of its engine. From the distance there came the lonely whistle of a train.

Captain Asa picked up the lamp and walked to the end of the trailer where Fernie was deep in slumber. He stood gazing at the girlish head on the pillow, her silvery hair gleaming in the soft light.

She wakened, and sat up in alarm. "What's the matter, Pa?"

The whistle of the locomotive blew again. The sound rose above the sighing of the pines, and drifted in haunting echoes down the valley.

Captain Asa listened.

The lamp flickered with a tremor of his hand. "You ain't going to leave me too, are you, Fernie?"

She pulled the covers tighter about her for warmth. "I won't ever leave you, Pa."

The train, coming nearer, blew for a crossing, rousing a dog in a farmyard to a shrill barking. The trailer rattled with a dull vibration of the ground. Some pine cones dropped from the branches overhead, and rolled across the roof.

Captain Asa spoke again. "I ain't been a good father to you, Fernie. I ain't been a good father to none of my children. If I'd have been a good father, they'd never have gone away."

He returned to his Bible and sat reading until daylight. He turned out the lamp, and slept.

When he arose the wind was slackening. A solitary crane flew across the water, stopping now and then to rest on a floating log. A belated flock of wild geese appeared in military formation, drifting off toward the swamps showing brown against the horizon.

Captain Asa took a chair at the table where Fernie had already set out his breakfast. The deep lines in his face had lessened a little.

He poured himself a cup of coffee. "I been thinking all night, Fernie. It's like Chick Waters says. I don't fit in the way things are nowadays. And I don't know nothing about keeping my children. I thought I was fixing things all right for you and Vergil when we got the show. But I didn't. Looks to me like everything I done's just been kind of wrong."

He finished eating, and shaved with an old-fashioned razor. Now and then a chilly blast from the dying gale swept through some cracks in the windows, where the panes no longer fitted the crudely-made frames. Taking a jackknife, he scraped the wood clean, and set about sealing the gaps with putty.

Fernie began to sweep the floor.

The knife in Captain Asa's hand came to a halt. He put it down, and confronted her suddenly. "What'd you like to do, Fernie? You tell me, and I'll fix things the way you want 'em."

She picked up a button from beneath her broom, and laid it on the bureau. Her voice was hesitant. "I guess I'm kind of tired of traveling, Pa. It was mighty nice for a while. But I'd like to settle down somewhere. In a city, maybe, where I can go to church socials and things, and have some friends, and kind of live like other people."

He put a preliminary daub of putty along another wide opening. "You stay in one of them cities and some fellow'll see you sure, and want you to get married. You're mighty pretty. He'll take you away, and I won't see you any more, like it was with Ula. Sometimes I wish both my daughters'd have been born ugly."

He pressed the doughy substance into place. "I guess if that's what you want, I got to do it. Maybe I can open up a little business or something. I was thinking about it last night. Chick Waters says this here's a business time today. Looks like with all the businesses there is everywhere, we could sure find something."

They set out in the car soon after. The wind died as the sun climbed in the sky. The air grew warmer. The road left the river, and wound through rolling farmland. Hens clucked in the patches of dried weeds before some tiny cabin, searching for a hardy worm, and pigs combed the mud with their noses. A fat rabbit scurried through the bushes, with upraised white tail waving in jerks, as though it were a flag of truce asking peace of any straying hunter.

Captain Asa's spirits lifted.

Fernie looked down the tree-lined road. "Where we going now, Pa?"

He drove the car carefully past a farm tractor clanking along the edge of the pavement. "We're mighty close to St. Louis again. Looks to me we better go back there and see if we can find something for us to do. They got fine people in that town. . . . You'd like to go, wouldn't you, Fernie?"

The wistfulness always present in her pale face deepened. "They got wonderful stores in St. Louis. I saw a place had a hundred ladies' hats, all in one window. If a person had plenty of money, there was one hat that'd be mighty pretty to buy. It was all blue velvet, with a little yellow bird made of real feathers sitting on top, and then a little gold veil coming over it all, just like it was a cage."

They reached the city in the morning. Timidly Captain Asa drove through the maze of traffic, his hand growing rigid on the wheel each time he neared a policeman signaling at a crowded intersection. With relief he parked the car and trailer, and set out with Fernie toward the middle of town.

As on their earlier visit, they stood admiring the luxuries on display in the glittering shops.

A woman wearing an expensive hat descended from a taxicab.

Captain Asa watched her disappear into an opulent department store nearby. "That there hat you was talking about, Fernie. How much it cost, you reckon?"

She turned from an ornate display where her eyes were feasting on some gold slippers. "It was three dollars, Pa. I seen the price on the little card."

Captain Asa counted the bills in his pocket. "Them ladies' things sure cost money, don't they? But I'm going to get it for you. You ain't had a bought hat for a mighty long time."

With eager steps she led the way to a showy building whose windows teemed with cheap millinery. They went inside. A bored clerk removed the hat from its stand, and placed it in a colored bag.

Fernie took the parcel in reverence, as a pilgrim might receive some holy relic at a shrine. As they walked through the streets, she halted now and then to open the bag and gaze inside, for reassurance that the gift had not vanished.

They reached the trailer. She looked around the interior, searching for a place where it could be deposited, as though its beauty could not be wasted on the darkness of a cupboard.

Her glance strayed to the stuffed dove moulting beneath its shiny dome, with a thin layer of white powder at the base. "Maybe I could put it there under the glass, Pa. It'd be mighty nice to look at it when I was doing the dishes and things."

Captain Asa nodded. "The dove's all wore out anyway."

Delicately she lifted the relic from its perch, while a smell of ancient perfume filled the air, then substituted the new treasure.

She stood gazing at it with folded hands, as though she were in prayer.

For a week Captain Asa wandered about the city, trying to find some little enterprise for which no large down payment was necessary. He was growing disheartened, when someone suggested that he cross the river to East St. Louis, where he could find many who like himself were native to the back country and the hills. His search was quickly rewarded. On a drab street in the Illinois town he found a tiny soda-water stand presided over by a lanky Texan, who had been ordered to return West for his health, and was anxious to be rid of his possessions at any sacrifice.

It was a shabby little establishment of the sort existing by the thousands throughout America, its area, scarcely as large as the trailer, being chiefly occupied by a stained marble counter for serving ice cream and sandwiches. Crowded along the wall was a rack filled with magazines and comic books, a narrow case containing some candy bars, and a second case displaying a few clockwork toys. Above these ran a long shelf bearing half-a-dozen faded typing tablets, several cartons of cigarettes, and a few dusty packages of electric-light bulbs. At the front was a pinball machine which emitted showers of sparks whenever a nickel was dropped into the slot alongside, and which bore prominently the sign "This Is A Game of Skill, No Gambling" and a smaller inscription "Give Your Winning Counters To The Cashier."

Several days before, Captain Asa had received a few dollars from the proprietor of the crossroads store in the South where he had left the horse to graze, and to whom after much negotiation he had agreed to sell the animal. Using the money as his capital for the new undertaking, he paid the rent for a month, and receiving the key, moved the trailer to a vacant lot beside a filling station a few blocks away.

They spent a day cleaning vigorously and making the necessary arrangements for provisioning the counter, then early next morning unlocked the door, and prepared for visitors.

Captain Asa looked with pride about the tiny interior. "We got a nice business, ain't we, Fernie?"

She hung up the new hat she had worn in honor of the occasion, and put on a fresh-starched apron. "It's a beautiful place, Pa."

Captain Asa moved behind the faded marble counter, and studied the row of tarnished handles for dispensing sodas. "Looks to me like maybe it's going to be all right. I had a cousin in Pineville once had a little store like this, and he made a pile of money. People's always eating ice cream, and they're always smoking cigarettes. And maybe I can fix up some of my stogies and sell 'em. People always says my stogies is about as good a cigar as they can get anywhere."

For the fourth time Fernie polished the sundae holders standing in a nickeled mountain on the counter. "I can make the sandwiches. The ladies at the church socials up in Clay Creek said people always tried to get my boxes, 'cause they liked my sandwiches. Maybe they'll like to get 'em here."

Captain Asa nodded. "There sure ain't nothing like a homemade sandwich." He shifted the cartons of cigarettes on the shelf an imperceptible fraction, and passing the pinball machine, studied the mechanism. "It's a up-to-date place, too. Ain't nothing old-fashioned about us now. A pinball machine's the latest thing there is. And people's always playing 'em. The Texas fellow said he figured if things went right I could get the rent from just the machine."

He stood in the doorway, looking down the street with its bleak little tailor shop, its paintless laundry with a scarred wooden box outside to receive bundles, its undertaking parlor where a purplish light burned gloomily and a seedy individual in a black suit sat at a telephone waiting for the call that meant another customer. At the end of the thoroughfare showed the approaches of the bridge spanning the river, the steelwork blackened with dirt and soot until it resembled a series of giant spiderwebs in some long-darkened cellar. Nearby, freight engines puffed and snorted, preparing to take their long trains across the Western prairies. Their smoke joined with the sooty bursts from some neighboring factories to form a somber canopy.

A constant procession passed before the store, a strange medley of cultures and races: stolid figures with dull, expressionless faces, brought by some profit seeker from a crowded slum of Europe to labor in the mills; tall, gaunt figures, drifted like themselves from the rural areas, who unable to cope with the complexities of modern life, were yet unwilling to return to the simpler existence of the farm; an occasional swaggering individual with coarse mouth and cruel eyes, a gangster who had fastened himself like a leech upon this outer flesh of the great city that lay across the river.

Captain Asa gazed with interest at the passersby. "They got some mighty nice people here, they says. You can make a-plenty of friends. The Texas fellow was telling me there's some fine Greeks and Polaks. And course there's plenty of hill people, come from down around the Ohio and everywhere. Wouldn't surprise me none if we met some folks from Clay Creek, maybe."

Fernie gave a final brush of her polishing rag across the cracked mirror, where a buxom pasteboard young woman urged the beholder to purchase a popular drink. "Maybe we ought to get some flowers, Pa. They always have flowers when they're starting a new store."

"That's sure right. I done forgot all about it. . . . Here's fifty cents, Fernie. You go out and get us a little bouquet."

She hurried up the street, returning with a dusty wreath of immortelles from which half the artificial yellow blooms had fallen. In the center was pinned a red ribbon bearing a faded "Good Luck."

With care she arranged the purchase to hide as many as possible of the missing blossoms. "They didn't have no flowers for the half dollar. But the lady looked a while and found this. A fellow ordered it once for a new dry-cleaning place that was starting, she said, but it burned down before he got it open so he never come for it. She let me have it cheap."

Fernie put it in the window. Captain Asa looked on with approval.

He walked past the game board with the metal balls once more, and dropping a nickel into the slot, watched the lurid sparks sweep from peg to peg like bolts of colored lightning. His face grew sad. "Vergil'd sure have a nice time a-playing the pinball machine."

The ice-cream man arrived soon after, carrying his metal cylinders, like shells for some odd cannon, and leaving a shiny trail of ice chips melting on the floor. Behind him came the first customer, a pigtailed little girl to buy a penny's worth of gum. All day there was a trickle of patrons: a truck driver to eat a frankfurter and drink a cup of coffee; some students on their way home from high school to buy sodas and sundaes; the pompous, gold-toothed proprietor of the tailor shop next door to purchase a cheap cigar.

They grew used to the store quickly. To save the expense of a rooming house, they continued to stay in the trailer.

Their lives were quiet, pleasant. With energy Captain

Asa would go about, tamping down the ice in the freezers, or putting some decoration in the window to attract customers—a pineapple sculptured in the shape of a rose, a trio of bright-colored sundaes formed of papier-mâché. Fernie stayed behind the counter, mixing sodas and making sandwiches, responding shyly to the customers who jested with her from their creaking stools.

Often after supper the tailor or some of the workingmen who lived in the flats upstairs would drop in for a chat. Sometimes late at night, when business was slack, father and daughter would go off to a picture show. Their profits were small, but enough to pay the modest rental.

Some of the patrons came with regularity now. Among these was a blue-eyed, clear-skinned young man of perhaps twenty with red hair set in a high pompadour, the son of a prosperous Czech baker in the neighborhood. Each afternoon he would draw up before the store in his battered yellow car, covered in juvenile fashion with painted signs proclaiming "Don't Be A Flat Tire" or "Stop. Look. But Don't Listen," and equipped with a horn that played a bar of a popular tune. He would come inside, and ordering a banana special or a piece of coconut pie, sit talking with Fernie as she moved back and forth before the mirror. He would take his departure at last, and the car would vanish in a yellow blur. A moment later far down the street there would sound the musical notes of the horn, in farewell salute.

Fernie would follow the course of the automobile with rapt eyes, then return dreamily to her labor.

The youth treated Captain Asa with deference.

He went away after a few weeks to stay with relatives in Chicago. Captain Asa saw him depart with relief.

There was another regular visitor, an amiable, stoutish

Italian known only as Joe, who came each week, exhaling a strong odor of garlic, to collect the nickels from the pinball machine. He would take out a yellow keyring in the form of a pretzel, advertising a local beer, unlock the metal compartment to gather up the coins within, test and oil the mechanism, and, wheezing a little from his exertions, sit down with Captain Asa at the single table for a friendly cup of coffee.

"Listen, Papa. I got a plenty good one today," he would remark, his words still touched with the accents of his homeland, and then relate some humorous event of the neighborhood, or some racy anecdote he had gathered on his rounds. Or sometimes, in a more serious mood, he would declare, "I tell you the truth, Papa. It's a plenty nice racket, the pinball racket. It's plenty money for me and Primo—that's my brother. But sometimes maybe I wish I was in Sicilia, raising grapes and plenty babies." And then he would add as an afterthought, "If you ever got trouble, Papa, call East 9965, and ask for Joe. I fix it for you quick."

Occasionally he would bring a present of an odd-shaped sausage or a fragrant Italian cheese.

Captain Asa looked forward to his coming.

The Italian was making his usual collection one afternoon, dropping the coins into a white muslin bag, when he turned to Captain Asa. "Listen, Papa. We got juke boxes now. You want a nice box, maybe? It's a fine thing when you got the ice-cream business. And then all the time you got plenty music."

Captain Asa shook his head. "I'd like the music fine. But I don't like them boxes."

The Italian puffed comfortably at a fat cigar. "I tell you the truth, Papa. The people got the candy place down near the bus depot, they're closing up when we put in a box.

And now they're carrying plenty money every day to the bank. You ought to do it, Papa."

Captain Asa agreed after considerable persuasion. The juke box arrived next morning, a monstrous marbled blasphemy in lurid green.

The stoutish Joe, who had come to escort the treasure, plugged the connecting cord into a socket. The glassy surface flamed into a series of blinding green waterfalls, over which there flashed a perpetual rain of greenish stars, pierced at times by dazzling emerald moonbeams.

The plump face of the Italian shone with pleasure. "Listen, Papa. It's the finest box we got in the house. My brother Primo, he wants it for his wife's sister keeps a saloon on the highway. But I do plenty talking, and tell him you need it for the store." He pointed to a steel plate fixed at the side that bore the details of the monster's genealogy. "That's the name, Papa, *The Irish Melody*. That's why it's painted green, Papa. It plays twenty pieces. Ten pieces crooners and big band leaders. Ten pieces hillbilly, *When Whisky And Blood Flow Together*, and cowboy songs. I tell you the truth, that's the way you got to fix a juke box in East St. Louis, Papa."

He pressed a lever. A rumbling like the warning of an earthquake sounded somewhere inside the machine's transparent vitals. It began to play.

Captain Asa listened with misgiving.

For the first few days his feeling toward it was an undisguised hostility. Then as a week passed, habit, that enables man to become accustomed to any environment, began to exercise its influence. Little by little his dislike of the instrument lessened. At times when he was by himself and loneliness would overcome him, he would drop a nickel into the slot, and listen.

Several more weeks drifted by, and he regarded the monster almost with affection.

"It's all in green," he would tell a chance visitor. "That's why they call it *The Irish Melody*."

He was alone late one night when the door opened and two youngish, swarthy figures who appeared to be brothers entered. They were clad in tight-fitting suits, and possessed cold, searching eyes in which the whites showed unpleasantly. They took seats at the counter.

"Gimme a shot of coke," said the first visitor, in whose cheek showed a crescent scar, as though from a knife.

"Make it two," grunted the second, his lips curling a little, like a vicious dog with a bone.

Captain Asa set the bottles on the counter with an uneasy hand.

The newcomers drank without hurrying.

"Ain't been in East St. Louis long, have you?" asked the scarred one, taking a cigarette from his flashy-tailored coat.

Captain Asa shook his head. "Been here a couple of months, I reckon."

The other struck a match in showy fashion with his fingernail. "Nice place if you know the right street," he declared in a cryptic voice.

The man with the curling lips arose, and walking to the pinball board, began to play. "You doing OK with Joe's machine?" he asked with a studied attempt at casualness.

Captain Asa went on washing some soda glasses. "I'm doing all right."

The man with the scar let the cigarette dangle uglily from his lips. "How about getting your machine and juke box from us? Joe's a small-time operator. We can do plenty better for you than Joe."

Captain Asa's bronze face grew stubborn. "Me and Joe is friends."

The man with the curling lip ceased his playing, and turned to glance in sinister inquiry at his companion. With the movement Captain Asa caught a glimpse of an automatic pistol slung beneath his coat.

The man with the scar shrugged his shoulders. He started with the other toward the door. "We'll be seeing you," he said.

They swaggered outside.

Captain Asa stood in silence as they vanished up the road. Next night when he came to the store the grave dog followed with watchful eyes at his heels.

Saturday arrived, the time for Joe's usual collection, and there was no sign of his appearance. More days passed without his arrival, and with no explanation for the departure from his usual custom. The coin compartments in the two machines were bulging.

Captain Asa questioned the tailor next door, whom he knew was the other's close acquaintance. The tailor's pomposity vanished. His face turned a greenish white, the color of his marking chalk. His expensive gold teeth began to chatter painfully.

He managed an evasive answer. From that time on, he avoided Captain Asa as though his neighbor were the carrier of some dread disease where even a word would mean a fatal contagion.

Captain Asa was filled with foreboding.

The plump Italian was almost two weeks overdue, when a little before noon the two swarthy, tight-suited visitors came swaggering into the store once more, their vicious faces confident now, and touched with a feeble attempt at cordiality. The man with the scar took out the pretzel key-ring Captain Asa had seen so many times before, and unlocking the machines, began to gather up their contents.

"Our boss bought out Joe," he grunted. He winked grimly at his companion.

The man with the curling lips nodded. "Joe and his brother didn't know the right street."

The scarred one put the coins in a new cloth bag. He twirled the key ring on his finger, and spoke in sardonic triumph. "If you need anything, phone East 9965. It's the same number, like it was before."

They swaggered away.

All day the lights on the pinball board danced, and the juke box blared out its harsh serenade. Captain Asa tried to busy himself with the customers so that he could not see or hear.

Night came. A drunken man sat down at the counter, and receiving change for a dollar, put twenty nickels into the juke box. On and on it played, in jangling monotony.

Captain Asa's face was gray. While the drunken man stared in foggy wonder, he disconnected the instrument and its flickering companion from the wall, then pushed them near the doorway.

He moved to the telephone and called a number. "You can come and get 'em," he said stonily. "I ain't keeping the machines any more."

The juke box and the gaming board were removed in the morning. But the episode left its scar on Captain Asa, like the mark of the knife in the swarthy man's cheek. Whenever anyone he did not know came late at night, he grew distrustful, following their movements till they had gone into the street. He brought his rifle from the trailer, and placed it in readiness behind a door. The days, however, passed uneventfully in regular pattern, the visit of the baker, delivering buns and long rolls of sandwich bread, the coming of the boy from the butcher's bringing hamburgers and sausage. Their trade showed signs of increasing a little.

Then one morning they noticed that most of the regular customers who came at the same early hour for their coffee and orange juice were missing from their usual stools. As the morning passed, the young men and women from some neighboring offices who always dropped in at lunchtime for a hasty sandwich, likewise failed to take their places. Three o'clock came, the time for the usual tumultuous entrance of the boys and girls from the nearby high school. The store remained empty.

Captain Asa was gazing outside in a bewildered attempt to solve the mystery, when an elderly, unshaven Southerner who worked in the railroad yards nearby, and was numbered among the regular patrons, shambled through the door. "Don't make it no Jumbo today, Sis," he drawled to Fernie, as he sat down at the counter. "Don't want nothing but a cup of coffee. I just come from that there new drugstore them big chain people opened down the street this morning, and I eat myself sick pretty near. You ought to go over and see it. Crowds is running around there like blind dogs in a butcher shop. They got a counter holds twenty-two people. Hope it ain't going to hurt you none."

It grew dark soon after. Captain Asa put on his hat, and turning the corner, walked toward the blaze of neon lights that marked the new establishment. The store had been some time in preparation, but it had not occurred to him that it might be a competitor. He halted before it, and looked into the plate-glass windows filled with candies and drugs and a startling array of crimson hot-water bottles seeming sufficient to warm all the aching stomachs of the Valley. Huge bouquets of flowers stood here and there, flanked by gilded signs of self-congratulation. In the aisles crowds were milling about, examining the toys and ladies' stockings and electric heaters and the other varied bargains on display everywhere. At one side, extending the entire length of the wall, was a counter of rose-colored porcelain, flanked by a succession of paneled mirrors that reflected the lights at the sides and in the ceiling till the wide interior seemed like a royal banquet hall. Behind the counter were a score of pretty but unsmiling girls in pink uniforms, handing out sodas and sundaes to the individuals on the glistening chromium seats alongside, like haughty royal handmaidens compelled to serve their inferiors. Beyond the sitters was a line three deep of standing men and women, like pelicans lining up behind a fishing boat, waiting to dive for the nearest stool.

A long time Captain Asa gazed at the scene, now and then recognizing one of his customers. He walked sadly away.

Several days passed, and a few of his more loyal patrons returned to their old places. But besides the glamor of the rival store, its prices were lower. The combination was too attractive for the neighborhood to resist. Captain Asa made new efforts to draw customers, constantly putting different attractions in the window—a novelty clock loaned by a dweller upstairs where two Negro boxers struck at each other with every tick of the pendulum, a jar full of dried peas with a prize of a pound of candy to the lucky one guessing nearest the correct number. The little shop remained empty.

He tried cutting prices, giving three scoops of ice cream where he had given two before, or reducing the charge for his pies and sandwiches. The number of customers increased a little. But when the week ended, he found that instead of the slight profit he had expected, his loss was greater than the week before.

He was compelled to raise the prices once more.

They extinguished the lights one Saturday night when the receipts had been particularly discouraging. Captain Asa halted outside the doorway and looked down the deserted sidewalk.

A heavy fog lay over the Valley. The street lamps had become faint moons, waning and waxing as a raw wind sent the mist drifting along the fronts of the shabby buildings. Automobiles crawled past, visible only where a dull blur marked their headlights. At a little distance, a shadowy span of the bridge loomed like a spectral mountain. Beyond it unseen switch engines clanked and rattled. A long sheet of white crepe paper drifted out from a trash heap and blew down the road, fluttering against the ghostly houses. It floated off toward the river, like a white crane returning home.

Captain Asa groped in his pocket for the door key. He found it, and slowly turned it in the rusty lock.

"I'm going to start looking for a job tomorrow," he said. "We got to give up the store."

CHAPTER FOURTEEN

He surrendered the key next day to a sister of the previous proprietor who had been receiving the rental, and went about the factories in the neighborhood looking for work. But his mountaineer hands were unfitted for the machines, that like animals with insatiable stomachs, swallowed up endless sheets of metal or bales of cotton. He would keep the employment only a few days, then would return home jobless. He began to grow dejected.

Winter was full upon them now. The nights in the trailer were bitter. The wind blew in icy currents through the cracks of the walls. The fire in the little oil stove seemed to have no effect on the freezing air. They went to bed early for the protection of the blankets. When they arose there would always be a thin layer of ice in the sink of their tiny kitchen. Occasionally a row of icicles would hang above the door like stalactites in a cave. At times snow fell, hiding the buildings nearby in a beautiful white cloak, then blackening under showers of soot.

At rare intervals there came a letter from Dallas, or a scrawled post card from a railroad town out West.

Captain Asa continued his rounds.

He abandoned his tour of the factories, and found a place not far away working with some older men as pin boy in a small bowling alley. With patience he would sit up on the wall of his little wooden coop, waiting while the bowlers sent the balls crashing against the polished clubs that stood in a triangle at his feet. He would hop down, set the toppled pins in place, then scramble back onto his perch to escape a new rolling avalanche. Now and then he would not be quick enough. A skidding ball or a flying pin would strike against his calf or ankle. He would go limping home at midnight, to find Fernie waiting with coffee and a steaming bowl of soup. She would bathe the bruise with hot water and bandage it tenderly.

The redhaired youth with the yellow car had returned from Chicago, and learning Fernie's whereabouts, was now a constant visitor. Each afternoon he would come to the trailer and take her off for a drive about the town. Captain Asa said nothing. But each tooting of the musical horn filled him with foreboding.

The job in the bowling alley went the way of the others. He began taking odd employment wherever he saw a sign in a window, working a few days as handy man in a shipping room or a store. His depression deepened.

He went one raw Sunday morning to a neighboring wagon diner, where at rare intervals he relieved one of the helpers in the kitchen, and finishing several hours earlier than he had expected, returned to the trailer. Fernie was out somewhere with the redheaded youth as was her custom each holiday. Captain Asa stretched out on his bunk and fell into a heavy sleep.

He was roused by the sudden halting of a car at the curb. Looking through the window, he saw Fernie and her escort walking hand in hand across the pavement. They stopped outside the door and began talking, the voice of the youth tense, eager, the voice of Fernie hushed, gentle. Their words came clearly through the paper-thin door.

Captain Asa turned pale.

For several moments the couple continued to stand there, then walked hand in hand to the car again, and drove away.

Captain Asa lay in his bunk numb with shock, as though he had been struck by a bolt from the light pole beyond the window. The world outside, the neon sign above the filling station next door, the police alarm box on the corner, spun in a series of fantastic merry-go-rounds within his brain. He rubbed his eyes and sat up dizzily. Climbing out of the bunk, he poured himself a cup of cold coffee.

The grave dog, lying in a corner, arose and whimpered to go outside. Several animals in the neighborhood had been injured by trucks, and Captain Asa had acquired the habit of not letting it run unaccompanied. Mechanically he put on his coat and hat, and went with it into the street.

A light rain had begun to fall with the approach of darkness, freezing as it touched the ground. Here and there the roadway was already covered with an icy sheen. For several blocks he walked with the dog, then retraced his steps. The sleet was coming down steadily now, clinging to his hat and his shabby overcoat. The streets were shining like mirrors.

As he drew near the trailer, he saw that the lamp was burning, and he knew his daughter had returned.

He went inside. Fernie was moving about the kitchen, still wearing her hat, as though she had just left her companion. She started guiltily as her father entered, her pale face flushed with excitement. She spoke with nervousness.

Captain Asa made no response. The colorless splotches had reappeared in his cheeks. He looked at her as though she were a stranger.

The sleet outside grew heavier. There was a continuous rattle on the roof, like falling pebbles. The windows were becoming sheets of ice through which the sidewalks were hardly visible.

Captain Asa began searching in a drawer of his table.

Fernie watched him with anxiety. "What you looking for, Pa?"

He pushed aside a matted tangle of string and rubber bands. "I'm looking for the car keys. . . . We're a-taking the road again."

She drew back in dismay. She started to speak, then checked herself, and stood near one of the windows, her long-lashed eyes fixed on the ice crystals forming over the panes. "You said we were going to stay here a long time, Pa. . . . Why you want to be leaving?"

He pulled out a new mass of pencil stubs and wire, then continued to search with doggedness. "You know . . . why I'm leaving."

He found the keys at last, and went out to the trailer parked at the rear, covered now with a thick layer of sleet so that it resembled the dwelling of an Eskimo. Knocking the ice loose from the coupling pin, he attached it to the battered automobile, and after some difficulty started the motor. He went inside again, his clothes glittering like glass. "Get your coat and come in the car, Fernie."

She made no move to obey.

For the first time in his life he spoke to her with harshness. "I told you to come and get in the car."

She trembled with emotion. "Charley ain't like Pretty Boy, Pa."

A patch of sleet fell from his hat onto the floor. He brushed it toward the stove with his shoe. "You ain't going to run off with nobody."

In the filling station adjoining a car drew up for gas. The bell on the pump clanged dully in the moist air. The neon sign over the doorway flashed in scarlet-and-green monotony.

Fernie spoke again, half-defending, half-pleading. "We were going to get married in Chicago, Pa. His uncle's got a big bakery there, and he's going to give Charley a job."

"How you know he's going to marry you? How you know he ain't just talking? He's one of them foreign people. And their ways is different than yours."

His coat came near the flickering stove. A cloud of steam rose up from the cloth. There was a faint smell of scorching.

He moved the coat away. "You ain't old enough to get married. You ain't even eighteen till September. And your mother always told me a girl don't know anything about getting married till she's twenty, anyway. The law says the same thing—you can't get married now unless I let you. You're going to do the right way—that's the way your mother wanted."

His sternness broke. His fingers plucked miserably at a torn, water-soaked buttonhole of his overcoat. "I thought you was going to be different than the others. . . . I thought you was going to stay with me . . . the way you said."

She hesitated, then put on her frayed wrap and followed him out the door. She climbed into the front of the car.

Captain Asa took a seat at her side. A look of desperation crossed her face, a look such as might come over a young deer when it first senses the trap which has made it prisoner.

Captain Asa kicked at the stubborn starter pedal. "He was a-coming back for you tonight . . . wasn't he?"

She made no reply.

He primed the engine and kicked the pedal again. The car gave a spasmodic cough, and moved across the curb.

Into a world transformed they traveled, an icy fairyland. The drab buildings were glistening palaces, dyed with magic color by the lights in the shop windows. The looped electric wires were rows of crystal chandeliers. Here and there showed a beautiful statue, a stately Venus or a graceful Apollo, before its reincarnation a bronze sign in front of a bank or a tall barber pole.

The car rounded a narrow corner, and went into a perilous skid.

The desperation had vanished from Fernie's eyes, replaced by stoic resignation. "You oughtn't be driving so fast, Pa. You'll turn us over."

Captain Asa swung the car forward. "He'll be following when he sees you're gone. . . . He ain't a-going to find you."

Through the suburbs they proceeded, past factories whose lofty, ice-covered smokestacks rose up like the pillars of ghostly temples. The sleet increased. The wiper on the windshield began to creak unhappily as it labored. Several times Captain Asa was forced to stop and clean the glass with a rag.

It grew colder. The dog lay close to the floor, taking advantage of the warmth of the engine.

Fernie covered the animal with a torn piece of carpet, and tucked the ends about their feet. "Where you taking us, Pa?"

He swung the car around a halted truck, looming out of the darkness. The brakes whined in shrill protest. "I'm going back to the hills. I don't fit nowhere else. Ain't no place left but home."

A car showed in the mirror, seeming to keep a fixed distance behind.

Captain Asa studied the reflection. "That there his car a-coming, Fernie?"

She shook her head.

The mirrored automobile changed direction at a cross-roads and vanished.

Captain Asa turned his eyes away. "They says it's easy to follow a trailer. I thought it was his car."

They were nearing the open country. Traffic was becoming rarer. At times a gas truck rumbled past, the chains at the rear emitting a stream of jewel-like sparks as they struck against the shiny road.

They stopped at a café to warm their chilled limbs.

A swarthy highway patrolman, sitting at the counter, looked at them in curiosity. "Bad night to be driving if you ain't got a reason," he remarked. "Plenty of wrecks by morning."

They went on again, the sleet continuing to fall. The road was deserted now, and a deep stillness lay over the countryside. They seemed to be traveling along a wide glacier on some distant planet, winding through a frozen wilderness.

In the mirror two headlights appeared, advancing swiftly, with two tiny parking lamps reflected beneath.

Captain Asa stiffened. "That's his car with them two little lights, ain't it?"

She did not answer.

Captain Asa pressed the accelerator. The car sped past a clump of glittering trees. On they raced, wildly. A filling station showed ahead, its pumps, covered with ice, standing like white-robed ski troopers on duty atop a snowy mountain. The car struck the slippery concrete that formed its approaches, and spinning in a giddy loop, sped toward the wide window at the front of the darkened office. It halted, with the bumper a few inches from the glass.

Captain Asa swung into the road again.

Fernie's voice shook a little. "You're a-going to kill us, Pa."

He did not hear, his eyes intent on the mirror, where the lamps of the other car grew constantly larger. The accelerator pedal was almost touching the floor. The rickety motor was pounding as though it would burst.

Past more gleaming trees they sped, the car behind gaining with rapidity. It shot alongside, the head and shoulders of the red-haired youth silhouetted in vague outlines at the wheel.

His voice called above the roar of the motors, in desperation. "Wait, Captain Asa! I want to talk to you!"

The answer was a new kick of the accelerator. Captain Asa's car made a wild lunge forward. Suddenly its lights flickered. The straining motor began an odd coughing. An instant later the lights went out. The rickety vehicle rolled to a stop in the middle of the highway.

Frantically Captain Asa stepped on the starting pedal. There was no response. A giant coal truck swerved past over the ice, the driver honking in fury. Captain Asa gazed after him with helpless eyes.

The red-haired youth brought his automobile to a halt behind the other and hurried forward. His clear-skinned, slightly Slavic face was somber beneath the collegiate hat he was wearing. "You'll get hit sure. I'll push you over to the side of the road."

Soon after the stalled car and trailer were resting on the icy shoulder. The youth took a flashlight, and peered into the compartment under the floor where a few rusty tools were lying. "You knocked a wire loose goes to your battery. I'll fix it for you."

He worked for a time with a hammer and pliers, glancing up occasionally at Fernie, shivering near the edge of the pavement. Captain Asa watched in silence.

The repair was effected at last. The motor gave voice to its usual noisy preliminaries. Captain Asa took his post behind the wheel. His daughter stood hesitant again.

He opened the door. "Get in the car, Fernie."

She waited a moment, her conflicting emotions revealed in swift succession upon her face, then sat down at her father's side. Her lover came forward in bitter protest. She pressed his hand, in silent entreaty. He walked away. The yellow car turned in the slippery road, and traveled toward the town. A moment later there came the sound of the musical horn in mournful farewell.

Captain Asa jerked at the stubborn gearshift. The wheels began to move over the concrete. The wiper creaked in doleful rhythm.

They halted for the night at the edge of a little town, frozen, soundless, like a city of the dead.

When they wakened the ice in the road was melting. The rows of crystal chandeliers above their heads were dissolving into wires and drooping trees. The glassy flowers fringing the highway were becoming lowly weeds.

They drove on steadily.

CHAPTER FIFTEEN

FOR several days they proceeded, through the dreary mining towns of Illinois and the snow-covered plains of Indiana, then crossed the Ohio into the rolling farms of the Blue Grass where sleek horses gamboled behind white-painted fences.

As the young man was left farther and farther behind, Captain Asa's sternness vanished. When he spoke to Fernie his voice was kind once more.

She answered in vague phrases.

The road began to grow steeper. Low peaks, streaked with white, showed everywhere against the horizon. The air grew sharper with the tang of the mountains. Log cabins began to appear, with lanky figures in overalls chopping wood before the door. Groves of pine trees climbed the rocky slopes, their branches covered with snow till they seemed rows of Christmas trees decorated with cotton.

Here and there a mine tipple appeared, covered with soot, and surrounded by a score of coal cars. With the machinery inside moaning and squealing, it resembled a great black sow calling her hungry brood to dinner. Occasionally the road wound through a shadowy forest, and there came the shrill whining of a sawmill. At times high up in some limestone bluff there showed the mouth of a gloomy cave.

They rounded a curve and saw the natural bridge linking the cliffs they had passed on their descent many months before, with the tiny stream flowing beneath.

Captain Asa lit a stogie. "We're getting near home."

They traveled on.

Great rocks lay alongside, as though hurled by quarreling giants. Often the highway twisted dangerously at the edge of a lofty stone wall.

A narrow river showed ahead, rushing between the snow-covered hills, then a blackish haze of smoke that marked the steel mill and the little town beyond.

Captain Asa turned into the creek that led off to his cabin. Over the stones they rattled, the wheels now and then breaking through a thin sheet of ice with a sound like tinkling glass.

They passed the cottage of one of their neighbors. The panes in the door were broken, and a great hole showed in the roof. The yard was overgrown with matted weeds that reached as high as the cobwebbed windows. Another home showed along the stream in similar desolation, and another.

Captain Asa's face clouded. "Something's happened," he murmured. "Everybody's moved away."

They rounded a bend and he saw their cabin, nestled at the foot of the saddle-like mountain. The pace of the automobile slackened to a crawl. The new stogie he was smoking went out.

All about the little dwelling, where the cornfields had shimmered and the pines had spread in dark green waves up the hills, there was now a vast extension of the steel mill, its furnaces belching soot and flame, the long black buildings beyond rumbling with explosions that set the whole valley to shaking. Everywhere were mounds of slag, smoking as with a thousand underground fires, and reaching their searing fingers farther and farther over the earth, like molten lava. The tiny home seemed like some doomed, encircled animal about to be swallowed up by a monstrous volcano.

They drew nearer, and the noise of the explosions increased. Giant cranes were moving about, tall as the masts of a ship, carrying huge ladles and immense metal pigs. Nearby a small railroad engine was puffing, pulling cars loaded with rusty scrap iron. At times from the tall stacks there came a sudden flash of flame that shot an immense distance into the sky, followed by a lurid crimson shower, spreading wider and wider till the earth seemed hidden in a series of fiery waterfalls.

They reached the cabin, its logs covered with soot, the ground before it thick with cinders. Unfastening the rusty padlock, they went inside. Silently they walked through the little rooms, looking at the objects they had left behind: a horsehair chair with a recent hole made by a mouse seeking stuffing for its nest; a small organ, flecked with the remains of some dried pussy willows which had been standing on the top; the handmade spreads on the beds, dimmed by dust, but still revealing the patterns of the Rocky Road to California and the Jaybird and the Crow.

They set about opening windows and brushing off the furniture. Outside the rumbling of the mill continued in a steady monotone.

A marked change had come over Fernie since the parting with her lover. Whatever her father requested, she obeyed without comment, without complaint. But her long-lashed eyes were strained; her movements were listless.

Darkness settled over the hills. Fernie took out a jar of home-canned succotash she found in the kitchen cupboard, and began to prepare supper.

Captain Asa tried to appear cheerful. "Looks like we're home, Fernie. Guess home's the best place after all."

She set his plate on the table, and looked at him oddly.

He began to eat, and made a renewed attempt at rousing her interest. "Didn't get nothing good as this since we been gone. Ain't anybody cans succotash like you."

Fernie reached into the oven. "I'll cut you some corn-bread, Pa." Her voice was far away.

They sat a long time in silence.

He buttered the golden square beside his coffee. "Things ought to be all right now we're back. Guess we shouldn't ever have left in the first place. Maybe if I look around in the hills I can find a wife that'll be a mother to you and make you happy. 'Cause I know there's a-plenty of things I can't do."

They finished the meal. Outside in the mill new showers of sparks were shooting from the shadowy stacks, like colossal fireworks. The glow lighted their faces.

The pounding of the machines in the cavernous buildings grew louder, like the booming of artillery.

Fernie began making a dish towel of a piece of cloth she found in a drawer. Often she would cease her work and stare off into the distance.

Her silence, her remoteness made Captain Asa uneasy.

A light showed up the valley. He took his hat. "There's somebody home at Marty Powers'. Let's you and me go over."

They put on their coats, and walking out in the moonlight, neared a cabin at the foot of a snow-streaked ridge. From it there came the tuneless wheezing of an organ, and the sound of chanting voices.

Captain Asa listened. "Sounds like they're having a singing. Marty was always getting people for a singing."

They walked onto the rickety porch. Through the door they could see the proprietor of the dwelling, a tall mountaineer with a drooping silvery mustache, holding a paper songbook in his hand. Near him a stiff-clad girl was playing the asthmatic organ they had heard outside. About these two figures a dozen rustic men and women were gathered, intoning a song with that peculiar broken rhythm so characteristic of the mountains, half-yodel, half-sob.

The music broke off as a new fiery eruption burst from the mill. The valley rocked as with the detonation of a series of giant bombs.

Captain Asa and Fernie went into the cabin.

The mother of the host, an owlish little old woman wearing a crocheted cap, sat jerking back and forth in a rocking chair as she watched the flaming sky.

She shook her head gloomily. "It's the sin of the Fire and the sin of the Fury. It's a abomination unto the Lord."

The glare and the noise subsided.

The silvery-mustached one greeted the newcomers with cordiality. "First singing we've had this year. Don't have 'em way we used to before the mill come. Too many people's moved away."

They took seats on boxes with the others.

The host picked up his paper volume again, and studied the pages.

A friendly woman with frizzy hair turned to Captain Asa. "It's a wonderful new songbook. I heard 'em talking about it on the radio, and Marty sent off fifty cents and got it. It's what they call the *Mother's Favorite Hillbilly Songbook*. Songs that's old and new. You got to send the fifty cents away off to Texas."

A lanky mountaineer next her nodded. "Marty'll send off anywheres for a songbook. He's got more songbooks than anybody in the hills."

The silvery-mustached one pressed back a page with his thumb. "Let's sing Ninety Seven, *My Wedding Ring It Is Tarnished*. That's a mighty pretty piece."

The woman with the frizzy hair nodded to Captain Asa in approval. "That's a beautiful piece. They played it on the radio when they was talking about the book."

They began a tune again, in flat voices. Fernie did not join in the singing.

The music ended, and the guests moved to the doorway. Off in the mill there came another blinding sheet of flame.

The owlish woman with the cap rocked gloomily once more. "It's wrote down in the Bible. In Joshua and Revelations. It's a abomination unto the Lord."

Captain Asa and Fernie walked home. It was late, and time for the changing of shifts at the mill. The leaping flames subsided. The noise of the machinery died away. A strange quiet lay over the moonlit valley, like the lull on a battlefield when two armies, weary of fighting, halt to await new strength and new ammunition.

They went to bed as the pandemonium recommenced. All night the windows rattled, and the beds shook as though in the grip of a giant hand. They slept little.

Night after night passed, while the columns of fire continued their lurid dancing. They lived chiefly on the home-canned provisions stored away.

Winter drifted into Spring. The ice in the creek melted, and the first wild flowers appeared on the bank. Here and there a ridge would be white with dogwood. But in a few days the blossoms darkened with soot. The budding leaves, seared by the smoking slag, blackened and fell to the ground. Bluebirds arrived, and cardinals, with feathers of such vivid scarlet they seemed artificial. They avoided the bleak area about the mill as though it were a land under a curse, where to enter was to die.

The constant smoke, the incessant pounding of the machinery began to affect Captain Asa's nerves. The lines that had appeared in his face since Vergil's departure deepened. He tried to farm, borrowing a horse for his plow from a neighbor. As he worked showers of soot would rain down upon him, and glowing cinders would scorch his overalls. If there was a wind, often a burst of pungent fumes would sweep out from the furnaces, stinging his nostrils as though they had been burned with acid. A wave of ashes would follow, coating horse, plow, and plowman till they seemed figures sculptured from pumice stone.

Several times sparks from the little yard engine that chugged across the track at the edge of his land started fires in his fields, endangering the crops of oats and corn. He went off to the mill to complain. Passing the rows of clerks and accountants bent over their desks in the brick building near the gate, he went into the office of the superintendent, a huge, bushy-haired man up from the ranks, with the body of a bull and the voice of a lion. The official, sitting behind a row of telephones and a red box that squawked like a voice in a nightmare, listened impatiently to his visitor. He spoke a curt negative, and turned to a telephone. Captain Asa continued to argue. The superintendent grew irritated. He pressed a buzzer, and arising from his desk, stood waiting near the glass door. A moment later a hard-bitten individual wearing the uniform of a guard entered, and hustled the unwanted visitor outside.

Captain Asa trudged homeward, burning with a fire as hot as the molten metal pouring from the furnaces.

His feeling toward the mill, before merely an undefined sense of oppression, hardened into bitterness. At times the blackened steel walls seemed to become the grim barricades of a prison. Often he would encounter some of the workers as they walked to the nearby settlement, or bought their provisions in the crossroads store. A genial broad-faced laborer would address him in phrases heavily accented with some foreign tongue. Captain Asa would turn away.

As the days passed, his nerves grew more and more affected. His anxiety about Fernie deepened. He was unwilling now to leave her out of his sight for a moment. Whenever his duties took him away from the cabin for a few hours, he was consumed with nervousness until his return. If she picked up pencil or paper, he looked on with suspicion, certain that she was writing a letter. She continued to wait on him faithfully. But her girlish face seemed aged by premature sorrow.

Now and then Captain Asa would try to arouse her interest with a jewel-like stone he had discovered at the entrance of a cave, or an unusual flower he had found in a meadow. She would take the gift, then return to her reverie. He saw in the town an announcement of a night of old-fashioned dancing, and brought her to the stuffy lodge-room above a clothing store that marked the scene of the festivity. For an hour they sat, listening to the trio of sweating fiddlers scraping at their instruments, and the bald-headed rustic calling the ever-changing dances. Before them passed a dizzy circle of overalled men and stiff-skirted women, leaping and whirling to a frenzied mountain tune.

Captain Asa spoke to her with hesitation. "Maybe you'd like to go out there on the floor, Fernie. It's mighty nice, the old-fashioned dancing. There's Todd Mason's boy sitting over there, ain't got a partner. He's a fine young fellow. And there's Big Jack Letcher's son, just come home from college in Lexington. If you want to, I'll go over and get 'em you."

Her eyes strayed absently about the crowde don't feel like dancing, Pa."

Soon after they walked back to the cabin. He further attempt at entertainment.

Then one evening, on returning from the fie ticed that a sudden change had come over her during his absence. Her pale cheeks were flushed with color. She seemed stirred by some suppressed excitement.

Captain Asa gazed at her in wonder.

They were eating breakfast several days later when a neighbor came with an invitation to a funeralizing to be held that afternoon, one of those strange mountain ceremonies where due to remoteness or lack of a minister, the funeral may be held as late as two years after the burial.

Captain Asa hurried back from his farming earlier than usual to allow time to change his clothes for the occasion. To his surprise, he saw no sign of Fernie in the kitchen. He walked to the porch at the rear. Here, too, no sign of her was visible. Thinking she might have gone down a gully nearby to gather wild flowers, he climbed a low rock and called loudly. There was no answer. Only the grave dog came out of the bushes, and scrambled up awkwardly onto the stone. Several times he called, again with no response. The dinky engine appeared on the mill track, and with its noisy puffing, drowned out the sound of his voice. He returned to the cabin.

He began to grow nervous. He looked at the kitchen again, then in case she might be taking a nap, tiptoed to her bedroom. With relief he saw that her hat with the yellow bird was still on the homemade dresser. Then he noticed a sheet of paper beside it, weighted down by a pincushion. [illegible]ked it up, and read the few carefully written words. [illegible] grew rigid.

[illegible] time he remained there, then went outside. He [illegible] now the fresh tracks of automobile tires in the [illegible]oil, coming up the creek and turning before the [illegible] stood looking off toward the bend of the stream [illegible] marks vanished.

A fat squirrel leaped onto a branch of a pine overhead, and began chattering in a shrill voice, as though to drive him from the vicinity of its nest. Another squirrel joined it, in indignant chorus. They continued their scolding until they grew weary, then bounded off into a neighboring poplar. A woodpecker swooped down in an arrow-like flash from the tree they had deserted, and began searching for insects in a rotten stump. It found a meaty prize, then flew off into the distance.

Still Captain Asa stood motionless.

The dog came to his side again.

Captain Asa spoke dully. "She's gone away with him, Ruby."

Rustic figures began to saunter up the creek, bound for the ceremony to which he had been invited. Some of the passersby shouted an urgent summons to attend.

He paid no attention.

The mail-hack passed, a wagon drawn by two horses, with half-a-dozen mountaineers occupying crude benches placed along the sides. A woman sitting at the rear saw him, and called out in reproach. "Ain't you coming to the funeralizing, Asa? Emma Berry was a mighty good friend of your wife's when she was living. You're sure a-coming to her funeralizing."

Captain Asa roused himself, and climbed up with the others.

The vehicle left the creek and moved into a narrow ravine, at whose foot a thread of water was trickling. The driver urged the horses up the steep trail, and traveling through a dark forest of pines, halted the wagon at a little family cemetery enclosed by a toppling fence.

Here a score of men and women were assembled around a mound covered by the grass of several summers, with the name of a mountain wife on an already weather-beaten stone. Behind it the deceased woman's husband stood with a solemn air, while his new young bride waited at his side, weeping silently. At the grave two wandering evangelists of the region were preaching as though the dead woman had just been interred, one a stocky individual with shiny trousers tucked into a pair of muddy boots, the other a tall, gaunt figure, like most of the men of his audience, with black coat-tails that flapped at every movement. On and on the evangelists droned, fervidly, breathlessly, their words blurred and unintelligible, when one wearied the other taking up without pause where his panting colleague had ended.

The gaunt preacher wiped his brow and began a new rhapsody. "It's wrote in the Book it's dust to dust," he chanted. "The Lord gives people money and jewels, and corn bread and turnip greens, and picture shows and radios. He gives people mothers and fathers, and gives 'em fine children. And then when He wants to He takes 'em back. If you and me done that we'd be a Indian giver. But Lord ain't a Indian giver. No sir. Because He ain't really giving them things. He's just a lending 'em, like you lend a plow to your neighbor. Amen."

The services ended. Captain Asa rode back in silence to his cabin. Entering his daughter's room, he read again the note lying on the dresser. His eyes wandered to her hat, the yellow bird beneath the golden veil seeming almost alive as it caught the glow of the setting sun.

He spoke to the dog, watching near the bed. "She said it wasn't right . . . to take it where she was going. . . . 'Cause I give it to her . . . to stay with me."

He went into the kitchen, and sat down by the window. Dusk obscured the nearby pines. The stars began to shine with brilliance.

He made no attempt to light the lamp or prepare supper, staring at the flames leaping from the furnaces. The hands of the alarm clock moved across the dial until it was long past the time for his retiring. He continued to sit in the darkness.

There came a faint crackling in the bushes outside, marking the presence of some animal. The dog scratched against the door, trying to push it open, and whimpered faintly. Captain Asa did not stir. Soon after there was a sound of racing paws as though the invisible prowler was scurrying across the porch, then a crash as it upset one of the gasoline cans filled with rubbish at the rear. The dog's barking became a frenzy. The unseen visitor scurried off.

Far in the distance there arose the sound of an automobile, advancing up the creek. The noise came nearer, becoming a series of reports like shots from a pistol as the motor labored to draw the wheels across the uneven stones.

Captain Asa raised his head to listen. He spoke again, his

voice touched with hope. "Maybe she's coming back, Ruby. . . . Looks to me like she'd sure be a-coming back."

The sound grew fainter and fainter.

Captain Asa resumed his vigil.

Some heavy clouds gathered in the sky. The pines overhead broke into a hushed murmuring. A loose board in the cabin wall commenced an irregular creaking. Suddenly a reed of the organ in the parlor sounded a deep bass, as though struck by an unseen finger.

Captain Asa lit the lamp, and gazed at the empty bench in front of the instrument. "They says . . . when a organ plays by itself . . . it's a sign of trouble. . . . Maybe she's had a accident."

He went outside and peered down the creek. "Maybe she was coming home . . . and something happened to the car. . . . It's mighty hard driving these roads . . . when you don't know the mountains."

Somewhere overhead a crow cawed noisily, frightened by a snake or other nocturnal invader.

Captain Asa shivered. "They says when a crow caws at night . . . it's a sign of terrible trouble. . . . She's sure had a accident."

He stood looking off toward the dark hills.

The clouds spread in gloomy tapestries across the horizon. The stars vanished. The wind increased. The branches of the pines began rubbing against each other with a curious muted sound, as though countless ladies clad in rustling silk dresses were walking down an avenue. Now and then a great cone dropped near him with a startling thud. A toad hopped up in fright at his feet. High in a tree a pair of tiny green eyes flashed through the obscurity, like twin fireflies.

He went inside and took his old seat at the window. The breeze died again. The air grew warm, sticky. Along the narrow valley frogs began to croak in perfect-timed chorus, as though under the baton of a brilliant conductor, some carrying the melody in a shrill tremolo, some booming out in sonorous accompaniment, like deep-toned bassoons. Far across the hills came muffled shouts and the excited baying of hounds pursuing a fox, blotted out soon after by a new rumbling from the steel mill. A whistle blew sharply. Inside one of the sheds a giant ladle, like a devil's cauldron, dipped as though under the hand of its Satanic master. The mill seemed about to be overwhelmed in a swollen river of fire.

There came the sound of a motor again. Captain Asa arose and pressed his face to the glass. A car was traveling toward the cabin now, there could be no mistake. Its headlights swept the banks in dazzling brilliance, cut off as with a knife by the black pines beyond.

Nearer and nearer it drove, and began slowing down before the porch.

Captain Asa had almost ceased breathing. "She's come back, Ruby."

He hurried to the door.

The car halted. A shadowy head was thrust out the window. A youthful voice thick with drink called loudly, "Where's Buck Robbins' place? We want to get some 'shine."

Captain Asa stumbled back into the cabin.

The car continued up the creek. From it there drifted a blur of youthful voices chorusing a drunken song. The lights vanished around a bend of the hills.

Captain Asa slumped into his chair.

There was a sudden clap of thunder. It began to rain in a violent shower. Streams of water coursed through the roof in half-a-dozen places. Captain Asa made no attempt to check the deluge.

Lightning swept the sky in blinding flashes, following so swift upon each other the feeble lamp shrank into insignificance. The cabin was filled with an eerie glow. Thunder echoed from hill to hill, like ghostly signal drums. The dog huddled against the wall.

The storm ended. The moon rose through the clouds in the saddle of the mountain, bathing the nearby peaks with melancholy light. Captain Asa sat as though he were a statue.

The dog came away from the wall, and stretched out once more at its master's feet. It gazed at him with troubled eyes, as though trying to solve the mystery of his behavior.

Its muzzle touched his hand.

CHAPTER SIXTEEN

FOR SEVERAL WEEKS Captain Asa went about in a daze. His neighbors, meeting him on the road, would call out a greeting. Many times he failed to answer, as though he did not hear. His appearance, his character were altering. Deep shadows marked his face. His once-friendly mouth was hardening with bitterness.

He cut himself off more and more from the mountain community. Often when he saw an acquaintance coming down the creek, he would hurry into the fields, fearing that the traveler would stop to pay a call. A pin broke in the motor of the automobile, making its use impossible. He did not attempt to have it repaired, leaving the car to stand in a patch of stony ground, exposed to the rigors of the weather.

His only companion was the dog, following constantly at his heels. At night as he sat in the lonely cabin, he would talk to the animal as though it were a person.

"They've left me," he would murmur. "All my children's left me."

The dog would listen with that curious intentness of an animal become man's intimate, its grave eyes fixed upon his face, as though it were trying to read his thoughts.

Then one day the mail-hack left a letter postmarked Chicago in the rusty tin box set along the creek. He read it word by word. His bitterness increased.

Some elaborate construction began at the mill, with new black-walled sheds, and a water tank with a huge pump alongside. He arose the morning after the pump's completion, and heard its steady thumping added to the clamorous voices of the mill, then went out to the well behind the porch that had served his family for generations. To his surprise, when he pulled up the wooden bucket, it was empty. Looking down the hole, he saw that the water was almost at the bottom. He managed to fill the pail with difficulty. Next morning when he looked again, the shaft was dry.

Beyond his cornfields the great pump pounded without ceasing. He hurried off to the mill.

He sought out the brick building housing the superintendent once more. A brusque young woman in an outer office prevented him from going any farther.

Captain Asa waited until late afternoon, when he knew the official would be returning to the town. He saw the husky figure stride toward his car, laughing and talking with a portly individual clad in an expensive golf costume.

Captain Asa came forward, and began to argue.

The burly man spoke a curt word to his chauffeur. The driver went off, returning in a moment with the same hard-bitten guard Captain Asa had seen on his earlier visit. The newcomer clutched the mountaineer's arm, and hurrying him along the cinder path, thrust him roughly beyond the high wire gate that formed the plant entrance.

Captain Asa stood in the roadway, looking at his arm that bore the mark of the guard's fingers.

A watchman who sat like a prison sentry in a tiny cubicle came toward him in sullen suspicion.

Captain Asa moved away.

Soon after he took a pail off to a spring a quarter of a mile distant, and carried it back to the kitchen. The water was unpleasant-tasting, heavy with minerals. Each day he was compelled to make a similar laborious expedition in the hot sun or the drenching rain. His hatred of the mill redoubled.

Often as he plowed the field with the dog walking behind, he would look off at the waste of slag and fiery metal.

His lips would move somberly. "It's like Marty's mother says. It's a abomination unto the Lord."

Another letter postmarked Chicago arrived and another. He read them moodily, and did not answer.

His life became more and more that of a hermit, only the dog sharing his seclusion. His dependence upon the animal increased. When he ate, it sat beside him, waiting with patience for its share of the simple food on the table. At night it lay at the foot of his bed, alert, watchful, as though its master's separation from the others of his kind demanded special vigilance.

A tattered, white-haired old Negro moved into a tiny shack on some mill land not far away, and tried when passing to strike up a conversation.

Captain Asa avoided him like the others.

His solitude was broken one twilight when a wagon rattled down the creek, and a loud knock sounded on the door. Looking out, he saw the tall, silvery-mustached Marty Powers, carrying a songbook, and his owlish little mother, wearing her crocheted cap.

They came inside.

"Just going to town and thought we'd stop," Marty remarked cheerfully. "They're having a welcome meeting at the church for a new Holiness preacher come over from Pineville, and there ought to be some good singing. Don't like hymn singing near as good as plain singing, but it's better than nothing. And Ma likes any kind of churching. We been getting kind of worried about you, Asa. How you been? I ain't seen you for a mighty long time."

The hermit gazed at his unaccustomed guests with dim eyes. He wiped a layer of dust off the long-unused chairs. "I'm doing . . . all right."

The guests sat down gingerly.

Marty cut a slice from a plug of tobacco, and after offering it to his host, began to chew. "You're a-looking terrible, Asa. Your stomach ain't a-bothering you, is it?"

"Ain't nothing wrong with my stomach."

Marty whittled at the plug with his knife. "If it ain't all right, I know a place in Memphis'll fix you up quick. Tells you about it every night on the Memphis radio. You just write in and tell 'em what's wrong with you, and don't make no difference what it is, they send you the medicine you need. Every time you buy the medicine they give you a present free—a dish or something. I know a woman back of Otter's Creek has a plenty of sicknesses she's been needing cured. And she says she's getting the prettiest set of china you ever seen."

The old woman sat up stiffly. "If it's stomach trouble, let him drink sassafras. That'll wash the sickness right out of him, better than any of them doctors."

The conversation languished. Captain Asa went into the kitchen, and returned bearing a bowl of fruit.

The old woman burst into sudden speech again. "What you hearing from your daughter? The one that run away. Man drives the mail-hack says you got a couple of letters."

The bowl in Captain Asa's hand shook as he prepared to set it on the table. "She's done got married. . . . She says she wants me to come and visit 'em in Chicago. . . . I don't want to see her. . . . I don't want nothing to do with any of my children after the way they left me. . . . I don't want to see 'em as long as I live."

Marty explored the mousehole in the chair where he was sitting. He pulled out a long horse hair, and wound it around his finger. "Used to be when you had children you knowed when you growed old they'd take care of you. But things is different nowadays."

His mother nodded. "Children nowadays ain't nothing but trouble and pain. . . . You put that horse hair in a glass of water, and it'll turn into a snake. If it's a black hair it'll be a blacksnake. If it's kind of brown it'll be a moccasin. I seen it done plenty of times."

A whistle near the furnaces blew a succession of short blasts, as though signaling an alarm.

Captain Asa listened. "Sounds like . . . a accident."

An ambulance went up the mill road, its siren wailing.

Marty took a place near the window to watch. "They been having plenty of accidents. Them foreigners get burned terrible in them mills. They says when they want the best steel, they let a man fall inside one of them kettles."

His mother moved beside him, and peered out with

owlish eyes. "Ruining the land and maiming the people. The Lord's sent down the curse of the Fire."

The automobile of the superintendent passed, racing toward the furnaces. Marty's glance followed as it sped through the prison-like gateway. "That's sure a hard man. Drives people same way he does them machines. Wonder to me somebody ain't killed him, all the good shots there is here in the mountains."

The old woman muttered gloomily. "Lord'll destroy him. Lord'll destroy all them that's abominations. Seven Heads and Seven Horns and the Beast coming out of the sea."

They drove off.

The construction at the mill continued. All day trucks bumped over the slag-covered roads, loaded with cement and fantastic machinery. New furnaces began to arise. New railroad tracks spread out from the mill entrance across the countryside, to tap the black seams of coal showing in the nearby hills. The twin ribbons of metal came closer and closer to the farm.

Captain Asa had come in from his work for an early lunch one morning when he saw a crew of laborers laying a track squarely across his farthest cornfield, separated from the rest of the farm by a narrow gully. His face grew gray. He took his rifle, and hurrying over his property, halted where two tall Negroes wielding scythes were cutting down the corn to clear the way.

He blocked their path, his hands gripping the rifle. "Get off my land," he commanded.

The Negroes backed away in fright.

The foreman approached, a youthful-looking individual with several days' growth of beard. He argued a moment, then seeing that his words had no effect on the stern figure holding the gun, disappeared in the direction of the mill.

The track laying ceased. The black laborers slung their spike hammers onto the ground and stretched out lazily, smoking cigarettes or dozing in the sun. A group gathered in a circle, and began to shoot dice. Captain Asa paced up and down, crackling through the fallen corn.

The foreman returned, bringing with him the wide-hatted, deputy sheriff bearing the mark of an ancient bullet wound on his wrist.

The newcomer spoke amiably. "That land don't belong to you, Asa. All that land this side of the gully for a couple of miles belongs to the state. People's been using it so long, I reckon they've begun thinking it's theirs. But it ain't. The mill's done leased it for ninety-nine years. . . . You're a law-abiding man, Asa. You got to do what the law says."

Captain Asa strode back to his cabin. Soon after he went off to get advice from Big Jesse, a neighbor considered a sage of the area, part blacksmith, part self-educated veterinary, who spent most of his time repairing the automobiles worn out by the trials of the rough mountain roads.

He entered the shop, where the smouldering forge was lost among the dismantled automobile bodies that lay like dissected corpses on the floor. The proprietor was a powerful, big-boned man, with a broad, thoughtful face. As he leaned over the broken fender he was mending, his large hands moved with the deftness of a sculptor moulding clay.

Captain Asa related the events of the morning.

The other took a strip of metal from a pile, and began to heat it in the glowing coals. "Ain't going to do you no good fighting the mill, Asa. You know them big companies has the politicians up at the State Capitol doing anything they want. One man by himself can't fight them fellows. Takes a lot of people fighting together." He worked the bellows a moment. "Even if there wasn't no politics, it wouldn't help none. It's like that show fellow you was talking to me about when you first came back told you. Times is changing. Steel mills and all them other factories are going to keep coming here more and more. Ain't no use trying to farm your place now. If I was you, I'd sell it to the mill and get out fast."

Captain Asa's drawn face was touched with stubbornness. "I ain't going to sell. My father had my place before me, and my grandfather had it before him. Ain't nobody going to put me off it."

Big Jesse took out the strip of reddened iron, and began to beat a rhythmic tattoo. "I'll be sixty-eight come Old Christmas, Asa. I done plenty of thinking. You can't fight new things that comes like the mill. You can't fight your own family like you been doing, just 'cause they got different ways of acting than yours. Humans was made for changing. Babies is born and grows up to be men and dies, and then new babies is born after 'em. And ain't one of 'em, old men or babies, is ever the same as they was the day before."

He dropped the hot metal into a tub of water. It hissed noisily. "I used to be a blacksmith, didn't know nothing but shoeing horses, and maybe doctoring animals a little. And then the autos come, and I took up fixing cars. Or I'd have starved sure. If you want to live on this earth, you got to take things as they come, and change with 'em. It's 'cause humans can do it that they're bossing things, instead of the ants, I reckon. If they don't change, they're going to hurt themselves . . . mighty bad."

Captain Asa returned home.

The laborers were laying the track again. He could hear the clink of the hammers as they drove the spikes into the ties; he could see the two Negroes wielding the scythes, like black winds laying waste the corn.

A wagon pulled by four horses rumbled down the creek, loaded with logs for the sawmill in the town. The over-alled driver was singing some verses of *Sparrow On The Mountain.*

The plaintive words echoed across the valley:

Little bee makes the honey,
But the big bee takes the comb.
Little man fights the battle,
But the big man stays at home.

Captain Asa listened. He looked at the mill spread along the horizon as far as the eye could see, its laborers dwarfed to the size of insects by the huge machines they were serving, as though they were beetles being fed to the monsters in some colossal zoo.

His lips moved drearily. "Ain't no place for a little man in the world no more. Little man might just as well be dead."

The track was laid in haste. The dinky trains loaded with coal and scrap and metal pigs began to rattle across the meadows. Whenever they passed, Captain Asa's dog, as though resenting this invasion of its master's former property, would lose its gravity, and dashing down to the track, bark in fury as it raced beside the engine. It had a frequent companion now, a little yellow-haired mongrel. The smaller animal's eyes had a quality of extraordinary alertness. Its thin ears, too long for its short body, seemed sensitive as the feelers of a butterfly, quivering to catch the faintest sound. Often the newcomer would join the older dog in following Captain Asa home. Halting outside, it would wait with the wistful air of an Oriental beggar, hoping for alms or shelter.

At times the train crews, irritated by the pursuing animals, would hurl down lumps of coal. On several occasions Captain Asa's dog was struck. Once it came back with a great bruise on its head. Captain Asa soaked the injury with liniment. His fingers were white as the piece of shirt with which he applied the medicine. That night, going through a cupboard, he found a long-unused pistol. He hesitated, then laid it with care in a bureau.

The days dragged past. His hatred of the mill was now an obsession, occupying every moment of his thoughts. Sometimes he would go down the creek on his way to town, and rounding the bend, see the river and the older section of the steel mill on the bank, with the dingy area known only as Milltown that lay in its shadow. He would plod along, staring at the blackened dwellings where men and women with odd-shaped faces sat on the porches, talking in outlandish voices. His lips would grow grim.

But it was on the burly superintendent that the full violence of his enmity centered. Each day when he saw the official pass in a luxurious automobile, Captain Asa would be swept by a cold wave of hatred. A curious constriction would come into his throat.

June arrived, and July, bringing with it the burning days of midsummer. The thirsty corn in the fields began to droop, the shrunken ears seeming scorched as though by the flames of the furnaces. The grass before the door shriveled. Great cracks appeared in the earth, where brown lizards darted, searching for flies. Heat waves shimmered everywhere, through which the trees and the mill showed like the creations of a mirage. The dog lay in the shade of the pines, panting. Even the songs of the birds seemed hoarse, as though their throats were choked with dust.

Captain Asa's nerves grew more and more taut. Some workmen from the mill had begun blasting near the cabin, shaking the walls and at times sending a faint shower of stones upon the roof. Each muffled explosion seemed to occur inside his brain.

He had started off to the spring on a trip for water one particularly hot afternoon, when the dinky engine came rattling down the track, pulling several cars of coal. The dog bounded off on its usual chase. Captain Asa filled the pail, and carried it back to the cabin. He missed the animal, and whistled sharply. It did not appear. He whistled again, then walked to the track, and began making his way across the ties. At first he saw nothing, only a faint trail of smoke where the dinky was disappearing behind the mill. He halted as a brown shadow showed near the stump of a toppled pine. He hurried forward.

The dog lay flat on the sun-baked earth, breathing heavily. It tried to raise its head in greeting.

He carried it off to the blacksmith shop and found Big Jesse, straightening an axle.

The broad-shouldered mountaineer took the animal to the back of the room, where some simple veterinary instruments lay on a wooden table.

Captain Asa's voice shook with emotion. "He's hurt bad, ain't he, Jesse?"

The other hastened to clear a space. "I'll do what I can, Asa. Ain't much chance for a dog that's been hit by any kind of train."

He lifted the animal, breathing almost imperceptibly now, and laid it on the boards. He set to work, his large hands manipulating the instruments with expertness.

Captain Asa moved to the entrance of the shop and stood gazing over the scorched valley. The day was still, deathlike. On the rotting doorsill at his feet a double line of ants was marching, carrying off minute bits of wood taken from the mouldering interior, or returning for another load. A wasp darted about in brilliant streaks of yellow, hovering close to the earthen floor as though searching for mud to build its nest.

From the back of the shop there came the sound of a glass stopper scraping in a bottle, then the sticky-sweet odor of chloroform.

A car drove up, with a cloud of steam arising from the radiator. An insignificant little man wearing clothes that marked him as a city dweller descended, and unscrewing the metal cap at the front, waited for the water to cool. He came over and began to talk garrulously. Captain Asa replied in monosyllables.

The white-haired old Negro who was Captain Asa's neighbor walked past barefoot, carrying his shoes over his back, to protect them from the rough stones.

The little automobilist was determined to make conversation. He chuckled. "Niggers are sure comical, ain't they? Saw a funny thing in Memphis last week. Nigger girl got killed by a nigger man that was living with her, and he ran away. So all the girl's family went down to the river, and laid her body on the water, with a fresh egg in each hand. They said that way the fellow that murdered her had to come back, and then the law could catch him. A nigger's most comical thing there is."

Captain Asa made no response to the other's observations. His eyes strayed off to Big Jesse, bent low over the table.

There came a tinkle of metal as the great-limbed mountaineer laid down an instrument; a second heavier wave of chloroform filled the air.

The newcomer followed Captain Asa's gaze. "Your dog hurt?"

Captain Asa murmured a reply.

The little automobilist took out a cigar, and offered it to him as though in compensation. "That's too bad. Dog's a mighty fine thing. Man's best friend, ain't he? Everybody ought to have a dog. 'Specially a boy. Gives him character, they say. Had a dog when I was a boy, and it helped me plenty to get where I am today."

He went off to fit the nozzle of a hose into the radiator so that a stream of cold water would pour through the coils.

The shop grew quiet again for a moment, the only sound the hushed creaking of Big Jesse's shoes as he hurried to take a surgical needle and some gauze from a drawer.

The little man returned, and glancing off at the back of the shop again, resumed his discourse. "I like all kinds of dogs myself. Airedales, wirehairs, don't care what. All except those nasty little dogs the rich women are always keeping. One of those dogs bit me over in Nashville. Belonged in one of the big houses near the University. Ran out and grabbed me by the leg, and bit clear to the bone. I went to the doctor with it fast. They say a bite from one of those little dogs is twice as bad as a big one. . . . Well, guess I'll be going. Spreckles is the name. Initials Harry C. Same as the refinery people. But I guess I haven't got their sugar. I'm selling for Delta Seeds and Hardware out of Memphis. Glad I met you."

He drove up the road.

A hush fell over the shop again. Beyond the window, martins flew in and out the pierced gourds set on poles to form birdhouses. The fluttering of their wings was hushed, mysterious. In the hot sky three crows cawed in melancholy. Above them a solitary buzzard drifted in funereal circles. In a stall somewhere at the rear a horse whinnied nervously.

Big Jesse came to the doorway. "I done my best, Asa. But a dog ain't no different than a human."

Captain Asa stumbled with his burden out the door. The solitary buzzard swooped lower, its gloomy circles growing narrower and narrower. It began following the bowed figure up the creek.

Captain Asa dug a grave on a low rise overlooking the valley and covered it with stones.

The tattered old Negro came from his shack nearby and looked on with gentle eyes. "You wouldn't want me to preach no sermon for him, would you, Boss? Down in Mississippi where I come from I done preached a-plenty of sermons for horses and dogs that died. I preaches a mighty fine sermon for a dog for a quarter."

Captain Asa shook his head.

The old Negro shuffled away.

Captain Asa went back to the cabin. He slumped into a chair.

The sun dropped lower and lower in the sky. The mill whistle blew for the changing shifts. The flames of the furnaces slackened, then burst into new sweeping rivers of fire. The dinky engine began chugging once more up and down the narrow tracks.

Captain Asa watched with expressionless face.

CHAPTER SEVENTEEN

DARKNESS swept the scorched countryside. Frogs began to croak in delirious chorus. Huge fireflies shone, like floating green lanterns.

Captain Asa took the pistol from the bureau and put it in his pocket. He walked out the door, his steps rigid, mechanical, as though he were moulded from one of the great pigs of metal piled here and there beside the mill.

He walked across his fields, and halting at the plant entrance, looked off toward the brick building where the office of the superintendent was situated. He had seen the car of the official before sunset, and knew that for several weeks he had been working until late in the night. The gate in this section of the mill was shut at sundown. Captain Asa stared at the high-barred fence as though considering an attempt at scaling it, then turned and set off down the creek.

Along the bank he plodded, the shrilling of the frogs and cicadas so constant he seemed to be moving through a solid wall of sound. A full moon arose, crowning the distant peaks with a radiant halo, and touching the rare pools of water with a glow so brilliant they appeared to be sheets of mica. Occasionally in a pool deeper than the others, fish jumped in golden flashes.

He rounded the bend and began walking along the river. Beyond the mill he could see the glare of the little town, with a line of light leading up the hill that rose behind, marking the homes of the richer residents.

He plodded on.

Beside the mill he continued, the great furnaces towering above him, and bursting into spectacular fountains of fire. He halted several times to gaze with lifeless eyes. A hard-bitten individual wearing the uniform of a company policeman paced up and down in the obscurity, watching him with deep suspicion.

The officer came forward, and spoke in accents foreign to the region. "Where you heading?"

Captain Asa's voice was leaden. "I'm . . . going . . . to town."

The officer shrugged his shoulders. "O K. Get going."

The road widened a little. The shabby houses of the workers began to appear, growing closer and closer together. The cinder path he had been following became a wooden sidewalk with a plank broken here and there that made traveling perilous. Amid the little dwellings there showed now and then a dim-lit grocery where some stout women stood waiting, or a little café where heavy-faced men sat drinking beer.

The odd tightness began to constrict his throat again.

The moon climbed higher. The night seemed to grow hotter with its rise. Somewhere off in the distance a dog began to bark mournfully, as though sensing a calamity.

The mill entrance showed ahead, with a guard standing outside. Captain Asa halted in the shadows.

A truck pulled up near the curb. Captain Asa waited until the guard's attention was concentrated on questioning the driver, then hurried through the dark gateway.

The mill was spread out before him, colossal, terrifying, its black buildings illuminated with flashes of crimson lightning and booming with peals of metallic thunder. Down the sooty street he walked, past the blast furnaces where conveyors creaked weirdly as they brought up coke and iron and crushed limestone to slake the fiery appetites. A laborer naked to the waist tapped a furnace wall. A stream of molten metal swept out from the opening, silhouetting the workers nearby like demons in an inferno.

Captain Asa continued to trudge forward. Dinky trains rattled by, carrying loads of flaming iron, their bells clanging, their whistles blowing. He moved numbly out of their path.

He passed a vast structure where row on row of immense machines were rolling white-hot slabs of steel, with a noise like collapsing mountains. Opposite it he saw the building that housed the superintendent.

The constriction of his throat intensified, as though it were bound with tightening wire. His head began a violent throbbing, like the vibration of the black monsters pounding and crushing the fiery billets. The arc lamps overhead and the moon in the sky seemed to begin a rhythmic flashing, as though they were in some fashion connected with his body, and were pulsating in sympathy.

He stood staring at the brick portico fronting the offices. A gnat stung his face. He brushed it off with a mechanical movement of his hand, and went into the vestibule.

The building, which had been so busy on his daytime visits, seemed deserted. Only a faint glow showed here and there down the long hallway. He reached the quarters of the superintendent, and saw that beyond a door at the rear a light was burning.

He entered the darkened outer offices, filled with typewriters and adding machines funereal beneath their black hoods. Moving behind a filing cabinet, he peered through the glass partition.

The burly official was sitting at his desk, working over some papers.

Captain Asa's hand went to his pistol.

There was a step down the hall. Captain Asa drew farther back into the shadow of the cabinet. A figure clad in overalls entered, carrying several samples of steel. He laid the metal on the other's desk. They talked earnestly a moment.

The man in overalls departed.

The superintendent settled back in his chair.

He was troubled over a problem in his papers. He made some calculations, tapping his fountain pen with a nervous hand. Obviously a man who drove himself as hard as he drove others, he was beginning to show signs of age and strain. His broad face, crowned by his bushy hair, was growing puffy, and possessed an unnatural flush, as of approaching heart trouble. A tumbler filled with an unpleasant-colored medicine stood on a blotter. At times as he worked he would stop and sip it with distaste.

There were no more interruptions. The superintendent sat intent over his notes, a perfect target.

Slowly Captain Asa raised the revolver. His grim face

seemed sculptured from the slag that lay along the road.

In the distance a crimson flash swept the sky as a new furnace was tapped, and another rushing torrent of fire swept out into the night. A giant overhead crane swooped past the window, carrying some vague object on a hook, like a ghostly bird of prey.

Still Captain Asa stood motionless, his fingers locked on the trigger of the pistol, as though he were frozen in some strange paralysis. Suddenly the stoniness of his face collapsed, like the shattering of a mask. He shook his head miserably. The pistol dropped to his side. Numbly he put it back into his pocket, and stumbled out the door.

Through the leaping shadows of the mill grounds he plodded, and made his way beyond the gate again, into the road along the river. He set off toward the town, and walking down the main street, dazzling with the lights of a picture show and an all-night café, continued until he reached the older section of the settlement. Past a shabby drugstore he made his way, where a jar of horehound drops stood in the window, past an old hotel with straw chairs on the porches where two prim old ladies sat in rocking chairs.

The courthouse lay beyond, its wooden columns marred by time and the holes left by half-a-dozen bullets. In the basement showed the sheriff's office, the cobwebbed bulb in the ceiling drearily lighting the paintless furniture and the iron-barred door. Behind a railing the deputy with the scarred wrist sat propping his feet on a chair, idly reading a newspaper.

Captain Asa went inside, and laid his pistol on the desk. "I come down to kill a man, Rafe. You better put me in jail."

The deputy studied the bowed figure a moment. He dropped the pistol into a drawer.

He spoke in a thoughtful drawl. "You go on home, Asa, and get some rest."

Captain Asa moved outside.

Back toward the cabin he plodded, along the main street again and through Milltown.

A burning thirst seized him. He stopped in one of the dingy cafés filled with men talking in strange voices, and asked for a drink of water.

A brawny steelworker standing at the bar filled a glass from a bottle of wine before him, and hospitably thrust it forward. "Wine good for stomach," he declared in cheerful tones.

Captain Asa shook his head. He drained the tumbler the bartender filled from a faucet. The others addressed him in friendly, broken phrases. He moved into the street again.

He passed a little dwelling where a family was gathered on chairs in the yard, when his foot went through a loosened board in the wooden sidewalk. He fell headlong.

A blond giant with a squarish face and a plump little woman came hurrying from the shadows of the cottage to aid.

The blond giant brought a lamp. By its light they helped him limp inside their tiny home. A half-dozen children were playing about, some talking English, some chattering in an odd Slavic tongue. The plump little woman led him into the kitchen, shining with cleanliness, and sat him in a chair. She looked at the dark swelling near his ankle, and hastened to heat some water in an iron kettle. She put his foot to soak in a tin tub.

The blond giant gazed at the visitor genially. "My wife she doctor," he murmured. "Children sick. Next door sick, down street, everybody sick. Wife fix good."

The plump little woman brought out some queer-looking cakes and set them on the table.

Captain Asa ate a sugared fragment. Its flavor was strangely pleasing.

He sat bathing his foot, while the children frolicked about the room. Their faces were bright, pretty. In the parlor he could see a cheap piano of the sort bought on payments. The eldest child, a girl of perhaps thirteen, moved to it and began a plaintive foreign melody.

The blond giant picked up a pipe with a huge meerschaum bowl, and smoked a violent-smelling tobacco. "You no work in mill?"

Captain Asa shook his head.

The little woman gazed at her husband with pride. "Anton makes plenty money. Works open hearth."

The giant nodded in jovial agreement. "Open hearth hot. Too hot, maybe. Takes plenty muscles." He moved his great arms up and down to exhibit their massiveness.

His wife poured more hot water into the tub. "Next year Anton buy new house. Out in country. Get cow maybe. Mama in old country always want cow."

The giant flexed his muscles with childish joy again. "Takes big man make steel."

It grew late. Captain Asa made his departure.

The swelling in his ankle had lessened. The throbbing in his brain had ceased.

He limped slowly along the road.

He was beside the mill once more, at the heart of its smoking furnaces, its grim walls that rose like a vast penitentiary. But at the edge of its ugliness, its desolation, men sat in their tiny cafés drinking bottles of fragrant wine. Between the gray piles of slag, children were playing happily, some with faces of dark beauty. A block party was in progress on a side street. In the roped-off area young men and women were dancing to the music of a noisy band.

Here and there a boy and girl stood watching, holding hands, their faces bright with the magic of first love.

He reached the cabin, and gave a start as a swift shadow dashed toward him from the bushes. Quickly he saw it was the little yellow mongrel with the too-long ears that quivered like the feelers of a butterfly. The animal halted at the doorway, its eyes wistful, pleading for admittance. Captain Asa went into the cabin. He lit the lamp, and began to study his Bible. There was a scratching at the door, and a faint whimpering.

He continued reading. The scratching ended.

Hour after hour Captain Asa sat holding the tattered volume. His fingers turning the pages moved slower and slower. The crackling of the paper ceased.

The moon became a pale ghost, as though exhausted by the pouring of its rays upon the earth. The distant peaks became gray shadows, suddenly shot with streaks of crimson. The sun began to show above the horizon, as though it were a glowing disk of steel floating up from the furnaces.

The weather had changed during the night. The air was cool, fragrant. A heavy dew lay over the cornfields. The green ears glistened like jewels.

Captain Asa arose and made coffee.

There came the scratching on the door again, loud, insistent. He went outside and saw the little dog, its curly yellow tail and the whole rear end of its body wagging in an ecstasy of entreaty. He hesitated, then let it come into the cabin.

It scurried about, sniffing in a frenzy of excitement. He gave it some scraps from the table. It swallowed them in a single gulp, as a vacuum cleaner sucks up a leaf or a bit of paper lying on the floor.

Captain Asa took out a pen and a sheet of paper. With

painstaking strokes he wrote a letter and put it in the box before the cabin. The animal followed, darting about him in the absurd circles to which dogs are given in their merrier moods, as though it were observing a ritual of some canine religion.

Captain Asa put on his hat, and walked down the valley. The sun shone with brilliance in one of those matchless mornings of a mountain summer. Behind the peaks white clouds towered, as though they were a farther range of mountains, covered with snow. On the banks bluejays screamed and bobwhite whistled. Somewhere in the trees an unseen thrush sang a faint, delicate song. A mockingbird, perched on a stump, was trying to imitate the melody, emitting odd throaty notes, as though it were a clumsy amateur, studying under some practiced professional.

Captain Asa reached the blacksmith shop where the tall mountaineer was busy at his forge.

He spoke quietly. "My car's needing some fixing next time you're up the creek, Jesse. I'm going off to Chicago soon as I can."

CHAPTER EIGHTEEN

LITTLE BY LITTLE, as though he were recovering from a long illness, Captain Asa's face lost its pallor. When he encountered the neighboring mountain folk again, he greeted them with his old friendliness. His voice grew warm, cheerful.

He decided to take Big Jesse's advice, and sell his property to the mill. The transaction was completed without difficulty. When the money was in the bank, and the last of his possessions that he could not carry given away to his acquaintances, he hooked the car onto the trailer. While the little dog sat on the front seat, barking in excitement, he set off down the stony creek.

Along the river road he proceeded, casting a farewell glance at the smoking furnaces, then turned into the dark-timbered hills. It was September now, and the mountain air was touched with the approach of autumn. But the squirrels still chattered in the trees. The cardinals still sang merrily as they flew out of the bushes, like flashes from a phantom fire.

All day Captain Asa traveled, the mountains growing lower and lower. Past Big Creek he drove, and Burning Springs and Elvira, past Sand Gap and Clover Bottom, into quiet Berea.

The road grew straighter. The hills became the rolling pastures of the Blue Grass, where graceful horses stood proudly near their grooms, like royalty watched over by their worshiping courtiers.

Captain Asa halted for the night and studied the road map. A letter had arrived from Chick Waters, saying that the showman was coming to Louisville to take advantage of the crowds arriving for the autumn races. Captain Asa decided to meet his friend in the Kentucky metropolis.

He saw the haze marking the city late the next afternoon, and drove through the busy outskirts. A score of men and women were gathered along the highway, gazing at some object in a parking lot. As Captain Asa approached he saw that the crowd was occasioned by a huge, dejected-looking ox, with battered horns which had once been covered with gilt paint. From its heavy neck hung a cardboard sign, "Get Your Photo On The World's Largest Ox—Twenty-Five Cents."

On the back of the animal a frightened small boy was sitting, while the pleased father stood alongside, supporting the child in a crude saddle. Before them the green-suited Mr. Waters was standing, adjusting his ancient camera.

The photographer saw the trailer, and waved in greeting.

Captain Asa joined him when the childish patron had departed.

Mr. Waters exhibited the shabby animal with pride. "Bought him from a butcher down near Brownsville, Texas," he declared jauntily. "Couldn't get a bull so had to take a ox. He's a Mexican. I call him Big Ike. Getting him trained, too, so he can shake hands with the kids. Shake hands with my friend, Ike."

The ox stood motionless, staring at Captain Asa stolidly out of its great red eyes.

Mr. Waters shrugged his shoulders in apology. "Them Mexicans learns slow."

The little dog stood off at a safe distance, its long ears fluttering nervously.

Mr. Waters took a few more photographs, then as it began to grow dark, led the ox off to a trailer camp near the race track that rose like a vast Colosseum in the twilight.

Here his car with its battered tent was parked, to which was now added a crude wooden carrier for transporting the ox.

Captain Asa pitched camp.

They ate supper, then sat smoking at the table. Captain Asa recounted his experiences since their last meeting. In the trailer adjoining, two sportily-dressed men sat drinking beer, arguing loudly about the winners of all the Derbys of the past decade. In a trailer beyond a woman was heating a bottle of milk on a stove. There came the plaintive cry of a baby. Before the camp office an old Negro stood on a rickety ladder, replacing a burned-out electric globe that hung over the door.

Captain Asa was silent for a long interval, puffing at his stogie. "You were sure right what you told me. And Big Jesse was right, too. If I'd have listened to you, I guess plenty that happened would have come out different than the way it done. But I've sure learned my lesson now. Things are always changing, and you got to change with the times. What a fellow's got to do most, looks like, is to keep from getting set in his ways."

Mr. Waters chewed a toothpick. "I didn't expect you to listen. You can't tell people nothing. Even if it was fixed so that every time a man was going to get in trouble something inside him'd buzz like a rattlesnake, he'd get bit just the same. People's got to find out things for themselves."

Captain Asa nodded. "I seen a piece in the paper a while ago, where a fellow said the way to live right is to keep your mind swung open, just like it was a gate. And that's sure the way I'm going to be."

The ox, standing spectrally in the shadows beyond the door, lowed in melancholy. Mr. Waters went outside and tossed it some hay. He returned, and took his seat opposite Captain Asa once more. "What you figuring on doing now?" he demanded.

Captain Asa poured himself a glass of water. "I been figuring plenty. And I think I got it figured right. After I go to Chicago to see Fernie, I'm going to visit with Ula in Dallas, and then I'll stop with Vergil in Denver, where he's a-working for the Santa Fe. If my children won't stay with me, I'll go and stay with them a while. And then I'm going on to California and buy me a farm with the money I got from the mill. That's where they got the most up-to-date farms there is today, everybody says."

In the distant trailer the baby began to cry again. They could hear the mother murmuring to it in soothing tones.

Captain Asa watched her silhouette moving back and forth in the window. "And I'm going to start really looking for some nice woman and get married again. Way it seems to me, what I need more than anything else is a good wife to keep me from being lonesome."

Mr. Waters found a rubber band on the table, and aimed it at an autumnal fly buzzing near the sugar bowl. "Easier to find a good woman than it is a good ox."

The rubber band went wide of its target. He snapped it idly. "Think I'll go some of the way with you. Been here about long enough, I guess. Louisville's a nice town. But it's a horse town. A ox don't do so good."

They set out together in the morning, Captain Asa and his trailer in the lead, Mr. Waters and the carrier with the ox following close behind.

They crossed the bridge spanning the Ohio and moved through the Indiana countryside where farmers were busy at their harvests. A dilapidated crossroads store showed ahead, with a rickety porch leaning far from the perpendicular. They stopped before it, and went inside to make a few necessary purchases. The windows were cobwebbed, and here and there a pane was stuffed with newspaper. The shelves were empty and thick with dust. Behind the counter a gnarled old man was standing, like a dwarf in an ancient cave. He served them funereally.

"That there's a fellow I call up-to-date," Mr. Waters remarked with irony, as they walked into the road. "He acts like he's waiting on you from his grave where they buried him a hundred years ago."

Captain Asa brushed off some dust clinging to his coat sleeve. "Guess that's the way I'd have been before long, the way I was going. It's like the fellow wrote in the paper. You got to keep an open mind."

Captain Asa looked at the road sign, and consulted his map. "There's a little tourist camp this side of Terre Haute I'd like to stop at when we're passing. A lady that married

Marty Powers' brother Will that come from up Clay Creek keeps it. She's been a-running it by herself since Will died. Marty asked me to stop and see her if I come this way. He said she'd cook us a mighty good meal."

A camp appeared not long after, a half-dozen blue-and-white cottages so trim and polished they seemed made of china. A pleasant little dwelling of the same porcelainlike appearance was situated nearby, with a farm beyond where a herd of sleek Jersey cows was grazing peacefully.

Captain Asa slowed down to glance at the name on the mailbox, and halted the car at the side of the road. He waited until Mr. Waters and his impassive cargo drew up at the rear.

They started across the scrubbed stone walk. "She's a Indiana lady they call Miss Mollie," Captain Asa informed his companion. "Married Will when he went off to work in a factory in Terre Haute. They made a-plenty of money up there some way, and started the cottages. I ain't never met her. But Marty and all of 'em says she's a mighty nice lady."

He knocked on the spotless door.

Miss Mollie appeared in answer, a pretty little woman whose blue silk dress was cut in a fashion that attempted to conceal a tendency toward plumpness. Her rich auburn hair was set in a glossy, too-perfect wave. With her rounded face that bore no sign of a wrinkle, and her carefully painted nails, she possessed that slightly artificial look which comes to middle-aged women who make too frequent visits to a beauty parlor.

She greeted Captain Asa with delighted surprise on learning that he came from her brother-in-law. Her voice was rich and warm like her hair, her speech bearing the usual rustic accents of the neighborhood, but touched with a conscious attempt at refinement, which gave it a slight air of affectation. She ushered the visitors into a living room arranged in an endeavor to follow the latest fashion in decoration, then hurried to bring some cakes and orangeade from the kitchen.

They sat talking, Miss Mollie vivaciously asking questions about her relatives, Captain Asa looking at her in admiration.

He glanced at the red leather chairs and the thick-cushioned couch in the corner. "You got a beautiful place here."

She patted down her glossy-marcelled hair, and turned to him brightly. "I tried to make it pretty. It's just the way I saw it in a magazine. I always try to keep up with the magazines. I take six, not counting the Sunday-school paper. I guess I'm like Mama, that lives in Indianapolis. She takes eleven."

She went over to raise a window. As she did so a fastening of the Venetian blinds loosened, causing the wooden curtain to collapse.

She stood helpless. "It's been coming down every day for a month now."

Captain Asa advanced with gallantry. He brought a ladder, and with a screw driver and hammer restored the blind to its place.

Miss Mollie gazed at him with grateful eyes. "It's like having your own family around, watching you fix things," she said.

The conversation grew more and more agreeable.

She left the room a moment.

Mr. Waters flipped the pages of a newspaper. "A blind fellow can see that woman's crazy about you. She's a fine looking woman, too, with them six tourist cabins. And them cabins are always crowded nowadays."

Captain Asa shifted with embarrassment. "She's a wonderful woman, all right. But she wouldn't be interested in a old hill fellow like me."

Mr. Waters discreetly went outside. From the window Captain Asa could see him release the ox from the carrier and tie it to the fence, so that it might graze in the nearby grass. The showman remained in his car, busying himself with some photographic equipment.

Miss Mollie returned to the living room. She continued to talk happily to Captain Asa, her rounded face dimpling at times as he paid her some compliment. "It's so pretty today. Maybe you'd like me to show you the cottages and the farm."

They went through the door.

Gaily she bustled about, exhibiting the cabins with their soft carpets and their comfortable beds, the porcelain-like barn shining with the latest farm machinery.

Captain Asa beamed with pleasure. "It's the prettiest place I ever seen anywhere."

He opened the pasture gate.

She halted on the other side, patting down her glossy hair again, disarranged by the wind. Her mood became serious. "I wish you could be stopping here for a while. They've got wonderful farms in Indiana. Maybe you'd like to get a farm here instead of going way out to California."

He shut the gate delicately behind her. "It'd be wonderful having a place around here. Looks like mighty fine ground, and there's plenty of water. Out West in California and them places it's just a big desert. Nothing but sand, and no water anywhere."

She grew gay once more.

They found Mr. Waters at the cottage. Miss Mollie invited the travelers to stay for noonday dinner, and hurried off to prepare the meal.

The guests sat down in the living room to wait.

"What you think about her now?" Mr. Waters demanded.

Captain Asa spoke solemnly, as though he were a judge pronouncing some grave decision.

"You wouldn't meet no other woman like her if you kept on looking for fifty years."

Some time after they took places at the table in the dining room, set with colored napkins and pink-decorated china.

They ate the crisp-fried chicken and the succulent ham, the golden corn and the scalloped potatoes, all prepared with an expert's mastery.

Mr. Waters looked on while Miss Mollie filled his plate for the third time. "This here chicken's like swing music," he declared. "Makes you so excited your stomach gets dizzy."

Captain Asa nodded. "If you gave meals with them tourist cottages, nobody'd ever get where they was traveling to. 'Cause they'd never go away."

The marcelled hostess blushed with pleasure. She selected a plump drumstick and urged it upon him. "I like to have things taste nice. I learned about cooking from Mama. Everywhere she goes, when she eats something good she always asks how they make it. I always do it, too."

She resisted his protests and popped the chicken onto his plate. "Will took Mama and me to the New York World's Fair, and we ate in the restaurants they had from the different countries—French and Dutch and Polish, and I don't know what all. And we always tried to find out how they fixed everything. I guess you ate in some of those restaurants at the New York Fair, didn't you?"

Captain Asa's face fell a little. "I never was at any kind of World's Fair. But I know a plenty about the St. Louis World's Fair. That was the finest fair was ever opened."

Miss Mollie poured Captain Asa some coffee. "Mama said that was a nice fair. She and Papa used to talk about it when I was a little girl. A lot of people from Terre Haute went to see it. But it wasn't anything like the fair they had in New York."

She offered him the cream in a dainty pitcher. "We had a wonderful time at the New York Fair. There was something going on every minute. I guess you read about the Mechanical Man, didn't you? He'd smoke cigarettes and do all kinds of things. And the artificial lightning was terrible. It was like the end of the world."

Captain Asa slowly buttered a biscuit. His face was growing stubborn. "There was things they had at the St. Louis Fair people never seen before, and ain't never seen since. They had the biggest pipe organ in the world. It took a whole freight train to bring it to St. Louis, and it shook the ground so they had to stop playing it at night, 'cause people and horses ten miles away'd get scared in the dark and think it was a earthquake. And they had the whole Boer War with six hundred soldiers on each side, the same soldiers that done the real fighting. They never had any of them things in the New York Fair."

Miss Mollie did not notice Captain Asa's face. She went on with animation. "At the New York Fair we used to go every day to hear the big machine that looked like a typewriter and could talk just like a person. And Mama went twenty times, I guess, to see the Midget Village. But I guess it was the big things were the best—the fireworks at night, and the automobiles that took you off to the way things are going to be fifty years from now."

Captain Asa's lips were hardening with sternness. "At the St. Louis Fair they had the Philippine Village, with real head-hunters, and the Hairy Ainus from Japan. They had the Holy City, with camels you could sit on and go past all the places where Jesus was when He was living. You could travel Under And Over The Sea in a submarine and an airship, and go to the North Pole. You could look at the way things are in Heaven and Hell, and the Galveston Flood with the storm coming up and all the people drowning. And then you could see the biggest thing of all, what they called Creation, the Lord making the world in six days, just like it was in the Bible. And that's the finest thing ever was in a fair."

Miss Mollie went into the kitchen and returned with a dish that bore a huge strawberry shortcake, lost under a luscious mountain of whipped cream.

She served each guest a generous portion. "Mama told me about the Galveston Flood and the Creation. She said they were pretty. But she said you couldn't compare the New York Fair with the one in St. Louis. She said you could have put the whole St. Louis Fair in a corner of the New York Fair, and then you couldn't find it anywhere."

Captain Asa grew grim. He sat in silence, and left the snowy dessert untouched. Soon after he rose from the table.

The marcelled hostess looked at him in alarm. "You're not going already, are you? I was hoping you'd be staying tonight."

Captain Asa took his hat. "It's a long way to Chicago and California. I got to be getting on as far as I can."

He bade her a stiff good-by, and went out the door. Mr. Waters followed.

They reached the gate where the ox was munching stolidly.

Captain Asa turned to glance back at the cottage shining like a porcelain miniature in the setting sun.

He breathed a sigh of deep relief. "Looks like sometimes a ox has got more sense than a human," he said.